The Devil's Pitchfork

Hexen Book 4

Al Hagan

Contents

Prologue

First, the car wouldn't start, the piece of junk, even when Carlos cursed it and kicked a dent in the fender in frustration.

"Get it running and catch up," Javier had ordered through clenched teeth. "That thing won't be going fast." He waved a hand dismissively at the cargo truck. He wasn't happy at all, being assigned to boring escort duty, just grinding down the highway at low speed. But it was necessary. The *pendejo* cops had lost a shipment of gold coins, and paid for it with their lives. Now there was a new crew on the job. Them, straight up from Juárez, and not soft like those *norteamericanos*.

After more tries, the engine had whimpered to life. There was never going to be any roaring with this pile of crap. It had kept running, but it choked and stumbled. Carlos had floored it in irritation, and also to catch up to the truck they were supposed to guard. That actually seemed to help and it started to run better, the water in the gasoline or clog in the fuel line or whatever eventually passing through the engine.

And then they'd found Javier's car, riddled with bullets, in the weeds in the median between the lanes of the highway, the engine still ticking over. All three men inside were dead, and no doctor was required to make that call.

But where was the truck?

They jumped back in the car and sped down the interstate, now desperate to catch up to the gold shipment. And suddenly there it was, stopped on the shoulder, with an SUV in front of it. Carlos had slammed down the brakes on the junk car, skidding it to a stop.

The gunfire had begun immediately, before he even got it stopped all the way. Bullets cracked by, way too close, and he hunched down in the seat, fighting the urge to just floor it and run. His adrenaline had been up since he'd seen Javier's car and the bodies, but now it shot sky-high.

He'd never been in a gunfight, not really. Oh, he claimed he had, but the truth was that some shots had been fired down the street once, he and his friends had fired some back, and then everyone ran away. He'd even forgotten to use the sights, not that he had a clear target anyway. He'd just raised his pistol and pulled the trigger three or four times.

His story was that he'd been in a long, drawn-out gunfight with the *Federales* and had killed two, maybe three of the dogs, before they'd retreated. He'd been a hero, a man, instead of the teenager who'd fired random shots at nothing and then fled.

Today was going to be a different story.

He got the transmission shifted into park and jumped out, hunched down, dragging his rifle with him. Fully automatic gunfire was blasting off at close range. He hoped it was his guys shooting the thieves. And then they were out of his sight, running around the truck and SUV on opposite sides. There was more gunfire.

Every time someone fired, Carlos ducked. He couldn't help it. He'd only taken a few steps and was standing in the highway, with the engine between him and anything on the side of the road. Those shots had been fired off to his left, and then suddenly there were others over on his right. He froze, glancing first one way, then the other, terrified that someone was going to burst out from behind the vehicles and gun him down. He desperately wished that one of his guys would fire a shot and then laugh, signaling that the last of the thieves was dead.

But it was quiet, now, way too quiet.

After a few seconds he did hear something, just not what he was seeking. No, this sound was tires on pavement, an engine revving up as it was downshifted, and an air horn. There was a truck coming down the interstate. It was two lanes, but his car was stopped in one of them and he was standing partly in the other. He looked desperately back at the scene on the shoulder, afraid to step out of the way of the oncoming truck and into that gunfight. Instead, he crouched down where he was, pressed his body against the fender he had dented earlier, and waved frantically at the truck to go around him.

The driver steered way over, as far as he could and still keep on the pavement, then accelerated off rapidly once he got past.

As the truck rumbled off, the ominous silence returned, even more frightening than before.

He could feel his heart, seemingly thudding against his ribcage hard enough to leave bruises, as if someone was punching him from inside. His throat was desert-dry. He softly called out the names of the men who had been in his car, one by one, waiting for a reply between each one.

There was only more silence. He started to call out the names again, when he thought he heard a noise and he panicked, jamming his finger against the trigger of his M-16 and swinging it wildly from side to side, emptying the magazine. Then he threw the weapon down on the hood of the car, jumped in, and floored the accelerator.

They were dead. They had to be. The thieves had killed them all, and he wasn't going to run into whatever buzzsaw had chopped them up and get killed, too. He was going to save himself. To hell with the gold. To hell with Javier. To hell with everyone and everything. He even laughed in nervous relief. He was safe!

And then he saw in the rearview mirror that something was coming up behind him, coming *fast*.

Chapter One

As the train pulled into the station, Antonio's heart rate went up. He fully realized he might be risking his life here. That was a thing that a young man could do, but his wife and kids were with him, too. He had a fleeting thought to just keep going, or to try to gain entry without saying anything. Don't call any attention to himself, check things out quietly, get the lay of the land, and then decide on a course of action.

Or just go right in, balls to the wall. The problem was that the quiet approach would make him look like a spy and would probably get him killed if he was wrong. At least with the straight-on option he could always be honest and say he was mistaken, if that was the case. No one could fault him for an honest mistake, could they?

He was possibly betting his life and the fate of his family.

He and his wife Megan got off the train like everyone else and made their way into the station. There was an empty bench near the door against the wall, so she sat. She was carrying a baby and leading a toddler, so her hands were full. He rolled the suitcase to the bench and set his duffle bag and the diaper bag down beside her.

She looked up at him uncertainly, one last time. This would be it. There was no going back if they didn't do it right now. He smiled at her.

"It's fine. It's either her or it's not. If not, then this is still a nice-looking place. The people on the train said so many good things about this place. You talked to them."

She just nodded wordlessly. The last few years had been horrific, but things were calming down. If they weren't great, at least back in the Valley it was the devil they knew. This was not. They had no real idea what this was.

Antonio squeezed her shoulder, winked at his little girl, and walked to the Station Master's window in the middle of the station. He spoke to the man briefly and asked how he could do what he came here to do.

The Station Master started with a smile since he loved trains and loved his job. His face went to surprise and then back to a smile, although less of one. He could have answered some of the man's questions but he was suspicious of con men and wasn't going to give him any ammunition.

"The best thing would be for me to get someone from Headquarters down here to talk to you," he said, lifting the handset to a wired phone. "They can be here pretty quickly. Why don't you have a seat and I'll get someone to come talk to you?"

Antonio thanked him and sat back down on the bench. Meagan looked at him and he leaned over to kiss her.

"It'll be good," he reassured her, while silently praying that he was right. He leaned back against the wall and surveyed the scene. It brought to mind something he had seen in numerous movies, everything from Westerns to Sherlock Holmes to *Murder on the Orient Express*: a bustling train station where rails were the most viable method of long-distance transport.

The Station Master himself was part of that illusion. He was dressed in a kind of costume, complete with vest, garters on the sleeves of his striped shirt, a pocket watch on a chain, and a stiff-brimmed little cap, to go along with his round glasses and walrus moustache. He looked like he could have stepped out of one of those movies where trains still ran on steam.

The station itself was immaculately clean. There were professionally-done signboards with maps and directions for newcomers, job and notice boards, and some advertising. While all of that may have been boring and even tiresome before the apocalypse, it was a welcome sight now. It indicated a thriving community, something that was all too rare now.

People moved back and forth through the station in a variety of clothing, mainly sensible work clothes, with a rare business suit. Many openly carried rifles and pistols. He saw one young lady that was nicely dressed in high heels, slacks, and a matching jacket, carrying a briefcase, with an H&K MP5A1 slung casually over her shoulder.

A briefcase and a submachinegun, he thought. *What a weird world we live in, now. I wonder if the conference room she is probably headed for provides a rifle rack or if you just lay your weapon down beside your notebook and coffee.*

He noted that they did have coffee here. There was a shop in one corner of the station, with glass display cases of baked goods, but it was too far away to see exactly what they had. It was obviously well-stocked, however, which was an excellent sign. The pastries or whatever could be locally sourced, but someone had to have established trade with Latin America to import the coffee. He considered walking over and at least seeing what they had and at what price. He didn't smell smoke, which meant they had some way to generate electricity to heat the coffee, another good sign.

One thing he didn't see was beggars and panhandlers. There was one girl off to the side, playing a guitar for tips, doing a decent rendition of Fleetwood Mac's *Rhiannon.* She didn't have the pipes to match Stevie Nicks' vocals but her guitar work was pretty good. Then he realized he was wasting time identifying the song and had also lost the opportunity to check out the coffee shop.

The reason they don't have panhandlers is because they have an active police presence. Like that one right there, he thought. A uniformed cop strolled by, glanced at them and gave a partial smile and nod and kept going.

But not far. He walked a little way and then eased around into an oh-so-casual U-turn and took up station off to the side. He wasn't staring directly at them but he could see anything they might do. He was close enough that any move

Antonio made, the cop could be on him immediately. In less than a minute another cop eased up on the other side of them. Antonio nodded to himself.

It's a sensible precaution. I'd do the same thing. The Station Master must have alerted them. I stirred up something. I just have to pray at this point that what I did was a good thing.

***

A few miles away, the call from the Station Master had come into Headquarters and lit a fire under some feet. The duty NCO immediately realized that this was something way above her pay grade, so she had alerted Taylor to take the call. She walked out into the main office, what they called the bullpen, and got on the phone.

"This is Taylor... He said *what*?" She paused for the other party to speak before coming out with one word full of meaning: "Really." That last word was said in the tone that a woman takes when a man has done something bold and she is deciding how much trouble he is in.

"No, that was great. Don't give him any info. We'll be there as soon as we can get there. Can you put some security on him? Just to watch — oh, good job. Tell them to restrain him if they need to. Cuff him, whatever it takes to keep him there, I don't care. We're on the way."

She hung up the phone and murmured "shit" under her breath. Everyone in the office was all ears and staring at her. Of course, things had to happen when there were a lot of people in the office. She pointed at the duty NCO.

"I want Security at the train station. Two people. At least one female SP. No siren. No drama. Meet us at the front." She swept an index finger across a couple of people. "You two in the SUV with rifles. Fire it up. I'll be there in a minute." She spun on her heel, moving fast, and went back to her office.

"Ted, I'm sorry. Something came up. I'll either be back in an hour or not at all today. But we still need..."

7

"Not a problem. I'll have it all done tonight. We can't starve the state bureaucrats of paperwork, now, can we?"

"I'm sorry to make you work late." She gave an apologetic smile.

"Ah, it keeps me from dancing on tables and chasing loose women."

"Oh, Ted, you are such a wild and crazy guy," she observed dryly, smiling, enjoying the banter, but as soon as she turned away her mind snapped back to this new issue.

It's an honest mistake, it's a scam, or it's genuine, she thought. *Or it's someone coming to harm her*. Some ideas flitted through her mind about how to deal with the first two possibilities and then another thought intruded: *Rumor control*.

She stopped in the middle of the bullpen, hands on hips, and slowly made eye contact with everyone there.

"Not. One. Fucking. Word. To. Anyone. Got it? Keep your mouths shut for thirty minutes or an hour and I promise I'll give you the scoop, okay?" There was a chorus of 'yes, ma'am'.

She hesitated, then blew out a breath. "Look, I'm not being a bitch, here. Dani has mourned her brother for years. She thinks he's dead. She has his name tattooed on her shoulder. If word gets out that he's alive, she's going to be extremely happy. Overjoyed. But if this turns out to be some asshole trying to scam her, then she's going to be devastated. Think about how badly she's going to crash, how disappointed she's going to be. So, nobody say anything until we know one way or the other. And if this is a scam, come bail me out of jail because I'm going to kill the bastard on the spot."

She hopped into the back seat of the SUV and buckled up.

"Lights and siren as needed," she instructed the driver. "Fast but don't be crazy. Don't run over any small children. And cut the siren before we get anywhere near the station."

Normally the driver would have a smartass comeback like "It's okay to run over big children, then?" but he kept his mouth shut today. He knew Taylor was not in a joking mood.

The young woman in the passenger seat looked back at her. "Do you think it's true?"

"I don't know. I need to think about this situation. I mean, it's not impossible for multiple family members to have survived. It's just uncommon."

She took the hint and didn't bother her for the rest of the trip.

Chapter Two

WHEN TAYLOR AND HER little entourage of two cops and the young woman from the office came through the doors, Antonio spotted them immediately, and knew they were there for him. He reached over to give Megan a reassuring squeeze on her leg and commented "The blonde is important."

The blonde strode through the building with complete and utter confidence, like she owned the place. Even above that, though, she projected an assurance that she could defend herself against anyone in the station. She might be locked onto him but she checked out the room, too, looking for accomplices that the others might have missed.

The station was emptying out at that point. Most of the incoming passengers were gone and the outgoing were onboard the passenger cars. He could hear men and machinery loading or unloading freight further down the track, so some people still milled about, probably waiting on a delivery.

Seeing Taylor and her escort striding in, though, caused a ripple of movement. Most people moved to the corners of the building, well out of the way, or even left the building entirely. Getting out of the line of fire, possibly. Some backed up a few steps and then stood to watch the action, their gazes going to Antonio as the obvious subject of anything to eyewitness. The busker stopped singing in mid-note and hurriedly cased her guitar. She was heading out the door as fast as she could.

The blonde was definitely trouble, and everybody knew it. And she was official trouble, the worst kind.

He knew she was there for him because of the attitude. He had touched a tender nerve with his question and she was borderline furious about it. He actually had second thoughts for a moment. He might get his ass kicked in a minute here if he was barking up the wrong tree. This girl was not about to tolerate any bullshit from him.

And there was no doubt that she was the driving force. This situation *meant* something to her. The girl beside her and one step behind was there as an extra hand, maybe a gofer. Her face showed interest but no attitude. Same with the two cops, one male and one female, all decked out in full camouflage uniform and gear. They were there to do a job but didn't have any real vested interest in whatever he might say. That didn't mean they wouldn't all enthusiastically join in to kick his ass, but it would be just routine to them.

He'd had his ass kicked before. He wasn't scared of that.

The blonde, now, she would *hurt* you. Like a permanent limp or an elbow that would never work quite right again or some extensive scarring. He realized his earlier thought about risking his life may not have been merely idle speculation. There was nothing he could do about it now, though. Not even run. He had spun this situation up, but it was out of his hands at this point.

On the bright side, the very fact that his questions meant something to the blonde indicated he was in the right place.

He stood and took a couple of steps forward, moving slowly, standing almost at the position of attention, but looser. He put his hands in front of his legs with the fingers spread to show that he held nothing concealed in them. The cops on each side of him had straightened up when the blonde walked in, but now they came out from the wall to give themselves more maneuver room and moved in closer to him.

The blonde turned her head to flash a smile and a thumbs-up at the Station Master. He was delighted with the recognition. He returned the gesture with a huge, toothy grin that made his eyes scrunch up into tiny little slits. The blonde was actually gorgeous and had a great smile with perfect teeth. But when she turned her face back towards Antonio, the smile was gone. Gone and dead and buried like it had never happened. Her jaw was set and her eyes flashed.

Antonio noted that she was naturally beautiful without a trace of makeup. She had symmetrical features, big green eyes, lips that were adequately full without being clownishly puffed up, and blond hair that fell past her shoulders. The hair was cut functionally, no complicated layering or styling, simply parted in the middle and swept back. Her clothing reflected the same no-frills, keep-it-simple philosophy: hiking boots, jeans, an untucked button-down shirt, and no jewelry other than a watch and a gold necklace. She was about five-eight, trending towards tall, with long legs, and athletic, not skinny. And not the 'athletic' that girls on online dating sites used to use as a euphemism for 'fat'. Athletic as in running and martial arts and kick boxing and weight training.

She was a predator. He recognized that straight up.

People always say that man is the greatest predator, and it's true if they lump the entire population of humanity together and put one label on it. If you break it down individually, though, few humans are actually predators. Few people in any primitive tribe were really hunters or warriors. Sure, people would defend themselves if attacked, but that doesn't make someone a warrior any more than swimming to keep from drowning makes them into a fish. The majority of any tribe is composed of women and children, for one. Beyond that, most men farmed or tended livestock. These were all prey. The real predators in their tribe contributed meat from the hunt but more importantly kept them safe from other predators.

It's always been like that, even in the twenty-first century, even if we didn't realize it. The specific jobs changed, but not the reality. The roles are still there. They function exactly the same way as they have forever.

This girl was dangerous. He didn't have a shred of doubt about that. And she was going to decide his fate in the next minute or two. Maybe less. He took a deep breath and let it out slowly.

Chapter Three

As she got closer and stopped a few feet in front of him at a normal conversational distance, he saw that she was barely controlling her temper. Her nostrils flared like a bull about to charge a matador.

"Talk to me," she said tersely through clenched teeth, her eyes stabbing into his with laser intensity.

He met her gaze unflinchingly.

"I'm looking for Dani Ruiz. Daniela Angelina Ruiz Vasquez from Houston. She's my baby sister. I am her brother Antonio."

There it was.

It almost took Taylor aback, hearing it firsthand like that. Her emotions seemed to split in two. On the one hand, she would weep for joy if Dani's brother was alive, and she desperately hoped it was true. On the other, she still had a deep suspicion that this was a scam, and if this guy was trying to toy with Dani's emotions just so he could get a free ride... well, if that were the case, she would put a bullet between his eyes with a smile on her face. But not really a smile because she would be so furious that Dani was hurt. She didn't even realize that her hand strayed closer to her Glock.

"I have ID cards in my pocket I can show you," he offered, pointing to his pocket but not reaching into it.

There were six people with guns close at hand focused intently on him so any suspicious moves would be stupid and quite possibly fatal. But the blonde held out a hand, so he slowly fished out his Marine Corps ID and driver's license and gave them to her.

He noticed that she held out her left hand. That meant either she was left-handed or she did it so that her right could stay near her weapon. He couldn't see a pistol the way they were facing each other but there was absolutely no doubt in his mind that she had one. He couldn't see her right hand, either, but it seemed to be at the five o'clock position, a common place to put a weapon.

She held the cards up so she could compare the photos to his face while she asked him to recite the information on them, full name, address, birth date, and so on.

His Marine Corps ID was a CAC, Common Access Card, with a photo and not much other information except for a rank of lance corporal. The main information in the CAC would have been read by computer, all of which were now dead. The card was in a clear plastic sleeve along with some other folded pieces of paper, which she pulled out and opened up. These sheets were abbreviated promotion orders, simply stating that on such and such a date he had been promoted, with an officer's signature. He'd gone through corporal, sergeant, and was now a staff sergeant.

It made sense to do it that way since there was no way to update the card and print out a new one, which required a functioning computer and printer. Going back to paper IDs was out, too, since repeatedly cutting out and re-laminating the photo to a new card would degrade the photo over time. Photography, like almost everything else, had been kicked back in time a century or two. There weren't many photos being made now and they were difficult to produce.

The photos themselves were not conclusive. How many people really look like their driver's license photos? The best she could determine was a maybe. She put the cards in her pocket and started in on her questions, anything she knew about Dani that her brother would know.

He was passing with flying colors when she asked him about his martial arts training. He looked down.

14

"Dani always followed me around and at some point, I started taking Tae Kwon Do classes. She wanted to learn, too, but my parents couldn't afford to send two kids. I showed her what I learned in class and we sparred. At first, I thought I could just hit her a couple of times too hard and she'd lose interest and stop bothering me. But no. She just dug in her heels and hit me back harder. If she got knocked down, she might get tears in her eyes but she'd wipe them off and get up and come back for more. I cherish every minute I spent with her now."

His voice shook during that last sentence and he looked up with eyes that were wet with tears.

"Please tell me. Is she here? Is she alive?"

Taylor cleared her throat, perhaps getting a little worked up herself, and replied more softly that she had previously.

"Of course she's here. If she wasn't, we wouldn't be having this conversation. You'd have been sent you on your way right off the bat."

Antonio used his sleeve to wipe away the tears that flowed now. Then he closed his eyes for a brief, silent prayer of thanks and made the sign of the cross. But he made it slowly, because those people with guns and suspicion were still there. No one had relaxed yet.

When he opened his eyes, Taylor was back to being serious, but much less angry.

"Do you have any weapons on you?" she questioned.

"No. In the backpack, I have a pistol and a knife. In the duffle bag, I have a rifle broken down."

Taylor turned to the Security guy nearest her.

"Take possession of their luggage. Lock it in your vehicle. Search the diaper bag and then she can have it back. Frisk both of them. Thoroughly."

Yep, the blonde was undoubtedly in charge, if there had been any question. People hopped to do what she told them.

While the cops were searching the bag and taking the pack and suitcase, the blonde stood with Antonio, not alone but with fewer witnesses than previously. She moved in closer to him for even more privacy and locked eyes with him. She was almost as tall as him, only giving up an inch.

"I love Dani very much," she said. "She's my big sister. I would kill for her, in an instant. I don't say that lightly. I've killed quite a few men and a couple of women. Don't hurt her."

She expected to get some pushback from her threat. Antonio was a Latino and a Marine and probably had a pretty aggressive personality. He completely took her off guard by smiling at her.

"Thank you for watching out for my baby sister," he replied in a soft voice. "I was stationed in California, so I couldn't do it myself."

His gentle manner took the wind out of Taylor's sails. She didn't have a reply to that. She was fully ready to fire back aggressively if he had done so, fully ready to throw punches and more if needed, but she wasn't prepared for gratitude. After a couple of seconds, she gave a curt nod, and then everyone was ready to go. As they walked out to the vehicles, Taylor's mind was humming.

That statement, above all else, convinces me that he really is her brother. The real proof will come from Dani, obviously, but I wouldn't bet against it at this point.

At the SUV, Taylor determined the seating, ordering exactly who sat where. She put herself on the driver's side in the far back seat, Antonio in the middle seat, passenger side, and Megan in the middle seat on the driver's side. Antonio thought about that for a moment and realized that she was positioning her field of fire. If he tried anything, she could shoot him across the vehicle without putting any missed shots into the driver's back, and it placed her weapon as far away from him as possible. Plus, she put the kids between him and Megan, so missed shouts could go into them. No father would risk that.

He mentally reversed the seating, doing a 'what if?' exercise. But then that would either put her shooting hand extended and open to being grabbed, or held tight to her body and therefore unsighted and inaccurate, literally shooting from the hip. The position they were in now offered the best compromise for shooting and weapon retention.

The girl may look young, but she is no amateur, went through his mind.

Antonio reflected that it's easy to act as if you own the place, and to put up a badass false front if no one challenges you and ruins the illusion. It's even easy to kill someone if you are just pulling a trigger. But this was training, or maybe experience. The blonde had been trained, or had been in these situations, or had thought and planned it out. He briefly wondered about her story, but he had more important questions right now. For now, he mentally marked her as a professional, which carried a lot of respect from him.

"So, Dani is really here? She's okay?" he asked.

"Yeah, her and her husband, and she just had a baby girl."

Antonio laughed in delight. "I'm an uncle! But I can't imagine Dani married. And with a daughter! Of course, she's an aunt twice over." He pointed to the children with his chin.

"How did you know to come here to find her?"

"Oh, there are stories, many of them, about a young woman named Dani involved in gunfights and ambushes and battles. I'm sure they're all either false or wildly exaggerated. We interrogated some prisoners, gang members. We were trying to keep order in L.A. but that was a losing battle. Long story. Anyway, these gang members had pulled out of Dallas because Santa Muerte kept killing them. Santa Muerte in the form of a beautiful young girl named Dani, with golden eyes. Dani has that unusual eye color. And all of the stories mention Texas. How could I not make that connection?

"In one of the stories, supposedly she set fire to a building where the gang was staying and killed all the gang members as they ran out. Then she did the same thing to an entire apartment complex that a gang had taken over." He smiled to show how ridiculous he thought the story was.

"Two," Taylor corrected.

"What?" The smile faded by half and his eyes widened.

"Two apartment complexes." She held up two fingers for clarity. Left-handed, again, to keep her right near her pistol. "And it was artillery strikes."

"What?" Antonio said it again, but his voice quavered this time. His smile was gone, replaced by an open mouth. The blonde didn't look like she was joking. She looked dead serious. His wife was staring at him with big eyes that asked what he was getting them into.

Taylor waved the hand. "Sorry to interrupt. That's Dani's story to tell you or not as she sees fit."

They stared at each other for a few seconds until Taylor prompted "You were talking about Santa Muerte."

Antonio's mind was racing. *Holy shit! She's saying the stories are* true? *Dani killed a bunch of people? Artillery strikes? And is Dani a follower of Santa Muerte? Is she acting as Santa Muerte? Or a priestess? There is a connection to this ranch, and a steady flow of followers to here. They have to know that. Is this Anglo girl here a follower? I find that hard to — well, maybe not. After Hexen, there's no telling what someone is going to believe. The usual saints didn't protect us from that, so a lot of people are turning to new ones.*

As if she could read his thoughts, Taylor spoke.

"Look, we have freedom of religion here, so whatever you believe, whatever someone believes, it doesn't matter. They aren't persecuted because of it. There are a large number of Santa Muerte adherents here, yes. Dani is not one of them. She goes to Mass at least twice a week. We have an Irish Catholic priest. But a lot of people seem to think that she *is* Santa Muerte, which comes from a thing she was trying to do to scare that gang off. Apparently, it worked, if they ended up in L.A.

"Anyway, she doesn't let people kneel to her or anything like that, but that just seems to make them love her even more. She provides them with jobs and houses and medical care and safety and, probably best of all, respect and the opportunity for advancement. That's very powerful stuff. People coming out

18

of the cities had pretty much nothing but the clothes on their backs. I know. I was one of them. I got here very early, one of the first. We secured an area, then brought in refugees to learn to ranch and farm. Then we secured a bigger area, brought in more refugees... you get the picture. You could say we imposed law and order on a wild territory."

"So, Dani and her husband own all of this? How much territory are you talking about?" Antonio asked. She had to mean something substantial. Immense. He thought the train station was on the ranch and they were still driving and hadn't gotten to their destination yet. Was all of this part of the ranch?

Taylor shook her head once to the side and back. "You'll have to get that from Dani." Apparently, she still had reservations about him until he was confirmed as Dani's brother.

They rode in silence for a minute or two before Antonio spoke again. "I guess my parents and my other sister and little brother... didn't..."

"No. I'm sorry." Taylor did soften, then. Softer, but firm. She obviously wasn't going to sugar-coat the fact that they had all died when Hexen stormed through the world. He appreciated her answering the question rather than letting him hang.

"Was Dani there, with them? Until the end?"

"Yeah, she was. Don't ask her for the details. She doesn't need to go through that grief again. She's been through it twice already. We went down to Houston a couple of years ago and brought the remains up here and buried them in our cemetery. Gave them a funeral Mass. It gave her a lot of closure, but it took a hell of a toll on her."

He had to take a long moment, then. He said another silent prayer of thanks that his family had been interred in consecrated ground, unlike so many millions, billions, around the world. There were just too many for the survivors to deal with. The overwhelming majority had never been buried.

After a few minutes he thought it might be good to ask something to take his mind off of his grief or he would be an emotional wreck when he saw Dani.

"You never mentioned your name," he prompted.

"I'm Taylor."

"Just Taylor?"

"Everyone knows me, but my last name is Marten. It's Eric's last name, and Dani's. They 'dopted me. That's the local slang. A dopt is a child that has been adopted and also the person or persons that adopted them. It works both ways."

"What's your title or what do you do?"

"I'm Dani's assistant. I make things happen. I do whatever it takes."

He almost asked her if 'whatever' included killing people, but his wife was upset enough and he didn't want to push that. If he had had to bet, he'd have said that it did. But then, did that mean that Dani was having people killed? Sitting in a mansion like a drug lord and ordering hits on the competition? He could easily believe that this ice princess blonde here had killed people, but his sweet little baby sister, too? Sure, if she was defending herself, but...

His mind swirled so much that he was getting a headache.

Chapter Four

THEY HAD BEEN PASSING mainly trees and fields. The fields had all sported either cattle or crops. Nothing was overgrown and fallow. It was all being utilized. Now they were coming into more and more buildings, and then they were past them and back into fields and trees. And it was clean! He was, sadly, accustomed to the absolute trash pile that Los Angeles and all of Southern California that he had seen had become.

Trash and ashes, that is. The Santa Ana winds swept in and carried a random spark all over the area, to ignite dry brush and houses alike. It occurred repeatedly. Not that that was unusual. All of the cities had burned to some extent, but in L.A.'s case, the long dry seasons combined with the high winds to create firestorms.

As Antonio and Megan peered out the window, Taylor said "This is called Crossroads. The houses and buildings around the train station are just collectively called The Station. We're back to the Middle Ages as far as cities go. It's a series of villages now, so people can live close to the fields and livestock that they tend. Obviously, we do have trucks now, so they don't have to live within walking distance, but there's no reason not to, either. Big things like schools and churches and businesses are concentrated in Mainside. The villages don't have little one-room schoolhouses and tiny churches of their own."

She thought for a minute before she went on.

"It's good. People are separated and not all jammed up together. We don't have ten people living in the same house any more. That led to a lot of personality conflicts. But then everyone comes together in one place for most things. Friday nights, Saturdays, Sundays, there are lots of things going on in Mainside then.

"You probably had the same thing in California, but without television and the Internet and video games, people make their own entertainment. There are concerts and plays and sports competitions going on all the time. And reading, if none of that appeals. We put a lot of effort and expense into our libraries. Dani is very proud of them. We have trivia competitions and spelling bees and crossword puzzle contests."

She went silent after that, not talking or naming off any more of the villages. They went through another three or four, depending on how big a cluster of buildings qualified as a village.

Taylor stopped the cars fifty or sixty yards from the house, since Dani was at home, taking a day off with her baby. The place was actually fairly small, maybe a thousand square feet or a bit larger, with two stories. But it was new and well-kept, with huge windows and crisp blue-gray paint with white trim. It was set in a wide clearing, surrounded at a distance by pine and oak trees, with a pond in back. There was a large garage off to the side with a matching color scheme. But Antonio didn't have much time to study his surroundings. The tough, no-nonsense blonde was back. She'd softened a bit on the drive but she had it dialed back up now.

"I want you to stand right here and face the house." She turned to the cops who had followed them. "Keep him here unless it's okay. I don't want him to charge Dani."

She took a deep breath and marched inside. The next few minutes might be rough on Dani, but it was going to be considerably rougher on the man claiming to be Antonio if he was lying. Well, she had warned him.

Stepping through the door, she called Dani's name in a low voice. She didn't want to be loud and wake the baby. Good move. Dani came out of the master bedroom upstairs and leaned over the railing with a finger to her lips to be quiet. She closed the door and padded downstairs.

She was immediately concerned when she saw the look on Taylor's face.

"What's wrong?"

"It may be something good. We have a man here claiming to be your brother." Taylor held out the ID cards.

Dani grabbed them and held them with fingers that now trembled. She looked at the cards and then clutched them to her breast in both hands. Eyes closed, she took a couple of deep breaths. When she opened them again, they were wide and wet with tears.

"He's here? He looks like this?"

Taylor shrugged. "It could be. These photos are the typical crappy ID card type. It's hard to tell. Look, grab the binoculars or something. I've got him standing out in the yard."

Dani ran to the window and parted the blinds. She stared for a few long seconds, then turned and ran up the stairs to the master bedroom. She slowed down long enough to ease through the door to not disturb the baby and emerged with a pair of binoculars.

Back at the window, she adjusted the focus and froze again. She stepped back, closed her eyes for a quick prayer, and then looked through the blinds again. She made a little cry and ran out the door, dropping the binoculars on the couch as she raced by. Taylor followed but stopped on the porch.

Antonio saw her and started to take a step forward but stopped when the cops beside him bowed up, ready to grab him or go for their guns. But then they looked at Taylor and saw that she was using both arms and making a wide 'come on' gesture like she was guiding an eighteen-wheeler backing up. By the time the cops told him he could go, it was almost beside the point. Dani reached him and crashed into him, barely slowing before impact.

Tears streamed down both of their faces. Dani kept her head buried in his chest for a minute, then pulled back, wiped the tears away, and stared into his face. She ran a thumb along a long scar that traced his jawline, one she hadn't seen before. He took her left arm and straightened it out so he could get a look at the tattoos that covered most of it. He shook his head in wonder at all of the changes, and murmured "My little Dani." His voice broke in the middle, and they both descended into body-shaking sobs while they clung to each other, mourning their deceased parents and siblings.

Taylor moved around in the background, as usual, making things happen. She thanked the Security personnel and retrieved the luggage.

"I imagine there are going to be people wanting to welcome Dani's brother, but I don't want them bothered tonight," she told them. "I think we need a Security detail on the driveway here. Turn people away, but courteously. Tell them we'll do a meet-and-greet on Saturday, late afternoon. They'll spend the night at the VIP guest house, so we'll need the detail to move over there later tonight. If you can arrange all that I'd appreciate it."

She and her people helped Megan get the kids and the luggage into the house and then rode back to the office in the SUV. She broke the news to the office staff and told them to put out the word that the right time to welcome Dani's brother was Saturday afternoon, not before. Then she made sure the VIP guest house was made ready — aired out, beds made with fresh sheets, and flowers on the dresser. There wasn't room for them at Dani's house, even if Taylor moved out of her bedroom. There was only a single bed in a small room there, hardly enough for a man and a woman and two kids.

Eric was in Austin, coming back tomorrow afternoon. Taylor got a message out to him, encoded as all of their communications were, via radio. Whether it would actually get to him was another question. He was always on the go.

She worked with Ted for a couple of hours on their project and then showed up at the house driving an SUV with an ice chest of beer and a couple bottles of wine in the back. She had supper wrapped in heavy butcher paper, tamales and charro beans from one of the local eateries. She had given a couple of other restaurants a head's up to cater the food for Saturday, barbecue brisket and sides, plus desserts from the bakery, and placed orders for the brewery and the winery to supply alcohol. They spread their business around to all of the local establishments as evenly as they could.

Dani and Megan were upstairs with all three kids, and Antonio was downstairs alone, sitting on the couch with a beer in his hand when she came through the door.

"Hi," he said. He looked considerably more relaxed than earlier. Not being worried that he was going to be beaten or killed in the next few moments may have had something to do with that.

"Hi, there. Can you assist?" Taylor pointed a thumb over her shoulder.

They got the ice chest and the food inside to the kitchen and then Taylor leaned up against the counter and looked at him.

"Antonio, I was hard on you back at the station but I'm not going to apologize. That's the way it had to be right then. I didn't know if you were some fraud or assassin or what. But I want that to be in the past. I want us to be friends."

"There's no hard feelings," he assured her. "Like I said back there, thank you for protecting my little sister."

He extended his hand and they shook. It wasn't an unfamiliar concept to him. His drill instructors in boot camp had been hard on him, but it had been the necessary thing to do at the time. And they hadn't apologized afterwards, either.

She turned to unpack the food and he grabbed a fresh beer out of the ice chest.

"A beer for you?" he asked.

"Yes. Thank you."

He opened one and set it on the counter within her reach. Then he watched her for a moment before asking, "What if I had been a fraud? A shallow grave for me?" half-jokingly. He had a couple of beers under his belt and she hadn't shot him earlier, so he was feeling his oats a bit.

25

Finished with her chore, she turned to meet his eyes, giving an abbreviated shake of her head.

"Strip the body naked. Leave it in an open field not too far from the tree line, maybe fifteen or twenty yards. The turkey buzzards get to it during the day. Coyotes and wild dogs and feral hogs will be on it during the night. There's nothing left in the morning." She shrugged. "Maybe some hair." Then she smiled back at him, a light, a soul, coming into her eyes that had not been there a second ago.

Antonio gulped. He felt like a mouse that has grown complacent and ventured out too far, to end up face to face with a cat. Taylor's big green eyes, staring unflinchingly straight into his, seemed a little too appropriate. And she was so quick and matter-of-fact with her answer that he was sure it was from actual knowledge, not just theory. His mouth seemed to have a mind of its own and he heard himself ask "You can do that here?"

"Oh, no. We have laws, courts, prosecutors, all of that. But I would do *anything* to protect Dani."

The soul-light was gone from her eyes again. For a couple of seconds, Antonio was completely still, not moving a muscle, still feeling like the mouse that is afraid to move, because then the cat would pounce. Sudden noises behind him made him startle and turn to look for the source. He wasn't a jumpy person but he had jumped then. It was only Dani and Megan coming downstairs. He glanced back at Taylor and she was looking past him with a smile and dancing eyes for Dani.

Beyond the age of twelve or fourteen, I don't think I was ever scared of anyone, he thought. *Cautious around some people, yeah. Scared, no. I knew some people might beat my ass, but that was just a fact of life. But this girl? Shit, I think I'm scared of her! I hope Dani's got her on a tight leash. She might need to be reeled in a little.*

Chapter Five

ANTONIO HAD PUT ALMOST six years into the Marine Corps and was technically on leave. The status of service members was finally being sorted out. For years they had been kept on duty regardless of when their enlistment was supposed to be up. There were plenty of horror stories in which people had a week or even a matter of days left before they were due to leave the military when Hexen hit. That national emergency had put all separations from service on hold and had called up the National Guard and Reserves.

After four years, it wasn't an emergency any longer. It was simply reality. This is how the world was, now. In Antonio's case, he had almost five months of accumulated leave built up. At the end of that time, he could return to his unit, join a different unit somewhere else, or simply not go back if he was so inclined. His enlistment would be up.

He and Megan did have to figure out what they were going to do, however. They already knew the fate of her family since she was a California girl. This trip was to find out about his, and more intriguingly, to run down the 'Dani' rumors.

***

That first night, they had talked for hours. Megan had gone to the VIP house early, to put the kids to bed. There were offers to have someone babysit, but she wasn't about to leave them with a stranger, at some other house a mile down the road.

Antonio didn't get there until close to midnight. He'd have stayed longer, but Dani had told him she had to go to sleep.

"Or try to sleep, I should say. You know what it's like with a newborn. But you're here now. We'll have plenty of time to talk."

They had hugged, and Taylor had given him a ride. She had emerged from her room a bit more casually dressed now, in a t-shirt that was a couple of sizes too big for her. It was likely something that she slept in, and she'd been getting a little nap. Her yawn would have been a clue.

As she walked into the open concept kitchen/living room area, she had both arms behind her back, one hiking up the shirttail and the other inserting her pistol into the holster. For a couple of seconds, the material was stretched tight against her breasts, and Antonio's quick glance seemed to indicate she wasn't wearing a bra. His male instincts operated naturally and he started to take a closer look, but then he mentally kicked himself, hard. He was a happily married man with two kids, and he most certainly did not need to be checking out his sister's... sister? Did that make her his sister, too? Relationships were complicated now. Maybe dopt, that odd word that was the local slang, was the right way to go.

But no, he did not need to think about the very hot girl that lived with his sister. Even if he had been single, she was probably pretty dangerous.

I'd bet that pistol is always on her hip, he thought. *Or on her nightstand, if she's asleep. That's a pretty wicked looking blade she carries, too. I wonder if there's anyone around here who's brave enough to be her boyfriend.*

Once in the truck, he smiled at her. "You're on call twenty-four-seven, aren't you?"

"It's actually better now than what it was when we first started," she replied. "Everything was down. Everything was broken," she continued. "We had to secure our ranch and take in refugees to work the nearby farms and ranches.

Dani told you that. But we also had to meet all of the local groups and set up agreements and diplomatic relations, for lack of a better term. Like legal jurisdictions. Y'all enforce the law over there on that side of the county road; we'll do it here on this side. Or we'll send our youngsters to your elementary school and you can send your older kids to our junior and high schools. Things like that.

"We had to set up everything. Road maintenance. Waste disposal. Police. Fire stations. Courts to enforce laws. A train station. Communications. And once people started setting up their own businesses like restaurants and breweries, we had to make sure things were sanitary and suitable for human consumption."

"And a bank? Dani mentioned something about running a bank?"

"We have three banks, actually. Marshall, Austin, and Wichita Falls. And the governor has a lot of assignments for Eric, so he's gone a lot. That leaves Dani to manage everything. That's kind of a tradeoff. He did the big land grant to us and has provided us with a lot of things, but he's also saddled us with groups of refugees. Like dropping a thousand of them on us at a time, with damned little warning. There was a time when my whole life seemed to be spent getting outhouses built."

She turned to look at him, and he could see in the illumination of the dashboard lights that she crossed her eyes and stuck out her tongue. He laughed, more in surprise than anything else.

The ice princess acts silly on occasion? he wondered, then thought *God, she's like eighteen years old. She should be a high school senior or college freshman. She deserves to act silly sometimes.* He focused his attention back on what she was saying.

"Trey, the governor, has kind of kidnapped Eric as a troubleshooter. He sends him all over the state, and even outside of it, to fix things. A lot of people in government just want to do studies and proposals and talk about things endlessly. Bureaucrats, you know. Eric is an action guy. He will tell high-level government people to stop talking and start working, right now. Early on, he threatened one group that he would draft them into the Texas Army National Guard and put them in the front line in a battle against a narco gang if they didn't make a decision by the end of the day. He got their boot sizes. At five o'clock, he showed up with two sergeants carrying boxes of boots."

Antonio laughed at that, too. "That's hilarious. I can think of people I'd like to do that to. A lot of people. Did they have a decision?"

"Damned right, they did. It didn't take many incidents like that before Eric got a reputation as a hatchet man and people started to make things happen on their own so that they would never meet him. The other side of that coin is that businesspeople just about stand in line to meet him because they know he can get things done. Plus being the governor's buddy doesn't hurt any. That means that we're ending up in a lot of partnerships, like with the banks and oil companies.

"We have Marten Oilfield Security that provides guards and food, mainly, to oil and gas operations. You have to feed your workers or you won't have any workers. Then you have to secure the product so no one steals it. And you have to police the workers so they're not fighting or whatever. We do all that, and since the oil companies couldn't pay us in money at the beginning, we took shares of stock. We've also bought more stock, so the Marten companies own considerable chunks of the major oil companies that are in the biggest oil-producing state in the U.S. If any oil companies make money, it's going to be these."

Antonio shook his head in amazement.

"Every time you or Dani tells me something, it's incredible. This ranch, the banks, the oil companies, just everything. I get the impression that my sister and her husband are very rich and influential."

"It's would take a couple hours just to tell you about all of the pies that Eric and Dani have their fingers in. A lot of it is things we don't even make any money on, but we're trying to help someone start their own business. But we all work our asses off. And here is the VIP guest house."

She cut the headlights as she turned into the driveway, leaving the parking lights on. There was a police vehicle parked in front of the house, and a uniformed young lady appeared, walking towards the truck.

"Hop out", Taylor told Antonio. "I'll get you cleared with Security. I put them on the house so y'all could get a good night's sleep, but I'll pull them off tomorrow at noon. You need anything, tell them. I have breakfast coming in the morning and I'll see what Dani wants to do. You coming here will undoubtedly screw up her schedule, but sleep late if you want. I'll come by at lunch. Oh, and the lights and showers work at this house. We manage to generate some electricity."

"Thanks. You really do take care of everything."

She smiled tiredly, twiddled her fingers at him, and turned to talk to the Security officer. They obviously knew each other, from the familiar greetings that they exchanged, and then put their heads together to talk.

I'll bet Megan thinks she's an A number one bitch, but she's just being fiercely protective of Dani. Antonio thought. *I like her. She's like some of the hardass sergeants I've known. The tough as nails guys, the ones who won't cut you any slack, but will damned sure deliver for you. They can make things happen. People like that are the backbone of any organization.*

But I am still curious about all of those stories about gunfights and everything.

Chapter Six

ANTONIO WAS DRINKING COFFEE on the porch of the house early the next morning when he heard gunfire. He was experienced enough to tell that it was target practice and not a gunfight. A gunfight is messy and sporadic and goes in waves. If the opponents are far enough away from each other, the sounds will come from different places, different angles and echoes. Range fire, on practice targets, is more orderly even when the shots from different rifles overlap.

It didn't seem like the range was too far away, maybe just beyond a field and a patch of woods. He'd spent a lot of time travelling lately, and he needed a good run to stretch his muscles out. He ducked inside long enough to tell Megan where he was going, told the Security guy in the driveway that he was taking a run, and started hoofing it.

About a mile down the road, there was a gate with a 'Range 1' sign and a red flag. That meant that the range was hot, with people firing at targets. He followed the road through a little patch of woods, to come out near a roofed firing line. Taylor was there, sketching something on a clipboard, with an attentive arc of young girls around her.

Suddenly, one of the girls noticed him and screamed "Stranger! Stranger!"

At the first word, Taylor let go of the clipboard and pen and spun, drawing her pistol. She had her sights on Antonio and her finger on the trigger before the clipboard hit the ground.

He threw his hands up and called back "Friendly! Friendly!"

Recognizing him, Taylor lowered her pistol, but it still seemed to point uncomfortably towards his balls. She turned her head and said "It's fine. He's a friend. Hands off weapons."

Antonio realized that two of the girls had gone for the rifles that lay on the shooting tables behind them. He thought he was probably lucky he hadn't been shot to rags.

Taylor holstered her pistol and straightened up out of the shooting stance she had assumed. "Girls, take a break," she ordered.

She walked towards Antonio with a little smile. It was a smile like he had probably given to young Marines when they had made an honest mistake because they didn't know the correct procedure and he was about to educate them.

"Walk with me," she said, and headed for the gate, leading him back out.

"Sorry, I didn't know I was interrupting," he apologized.

Taylor took a deep breath, held it, then let it out slowly, decompressing from the adrenaline shot she had gotten when she thought there was danger.

"No problem. These are some girls I'm mentoring. Everyone has their own horror story about Hexen. These girls either had some extra trauma to go along with that, or it just hit them particularly hard. They're twelve and thirteen years old. They were around eight when their worlds ended. I don't even know what some of them went through. If they don't volunteer the information, then you don't ask. You do know that, don't you?" She looked at him intently.

"Yeah, we had the same thing in California. If someone needs their alone time, their cry time, you let them have it. You don't ask about someone's family, not unless you know them awfully well and know that they have a newborn daughter or something like that."

"Good. Anyway, I think it helps these girls to accomplish something, and also to learn to defend themselves. So, I train them to shoot. We give everyone a firearms safety class, but this is beyond that."

Antonio smiled at her. "You're the mother hen, aren't you? Or the mother lioness, I should say. You're concerned about these girls, you're concerned about

Dani, keeping everyone safe." He reached out and squeezed her bicep. "Don't take the weight of the world on your shoulders. Especially not this world. It's too much. You'll worry yourself to death."

They took a few more steps before Taylor spoke again.

"Maybe you don't realize how fragile it all is. There could be a wildfire, a tornado, some gang bigger and badder than us, maybe mad cow disease that kills off all the cattle. We're on the high wire and there's no safety net below us. Things could change in an instant and we'd all be out in the cold. That's what happened with Hexen. We thought we were in such a great position, we were fat and lazy and just looking for things that 'offended' us. That was all gone in a couple of weeks. Here, now, we may look like we're safe, but things are balanced on a razor's edge. You're damned right I'm worried."

They'd reached the gate and she put a hand on it, looking off into the distance, turned partly away from Antonio.

Lower, almost to herself, she said "I'd have made a good big sister." She reached a hand up to her eye, maybe to wipe away a tear, but he couldn't tell. "No, that's not right," she continued. "Back then, I'd have sucked as a big sister." She turned abruptly to face him. Her eyes were blazing with determination even as a tear raced down her cheek.

"I have dozens of little sisters now and I am damned worried about keeping them safe." She turned and started back towards the firing line.

"Taylor, I'm sorry. I didn't mean to interfere or anything." His voice kind of trailed off as she kept walking, not interested in hearing what he had to say.

As he walked back towards the house, he thought *I'm an idiot. I thought Taylor was this tough ice princess and that was her whole personality. But really, she's desperately trying to keep people safe in this little Hell we've managed to create. She's a hell of a lot deeper than I gave her credit for.*

Chapter Seven

ONE OF THE EARLY discussions was about the gunfights Antonio was so curious about, and it was a painful one.

Dani had killed a lot of people. She was neither proud nor ashamed of that fact. She had very good reasons for each and every one of them. Men had tried to rape her, had attempted to kidnap her, had succeeded in kidnapping her once, and had threatened her and Eric and their people and everything they had worked for. With no police and no legal system in place, they had only themselves to go to for defense.

And they had defended themselves. Thoroughly. Eric's philosophy was that if a group or gang attacked them, they had crossed a line and the only answer was to kill them all. There was no running away for them afterwards or surrendering or negotiating a truce. No mercy for the enemy. If they had attacked you once, they could do it again. Kill them all now and be done with it. There was no sense in killing some and allowing the survivors to come after you in the future, once they had built up their strength and could attack when you were at a disadvantage.

Antonio seemed fascinated by the stories he had heard but had always been certain that they were wild exaggerations. He asked about them and Dani tried to brush him off. She wasn't interested in talking about them. She was much more interested in the upcoming deals that she had going, in the good works they were doing with training people in trades, with their schools, libraries, and clinics, and expansion of their territory.

"And the books!" she had said one night, excited. "When we made the agreement to sell Texas gold coins to Louisiana at a better discount, we included a long list of items we wanted. One important item was books, and we sent a small delegation to Baton Rouge to make the selection. Basically, we cleared out several book stores, three branch libraries, a couple of high schools, and a junior high school. That's how we built our library." Her eyes were shining. She valued knowledge and was justifiably proud of what they had built.

"You always were smarter than me," he admitted. "How did you get so good with a rifle so quickly, though?"

That was it.

If he had made that comment in isolation it would have been fine, but it was a probe, once again, after several others, and Dani had had enough. Eric knew instantly when Antonio had pushed Dani's patience past the breaking point but didn't know what he could do to quickly defuse the situation.

Dani went still and glared at her brother for a couple of seconds before she spoke.

"If all you want is to hear the stories, then we will tell you all of the stories. One time. One time!" She had one finger held up for emphasis and then she started waving it around. That was bad news, when the finger waving began.

"And you will listen! You want all of the stories; you'll get them all! And then you will stop asking!"

She turned to face Eric and took a moment to soften her expression. She wasn't mad at him.

"Please pour me a glass of wine." She had not been drinking since she was nursing, but Eric was not about to argue with her at this point. He got up and poured the wine.

Dani next turned to Taylor, who had been attempting to slip out of the room quietly.

"Taylor, could you do me a really big favor? Could you grab your journals and give my very annoying brother a summary of each and every one of the gunfights? All of them. Start with Eric's, right after Hexen. Don't stop."

After delivering the wine to his wife, Eric grabbed two beers, one of which he handed to Taylor as she came by. She took it without missing a step and mouthed a "thank you".

He'd been delighted to meet Antonio when he returned from Austin. He knew how devastated Dani had been after losing her whole family. His parents had both passed on, years before Hexen, but he'd lost friends, and that had hit hard enough. He couldn't imagine all of that grief, all at once. He liked Antonio, and valued him not only as a trusted ally, but as a fellow Marine.

He needed good people. He hoped this wasn't going to cause a rift.

Chapter Eight

HEXEN.

The avian flu had flared up in China and had spread incredibly quickly in the densely populated Yangtze delta, the Pearl River Delta, and on the Chengdu Plain of the western Sichuan Basin. It differed from previous avian flus in that it transferred easily from human to human via airborne transmission. It was also much more deadly: ninety percent fatality rates instead of the typical sixty.

The Chinese government had tried to suppress news of the disaster, which only made it worse, by robbing scientists of the opportunity to combat the threat. Whether that lost time would have mattered or not was something for future historians to decide. Judging by the speed of the spread of Hexen and the rapid fatality, probably not. The scientists at the Center for Disease Control had not even had the time to properly classify the virus. An intermediate, temporary name, HXN2, had been converted to "Hexen" and the name stuck.

Hexen infections grew geometrically. A single infected person walking down a city street, or in an airport, or in any area near others, would infect dozens if not hundreds. Each of those would then cut their own swath of destruction, through their commute or school or place of business.

Once the threat became known, panic ensued.

People fled the cities, or they sealed themselves in their houses and cut off all contact with others. Neither strategy worked. Those in their homes simply died more comfortably, usually in their beds, driven there by the headache and high fever that soon boiled the brain and killed them.

Those that fled usually found themselves in immense traffic jams that went nowhere. The roads simply weren't designed for so many people to be on them at the same time, and the inevitable wrecks and breakdowns plugged lanes and brought everything to an absolute standstill.

Then the EMP hit and killed all of the electronics. That meant all of the cars built since about 1990.

Electro Magnetic Pulse is formed when nuclear weapons are detonated at high altitudes. There is no damage from the blast and heat and concussion, but a pulse goes out over huge distances, a thousand miles or more in every direction, and fries all of the electronic circuitry. Our digital society went from the twenty-first century back to the eighteenth in less than a second. No lights. No Internet. No phones. No clean, safe, hot, running water. No newer computer-equipped cars, trucks, motorcycles, or aircraft.

The people who were driving away from contact with others now found themselves walking on the sides of the highways with crowds of people. Ironic. Many went off into the grassy medians or the woods or the desert or beach or whatever scenery was beside the road, set up camp, and died there instead of in their nice, warm beds. The rest walked to... wherever. Few made it.

Even four years later, no one knew much information about those two events, or if they knew they weren't telling. Hexen may have been natural or a bioweapon. On the one hand, avian flus had been growing more readily transferrable from birds to humans and there had been increasingly frequent cases of human-to-human transmission. On the other hand, the easy transmission and increased virulence may have been the result of an engineered weapon.

The EMP was less of a question. It was apparently manmade. It would have been a fantastic coincidence if a solar event had caused it in the midst of the Hexen outbreak. The popular opinion was that some military power had purposely detonated the device or devices. Perhaps China had mistaken Hexen as an American attack and had retaliated with the EMP. That led to the fear, which persisted for years, of Chinese tanks and troops coming over the horizon at any minute.

Fortunately, they never did.

The entire world had apparently been struck by both Hexen and the EMP. The more temperate countries suffered the worst effects of the virus, since it was perhaps inhibited somewhat by cold weather, but the colder climates then had the little problem of freezing to death in the dark once winter came.

Hexen ripped through the world in a matter of weeks, five or six for the most part, a couple of weeks more if you count the really remote areas. The first few weeks it was China, seeping gradually into Asia, and then exploding across the rest of the world. The EMP hit just as the virus burned out in the U.S.

The survivors were apparently naturally immune. There were no vaccines, no prophylactics, no regimes of isolation that had saved anyone. Ninety percent dead. No family, no race, no group was left whole.

The EMP was also apparently worldwide, which argued for multiple weapons, or one weapon with effects that went far beyond the theoretical capabilities. Of course, that was the central problem with EMP weapons — they can't be tested.

If a weapon affects everything within a couple of thousand miles, where can it be tested? In the 1950s and '60s, Soviet and NATO countries attempted tests that always seemed to have effects much greater than expected. Electrical power in cities was burned out, supposedly shielded test equipment was fried, and the physicists scratched their heads.

Chapter Nine

Eric Marten, in his mid-twenties, had been visiting an old Marine buddy and his wife in Katy, Texas, near Houston, when Hexen and then the EMP hit. They died. He did not. He had tried to care for them during the brief illness before death, but, as people worldwide found out, nothing could be done.

He started making his way back home and met Dani. Daniela Angelina Ruiz Vasquez was eighteen, fleeing a bad neighborhood in Houston with a backpack and her mother's biggest butcher knife for protection. Her parents were Colombian and had fled the violence of the drug traffickers and FARC guerillas. Although a licensed medical doctor in his home country, her father was unable to get a residency in the U.S. and so the family had to settle for lowered circumstances.

Eric saw three gangstas breaking into an SUV and fighting someone inside. He had no idea who, but knew that if he didn't stop the attack, no one would. This hadn't been a situation where some strong words would have deterred the men. If he had tried, they'd have casually shot him and carried on with what they were doing. He was faced with either avoiding the situation, or winning the fight.

He also knew that if you ever find yourself in a fair fight, then you have planned poorly.

That encounter ended badly for the gangstas, mainly since Eric was not a poor planner. He evened the odds by shooting two of them before they even knew he was there. He put the third one down seconds later, while the man was trying to draw a pistol.

Eric's jaw dropped open when a hot little Latina with long, dark hair and golden eyes stepped out of the vehicle. Then his mouth ran away with him, inviting her to come with him to his house.

She was scared of him at first because she had just seen him kill three men, but the reason he had done it was to save her. And she had determined, right then and there, that she needed someone to teach her how to defend herself. He had just shown some degree of skill in weapons and tactics, so she went with him. The fact that he was tall and handsome didn't hurt a bit.

From the Houston area to East Texas, two hundred miles, they'd walked and ridden bikes. And they'd talked and practiced shooting and maneuvering like a military squad. They'd put the training to use several times as they were attacked by bandits along the way.

Dani had actually been the winning factor in all of those encounters. She had been the first to spot the danger and had proven to be the decisive factor in defeating the threat.

Taylor had kept journals of all of the things that they had gone through. She knew that someday she would write a book, or several, with the history of Dani and Eric. They would be like the old pioneers. They would be the rebuilders. And now Dani wanted her to bring out her journals and read them aloud.

That had been an emotional night. Dani sat and drank wine and glared at Antonio for the longest time, but periodically she broke down into tears, reminded of the death of a friend or a tough time.

Eric sat beside her and held her. Megan excused herself early in the process and didn't return from checking on the three kids, who were all laid out on the master bed. She had heard enough pretty quickly.

Antonio was aghast and in tears himself at the end.

"Now tell him yours," Dani commanded Taylor, back to glaring at her brother.

"No, you don't have to —" Antonio had tried to stop her.

"Be quiet and listen!" Dani had hissed through clenched teeth, her eyes flashing, and so Antonio had gotten the entire story of Taylor's kills, too.

Antonio was drained at the end of it all. They all were, even with the sparse summaries that Taylor was relating, devoid of the majority of the details. She spoke in her normal voice, which was what Eric called her 'Dallas rich girl' accent. It was no accent at all, really, a precise way of speaking without a drawl or a twang, and without dropping any letters like the "g" at the end of a word or a "t" in the middle of one. She could have been giving the evening news or weather forecast on TV. But she wasn't. She was relating gunfights and the deaths of human beings.

"Eric and Dani were seeking water in a subdivision when a man with a shotgun got the drop on them and tried to kidnap Dani. She appeared to go along with him willingly until she got close enough that he had to raise the shotgun barrel. At that point she drew her weapon and shot him multiple times" did not convey the knee-shaking fear that comes with someone pointing a loaded weapon at you. It does not highlight the frustration and helplessness when a girl that you were protecting is being forcibly taken away to be raped. It omits the raging adrenaline, the loud gunfire, the blood, the weight of being responsible for the termination of a man's life. The summaries were a drop compared to the ocean of the reality of the event.

And the stories kept coming and coming and coming.

Antonio hugged Dani, who cried a little.

"I am so sorry," he said. "I am so sorry you had to go through all that. I had no idea. I thought the stories I'd heard were wild exaggerations. I could have never guessed that the opposite is true. The stories don't mention half of what you went through. I will never bring any of it up again. I can only ask for your forgiveness."

He apologized to Eric and Taylor, shook his hand, and hugged her. She seemed to have a tear in her eye, too, and she kept clearing her throat.

If this girl turns into an ice princess sometimes, she damned well deserves it, he thought. *Maybe she is a little bent, but who wouldn't be after what she's gone through? I saw full-grown Marines have mental breakdowns after going through less than this girl did when she was fifteen years old.*

He reflected on his own experiences. The time after Hexen and the EMP had been horrific for everyone — the deaths of ninety percent of the people around you, the dread that you were next, and the failure of everything electronic. Leadership was dead, dying, or confused and without orders or precedent for the situation.

He and his fellow Marines had been thrown about erratically, ordered here and there, trying to handle a thousand emergencies without the manpower needed for one. Food, water, and alcohol became items that, overnight, people were willing to kill to get or to keep. Next it seemed the thing to fight over was territory for drug deals or safety zones for armed civilians.

Then a lot of people seemed to view the whole situation as an opportunity to settle old debts, or vent their prejudices, or make the world a better place by ridding it of whomever, fill in the blank. And there were apparently a lot of anarchists that would snipe at any uniform, be it police, fireman, military, or UPS man. Not that any delivery drivers were dedicated enough to remain on the job after the end of the world.

Antonio had, therefore, been under fire and had returned it. He was sure of three kills and a probable fourth, but the situations had all been different from the ones that the Martens had been through. Theirs were much closer combat. His close combat had been less, since few people were crazy enough to take on a fire team or squad of Marines. A guy and a girl, sure, they'd go after them up close and personal. With Marines, they were more likely to pop off a shot at some distance and then run like hell or lay low until the Marines had left the area.

That made it more difficult to confirm a kill. Antonio's experience had been that he and his fellow Marines would shoot at someone and then they may find three bodies. Who, specifically, had killed them? With four or twelve or however many Marines shooting, who fired the fatal shots? Either that or they found only blood trails. Was that someone that was barely hit? Critically hit and crawling off to die somewhere, or being carried by companions? Was that blood left by one or two people? Or maybe the situation was such that they never investigated the shooter's location. In that case there was no telling if someone was dead or unhurt but discouraged from fighting or what.

Even if you tripled Antonio's kills, including the probable, the number paled against Dani's or Eric's. It was not even worth mentioning. Almost embarrassing, in fact. Taylor had twenty-two, over five times Antonio's number even if you included the possible fourth, and she had gotten those at the age of fifteen. And she had gone up against multiple opponents alone, more than once. Antonio had been in the midst of other Marines, all of them heavily armed, and he was confident of their training and knew how they would react.

It boggled his mind. He already respected all three of them, Eric, Dani, and Taylor. Now his level of respect went sky-high.

And pride in his little sister made his chest swell. Tears flooded his eyes, then, and Taylor quietly slipped out of the room to let brother and sister cry together.

Eric walked out on the little porch and sat, looking at the stars and fighting the mosquitos. The house only had two bedrooms. He couldn't really hang out in Taylor's, and Megan and the kids were in the other at the moment. That left him the porch.

That was fine. A few mosquito bites was a small price to pay for Dani getting her brother back.

Chapter Ten

ANOTHER NIGHT, ERIC ASKED Antonio about Los Angeles. He didn't have any particular ties to the city. He had been at Twentynine Palms for desert warfare training in the Mojave before deploying to Afghanistan but that was all. It was a general question he asked of anyone who had been somewhere else. The answers all seemed to boil down to the same thing: The cities were dead or dying. The larger cities, that is. The smaller ones were alive.

The first problem had been food. Grocery stores had about three days' worth of food in stock, which expands to thirty days if only ten percent of the population is still alive. But with no more coming in, at some point people have to produce their own. The typical method of doing that was to flee the cities for the countryside, where farms and ranches could provide a steady supply.

Some hardcore city dwellers created gardens and pastures in parks and other grassy areas but these were sufficient for no more than bare subsistence in the majority of cases. No one was going to grow enough food to start selling truckloads of it from a bunch of subdivision yards turned into a farm.

The second issue was transportation. Even if someone got an old truck to run, there were limited routes they could use, with the major roads jammed with dead vehicles. A truckload of cattle was no good to a city if forty miles of bumper-to-bumper traffic jam separated the two.

Next was electricity for things like elevators and water. No one was going to live on the twentieth floor of a building when they had to walk up that many flights of stairs to do anything, including carry water up that far. Some thought that a high perch like that would be secure, but that false security proved treacherous as soon as someone blocked off the stairs and starved them out.

Electricity also did useful things like keep cities from flooding. Washington, D.C., New Orleans, and Houston were all built on swamps and they seemed to be almost eager to return there as quickly as possible. Half of New Orleans is at or under sea level, with some portions twenty feet below. The city is surrounded by levees and, obviously, water has to be pumped out of this bowl when it rains. With the pumps dead, the levees now hold the water in, even in the parts that are above sea level but below the levee. Alligators swim the streets now.

D.C. also has pumps, but they are not as critical as New Orleans. Still, flooding is a reality.

Houston was in a better situation but is still low and flat, and the immense area that is paved means there's less land to soak up rainfall after a major storm. A mere one inch of rainfall can mean a one-foot rise in river levels. A good, slow-moving storm can dump enough precipitation to flood major portions of the city, to say nothing of what a tropical storm or hurricane can do.

Cities that relied on potable water from a distant source died out. Las Vegas, Phoenix, and Los Angeles started returning to the desert on day one.

Northern cities like Minneapolis, lacking electric heat or natural gas, which had been delivered by electric pumps, became largely uninhabitable in the winters.

Simply put, once the electricity died, the big cities died.

People had tried to stay in the cities but it was a losing battle. There was very little to eat there if you didn't like stray cat or dog. The concrete jungles offered little chance of growing crops or raising herds of farm animals. Some eked out an existence for a while, but all it took was one bad turn, one issue, and they were without food.

The states or cities or barons had carved out their territories and established rule of a sort in their areas. The areas outside of those fiefdoms, which covered most of the country, were open, frontier badlands. In many cases the badlands were not out in the boonies. The inner city of all of the major metro areas were badlands, pretty much. There were some forted up areas, called *barricadas* in Texas, even if the inhabitants weren't Latino. It was just the name that stuck.

In centuries past, people had given up farming and animal herding to move into the cities and produce goods other than food. This continued in modern, First World societies until the population in the cities vastly outnumbered the food growers. By 2008, less than two percent of the population of the United States was directly employed in agriculture. This shift from a majority to a tiny minority had taken centuries.

After Hexen and the EMP hit, the shift reversed in a matter of weeks, months at the most. The survivors flooded out of the barren cities into the countryside. Now, four years later, the population was spread out in a series of villages instead of concentrated in cities. The villages surrounded the cities starting at the edges of the far suburbs.

Inside the inner cities, only important facilities were kept functional. In Austin, the governor had deemed it significant to keep the capital building and offices active. Around Houston, Corpus Christi, and other cities, some of the oil and gas operations had been brought back up. Railroads and highways were maintained through the cities. Other facilities were brought up as needed but there was a heavy cost involved in turning people away from food-producing efforts to other things.

Chapter Eleven

THE ARRIVAL OF ANTONIO and Megan didn't bother Taylor. She didn't view them as intruders that took Dani's attention away. The baby had started that, truth be told. Taylor was not maternal at all, just like her mother. She'd never been around babies and didn't particularly like them. They made noise and messes and took up a huge amount of time.

Older kids were different. She liked teaching them. She really enjoyed training the older girls, in their early teens, how to defend themselves. She viewed that as empowering the girls, giving them the ability to survive without having to rely on a man. She also gave a lot of her time to the girls in any way she could, as a mentor, a confidant, a shoulder to cry on, a cheerleader to them whenever they needed one. As a matter of fact, with the baby keeping Dani and Eric up at night, Taylor had taken to spending a lot of nights at one or another of the girl's dorms so she could get a full night's sleep.

Taylor chose a time when Dani's attention was undivided. Megan had all of the kids and was out of earshot.

"I've been thinking about something," she began. "I think I want to take a vacation or something. Temporary duty, maybe."

Dani looked at her closely and put her hand on Taylor's arm.

"Is everything okay?"

"I don't feel like I'm doing a whole lot of good here. You have Megan here now to help with Elena, and I apparently don't have much maternal instinct anyway. As far as everything else, it's gotten kind of routine. We've nailed down a big enough territory that we're safe. The leadership positions are filled. What you need is a bright, responsible young girl that will be great at this job. I even have a candidate in mind."

"But I don't want you to go!" There were tears in Dani's eyes. "I want you to stay here. Look at all we've built. Yes, it's safe now. That means you can enjoy what you're worked so hard for. What you risked your life for, more than once!"

Taylor stepped closer and embraced Dani.

"Temporarily. Not permanent. Not for a long time. Maybe a few months. Maybe just a month gone here and there. I don't know. It depends on what the opportunities are."

"Opportunities for what?"

"Adventure, I guess. That's kind of the way I grew up, right? Never knowing what fresh hell would come over the horizon at any moment." She smiled grimly.

Once Hexen and the EMP hit, they had no information beyond what they had explored or could learn from someone they could talk to face to face. The situation wasn't much better today, but there were radio stations broadcasting to repaired radios or newly made crystal sets. Electrical power was slowly and painfully returning to the most vital areas. Newspapers were back in use, and the trains could carry them across the country. There was some phone service being restored, mainly local. The long-distance involved a lot of yelling and repetition so the other person could understand. Telegraph was better. Computers, cell phones, and the Internet were all things in both the past and the future, but they didn't exist now.

Dani's eyes took on a thousand-yard stare, and her thoughts were transparent. She was a mother now, and beyond that she was responsible, or felt responsible, anyway, for thousands of people. This wasn't a coalition or a cooperative, it was a business, and it was owned by two people: Dani and her husband Eric. They didn't want things to be adventurous. They wanted safe and warm and happy and without conflict. They had cried a thousand tears over the friends they had buried in their cemeteries, and they had both personally removed a number of criminals from this earth.

Taylor had done all that, too, and she also owned a chunk of stock in Marten Cattle Company. She had a vested interest in everything being nice and safe and cozy at the ranch. But youth has always wanted adventure, always wanted to explore, to see the world, to make a mark.

Taylor had grown up as a little rich girl who would probably have become a trophy wife and led a life of shopping and soirees. All of that changed when the world ended. At the tender age of fourteen, her parents were dead and she suddenly had nothing beyond a bike and some clothes in a little backpack. A neighbor woman led her and some other kids out of Dallas, walking past the dead hulks of abandoned cars, trying to find food and avoid rape.

Desperate and starving, she had approached Eric, who was taking on refugees to learn to farm and ranch. He had placed food out in the middle of the road for her to pick up later, like drawing in a feral kitten. The next day Dani had been there with more food, and Taylor and the woman and the other kids had been with them ever since.

Dani and Eric's brilliance had been in organization. The major problem was food. Without that, nothing else mattered. On top of that, with a limited or nonexistent police presence, many people thought that they could do anything they wanted, including murder, rape, and theft.

Eric didn't want to steal from anyone and didn't want to farm or ranch, so he fell back on his Marine Corps training. He organized farmers and ranchers who lived near his east Texas property as instructors and managers, brought in refugees from the cities to learn the skills, and recruited and trained a security force to protect all of them.

They aggressively grew their operation to the point where the acting governor of Texas learned of them. He used their model to push similar operations of his own, to keep people from starving and to give them a home. And as usual for a politician, he looked for ways to remain in office and increase his power.

It didn't take long to realize that virtually all of his rich supporters were either dead or bankrupt, courtesy of the Hexen/EMP twin disasters. That meant that he had to create some rich supporters to replace them.

He had granted title to hundreds of thousands of acres to Marten Cattle Company, MCC for short, and routed refugees fleeing freezing Northern winters to their operation. With more people, they could farm and ranch greater areas. He also paired them with a number of people with interests in rebuilding oil and gas operations, banking, and transportation. In return for providing food and guards, they received shares from the oil companies. They took a much more involved position in banking, opening and running three banks in an arc around the northern and eastern parts of the state.

What made the banks so fantastically lucrative was that Texas had a gold repository. Virtually all of the other states offered only paper money, which was backed by nothing other than trust in the state governments. That trust tended to run fairly low, or in the case of the federal government, nonexistent. The result was that people willingly accepted half or two-thirds of the paper money's face value in return for Texas gold and silver. MCC then took the paper money to the state of Texas, which bought it at a healthy profit. Texas then used the paper money at full face value to buy things from the state that issued the money. That state had to accept it. They couldn't claim that their money wasn't worth the full value because that would cause the real value to sink even lower. On the other hand, Texas could legitimately demand Texas gold as payment when it was selling its products.

When states like Louisiana and Arkansas and others tried to make deals to quietly buy Texas gold at a better exchange rate, the governor sent them to MCC. Dani proved to be a tough negotiator, and offered them good rates in exchange for "some items that were probably just lying around your state, not doing anyone any good." The truth was they actually weren't doing anyone any good now, but Dani's eyes were on the long term. In a couple of deals alone, she acquired more than a hundred million dollars' worth of trains, eighteen-wheelers, military equipment including armored vehicles and artillery, oilfield equipment and supplies, whole libraries of books, and heavy machinery. Of course, most of it wasn't worth that much now, but she had ideas for the future now that they had food and a safe haven. She had grown up poor and was not going to live the rest of her life like that if she could help it.

Taylor, adopted by Eric and Dani, had been right in the middle of everything. She worked as Dani's assistant and knew everything that was going on and that was planned. She and Dani had both been thoroughly trained by Eric and then others in everything that would make them lethal, every type of firearm, explosive, and military weapon that they could reasonably be expected to wield, knife fighting, martial arts of several varieties, and various skills such as first aid, camouflage, use of map and compass, rappelling and rope work, and many other skills. When danger really could pop up at any second, they were good skills to have. Realizing this and never wanting to be helpless again, the two girls had enthusiastically absorbed everything and practiced their skills daily.

Until Dani got pregnant and had to stop. But that wasn't the real reason. It may have accelerated things, but Taylor was getting bored.

And she hadn't killed anyone in a long time.

She wasn't a murderer. Every single one of the men and women she'd killed had been a criminal, most of them actively committing a felony at the time. The damned truth, the guilty pleasure, was that she enjoyed it.

She liked killing criminals. That last one, she had paused to savor the moment. Even now, if she stopped to think about it for too long, she could feel something stirring inside of her. Some movement in an inky black swamp at midnight, a claw or hook or something coming up out of the slime, water dripping down skin stretched tight against protruding bones and ropy muscles. She remembered an insistent voice whispering over and over in the back of her mind for her to enjoy it and she panted and squeezed the trigger and felt something like an orgasm but different.

That had scared her. She had questioned her sanity. She had prowled through the masses of books that Dani had acquired, even before their library was fully functional, to read up on the subject. That had led her to psychopaths, and she had to admit she did have some traits to a greater or lesser degree: charming, intelligent, somewhat arrogant, a belief that the usual rules don't apply to her, and a lack of remorse.

The one that hung her up was that psychopaths are master manipulators. She didn't feel that she was manipulative. She wasn't emotionless. She truly loved Dani and Eric. She would lay down her life for them!

But that had been the end of the gunfights for Taylor. It wasn't any conscious decision or anything, it was just circumstance. They had made their section of the world a safer place. The Security Police had had some small incidents but the area was as safe as anywhere. Prudent people still kept firearms within reach at all times, but that's what made it safe.

And boring.

She and Dani talked about it over the course of the afternoon, and brought Eric into it when he got home. When Taylor told him what she wanted, he stood and gave her a big, long hug.

"I don't want you to go," he stated. "I'd rather you stay here where I can keep you safe. But I realize that there are some things you feel that you have to do, and you won't be satisfied until you do them. I have tried to equip you with the skills and knowledge you need."

He could feel Dani glaring at him. He didn't need to look.

"Can I suggest you do something like going out for a month with Oilfield Security?"

That was the division that, obviously, guarded oil and gas operations, and also the convoys that brought food and supplies in and crude oil and refined products out. The original Marten Cattle Company had diversified into Marten Oilfield Security, Marten Financial Services for the banks, Marten Agricultural Products, and others.

"West Texas. I wouldn't want you to go to the Houston or Corpus areas. Too damned hot and humid. It's just nasty down there. Swarms of mosquitos, sweating all day long."

Taylor tilted her head to the side and back in kind of a head shake.

"Isn't that just a bunch of standing guard duty?"

"It's out on the frontier." He laughed. "What we consider the frontier now. Again. If nothing else it would give you a chance to get your feet wet. See what it's like. You could also do an inspection of the operations. Audit the books. You'd still be working for us. You'd have the authority. What's you next best option? Just wander down the road?"

She thought about that and it made sense. There would be a long train ride to Midland / Odessa in west Texas, about five hundred miles away. That would be something. She had spent all of the past four years in east Texas or in Austin, with a few brief trips to other states.

"The oilfield guys run AK rifles," Eric commented. "Grab five or six out of the armory and do some test-firing. Find one that you like. And I've got a seventy-five-round drum magazine that you can borrow."

Dani was still glaring at him. He might be in trouble later, but Taylor was going to do what Taylor wanted to do. When she had gone after the men that tried to ambush the gold convoy, she had just left a note and disappeared. Eric figured they could fight her or they could help her. She was going either way, so it was best to assist rather than hinder. And he was loaning her the drum, so she had to bring it back. There was a subtle method to his madness.

"What else do I need? Or need to know?" Taylor questioned.

"It's hot and dry. No humidity. Dusty. Make sure you have some big bandannas. If you're riding in a vehicle, like the bed of a truck or the gunner's position, you'll need goggles. Put one bandanna across your face like a bandit. Put another one across the other way, to keep dust off the back of your neck. And wear gloves. And a big hat." Eric had been in the Mojave Desert and in Afghanistan, so he was well-experienced with desert conditions.

"Gloves? You said it was hot."

"You have the choice of being hot or having dust stick to you. Most people choose hot. Find a pair of lightweight gloves."

They discussed equipment some more, mainly what to leave as being too east-specific, like a machete. That wasn't a tool much needed in the west.

At supper, Dani brought up the house plans. Eric's house was fairly tiny, really just something he had built for himself. It had one main bedroom upstairs and a small one downstairs, with one bathroom, also downstairs. Now that they were producing babies, they felt they needed more room. Rather than expand the existing house, they had debated building a new one nearby and using the current one as a guest house. Antonio and Megan would probably move in there. But Dani wanted to reassure Taylor that she would always have a home with them.

"Taylor, in the new house, how do you want to do your room? Or do you want a cute, separate little house nearby?" she asked.

Taylor smiled broadly and showed a touch of color in her cheeks. Pride, maybe?

"Is there going to be a garage?"

Dani looked at Eric to answer. He had just taken in a mouthful of beer, so he jokingly widened his eyes as much as possible and puffed out his cheeks as far as they would go. In answer, he gave a thumbs-up.

Dani turned back to Taylor.

"Yes, a garage."

"How about a garage apartment, then? With a little stairway up the side for a private entrance but I'm right there if you need anything. It doesn't have to be big. Smaller is better, in fact."

That was certainly a change. The house she had grown up in was about six times the size of this one. Her walk-in closets, plural, had been stuffed with clothes and shoes and, to tell the truth, junk. If she had a choice, Taylor would never go back to that lifestyle. She had turned away from it with a vengeance. She almost religiously kept her possessions to a minimum.

Chapter Twelve

Taylor ran shooting drills with her chosen AK, getting a feel for the platform. She had started with several AK rifles and narrowed the choice down to one, which she then started practicing with. The manual of arms varied between every model of rifle and she wanted it to become something she did automatically, without a moment's hesitation to remember which side the safety was on or how to run the bolt or change magazines.

The AR and the AK were very different as far as the controls went. The AR had the safety and the bolt release on the left, the magazine release on the right, and the charging handle in the rear. The AK had the safety and the charging handle/bolt release on the right and the magazine release on the bottom behind the magazine. This did allow for the 'AK mag change'. Instead of dropping the magazine with the right and grabbing a fresh one with the left, as with the AR, you grabbed the new magazine first and jammed it against the mag release to drop the old one and sweep it out of the way. Then the new one could be rocked and locked in, versus the straight-in and up of the AR. But the fact remained that the controls were very different between the two.

So far, she preferred the AR. The AK fired a bigger round and was potentially more deadly, but it was kind of a crude bit of machinery. The one thing she liked was the folding stock that made it a much handier package. The AR had a buffer tube that stuck out from the back and precluded a folding stock, or one that collapsed any meaningful amount. There were some aftermarket devices that allowed an AR to fold, but she just didn't like the idea of introducing a third-party hinge in the middle of a rifle mechanism. If it came from the manufacturer that way, then okay. Otherwise, no.

She took a break and thought about something Dani has said. She didn't want Taylor to go, but she was perhaps coming around to the idea. This morning at breakfast she had suggested going to see their Oklahoma operations. They subcontracted these operations to a company headquartered in Oklahoma City. Dani had mentioned that she could go up there for a few days to get a feel for how they ran things. Taylor suspected that the "few days" part was what Dani was really pushing. Give Taylor a little travel, a little change of scenery, and she'll come back with a new appreciation for the ranch.

That was fine, a great idea, in fact. Eric would be the first to admit that he didn't know everything and that he was always willing to see how else things might be done. She might learn something that would be great to implement here. She would suggest that she and Dani write a letter to go out on the train tomorrow to set up a visit. A week should be enough notice, and they could get a reply back in two or three days if she needed to reschedule.

Chapter Thirteen

Riding the rails was the best form of long-distance travel currently available. Sure, there were some older light airplanes that lacked newer electronics and still ran, or ones that had been retrofitted. The problem was that the entire flight-related infrastructure was gone or pushed back most of a century. There were no reliable weather forecasts and no GPS navigation.

Even avoiding bad weather and successfully using a map and compass didn't guarantee that the destination airfield was maintained, had fuel, or had any services at all. It may not even have something as simple as a windsock to show wind direction for landing purposes. And if you found the place and landed safely, the local commander of the Air National Guard or some other self-important official may confiscate your aircraft 'for the duration of the emergency'.

Things would get better, and progress was being made, but air travel was dangerous at best. Trains were a different story. Man had been able to run trains for well over two hundred years, figuring out how to share rails and switch tracks and schedule runs without cell phones and electronics. Weather didn't matter all that much, and GPS wasn't required since they had to follow the rails.

It wasn't that difficult to create passenger cars, if none were available, from existing boxcars. As long as you had the frame, the railcar carriage, you could build anything you wanted to on top. It was just like building an RV on a truck frame, and people had been doing that for almost as long as cars and trucks had existed.

And so, Taylor got a ride to Marten Station and rode to Oklahoma City, by way of Dallas-Fort Worth, on a train in a private compartment in relative luxury. Valentina was waiting for her, having received the head's up last week via mail, which also went by train.

Valentina Mendez Hernández was tall and slender and exuded a hot, smoky Latina sexuality just standing there with only a little makeup on, and dressed in comfortable work clothes, nothing that was tight or revealing. She kept her raven-black hair long, and had a ready smile for Taylor. They had first met when Valentina had taken an assignment from her boss to extradite a fugitive from Kansas and deliver him to the Martens in Texas. It had sounded like a simple task.

It was not.

The fugitive had friends that were determined to free him once he was out of the local police department's custody. The chief was only too happy to give the man to Valentina, since it meant he didn't have to fight the gang. Not that he would. They were all local boys, the chief included, and the only reason he had the prisoner in his jail was that the state police had put him there. Once the prisoner was taken out of his custody, he didn't care what took place. And if Valentina didn't survive the escape attempt, well, that was unfortunate, but not his problem.

Her bit of luck in the whole affair was that a drunk in a restaurant bragged that the gang would free the man, and then he attempted to break her arm. Maybe he was trying to be a hero for the gang, or maybe he thought it made him a man to threaten a young woman, still a teenager at that point, actually.

Whatever his motivation, he ended the night early, bleeding out on the floor from a severed carotid artery.

And Valentina, with her bloody little sleeve knife now at the chief's throat, strongly *suggested* that they get the prisoner and spend the night at his house. She figured that the man's friends would strike that night rather than wait for her to get out on the road and possibly elude them. She had a truck and was not tied to the railroad schedule, so they had no idea of her timing or route.

When the chief went out to supposedly feed the barnyard animals and disappeared, she knew that the gang was on the way. She filled the whole interior of the house in gasoline and propane, set up a muzzle-loading rifle with a string between a doorknob and the trigger, and hid in the barn.

Three or four men, maybe even five, showed up and determined that she was holed up behind the locked door of the chief's bedroom. That's exactly what she wanted them to think. She'd locked the door and climbed out the window, then jammed it shut with a nail.

They called to her, promising that they wouldn't hurt her, as two of them stood outside the window, one with a still-working flashlight and the other with a bow and arrow, ready to shoot her. The ones inside kicked the door in, which pulled the string, which pulled the trigger, which caused the muzzleloader to fire a double load of flaming gunpowder into a house full of highly explosive gasoline and propane vapor.

Valentina had not realized just how explosive it was, but she got an object lesson that night. The fragments of the house, traveling at high velocity, almost destroyed the barn, too. The roof lifted off of the house, relatively intact, sailed fifty or sixty in the air, and then came crashing down, knifing into the barn like an axe. If Valentina had been in that part of the barn, she'd have been speared by the rafters.

She had taken a single step towards the debris field that had been the house, intending to finish off the survivors, when she realized that there weren't any. Any explosion that would fling a washing machine off into the woods would have crushed the internal organs of a man like stepping on a tomato. And that would be after they were shredded by a couple of thousand fragments of glass, wood, copper wire, and other house components.

So, she'd taken her prisoner, found the gang's truck, since hers had been destroyed in the explosion, and took off. A couple of the gang had gotten ahead of her in a fast car and were waiting in ambush, but that hadn't ended too favorably for them, either.

She'd delivered the prisoner and spent a couple of days at the Marten's ranch at Dani's insistence. The Martens had contracted out the prisoner extradition rather than doing it themselves partly as a test. They were expanding their Oilfield Security operations into Oklahoma and had asked around about a good company to partner with in the area. With the slow pace of communications now, you had to have good people on the ground, able to take responsibility and make logical decisions on their own. The days of calling the head office on a cell phone from the field and being micromanaged were gone.

Dani had been impressed by Valentina and had immediately taken to her. She'd been able to evaluate new situations, think on her feet, and act decisively.

An Army veteran named Tony owned the company that Valentina worked for, Oklahoma City Security, but he had left some fingers and most of a leg in the Middle East, courtesy of a roadside bomb. Dani respected that, but she also needed someone who was completely mobile and could be onsite wherever needed, with no restrictions. When she and Taylor traveled up to meet with Tony, she had said that Marten Oilfield Security would be glad to contract with them and greatly expand their operations, provided Valentina was made a full partner.

"What that means is, you can have half of a watermelon or all of a grape," she'd said. "Your choice. Of course, my other option is to set up an operation in Oklahoma ourselves, but if we have to go that route, then I'm going to make Valentina an offer she can't refuse and have her manage it." Dani had crossed her arms at that point, which meant that the negotiation phase of the meeting was over. Now came the part where the other party gave Dani what she wanted.

Tony had cut his eyes over at Valentina.

"Don't look at her," Dani piped up. "She's not making any demands. I am. She didn't go looking for another job. I'm pushing her into it."

Tony had laughed a little, looking down and rearranging some papers on his desk to create some time to think.

"To tell you the truth, I was planning on doing that anyway. Making her a partner. I was going to give it a little longer. She just barely turned eighteen. But kids are growing up way earlier now than they used to. They have to." He turned to face Valentina fully. "I would like to offer you a partnership. Expenses and upgrades come out first and then it's fifty-fifty". He held out his hand for a shake.

Her face lit up. She'd been feeling a bit guilty. As Dani had said, she hadn't been looking for another job and she didn't want Tony to be mad at her. He'd helped her when she'd been alone and looking for food. He'd never taken advantage of her, never abused her, and she didn't want to betray him. For Dani and Tony, the two most important people in her life, to both show such confidence in her was amazing.

Chapter Fourteen

THAT HAD BEEN TWO years ago. They'd all met a couple of times after that, once at the ranch and once in Oklahoma City, and communications via written mail were frequent, so they weren't strangers.

After greetings and hugs, Taylor assured Valentina that she was not conducting an audit.

"I am not here to criticize your operations or give you a report card or anything like that. This is for me to learn, for you to teach me. I know how the ranch runs, how the cattle part works, and how the banks work. What I don't know is the security part, other than the ranch security. Not the industrial operations."

"Aww, really? I've had the guys swabbing the decks and painting rocks white and raking the dirt into nice little patterns." Valentina pouted.

Taylor looked at her, wide-eyed and speechless for a moment, until Valentina laughed.

"I'm kidding. I'm not going to put on a show to try to fool you. What we do is what we do."

"You had me going for a second."

They were approaching Valentina's vehicle at this point, a 1970-something Monte Carlo, the second generation with the swoopy lines. A young man standing by the car saw them and ran around to open the trunk and then the doors.

"Does he get a tip?" Taylor asked.

"Him? Oh, God, no."

They were at the trunk now, Taylor putting her pack in but keeping her rifle slung on her shoulder. No sense in carrying a weapon and then putting it where you couldn't get to it.

"This is Horn Dog," Valentina said with a sigh. "Don't shake his hand. There's no telling what he's had in it."

"Horn. Dog." Taylor repeated slowly, eyebrows raised, making each part of the name a separate sentence. The Marten operation was a bit more formal as far as names went.

"Yeah, his real name's Roger or Fred or Mephistopheles or something. I don't remember. He discovered his sexuality a few months ago and he's been dry humping the furniture ever since. It's embarrassing."

Taylor slapped a hand to her mouth to keep from bursting out laughing. She'd forgotten that Valentina had such a dry, snarky wit, and absolutely no filter.

Horn Dog put both hands to his heart and focused on Taylor. "I am delighted to meet such a gorgeous young lady as yourself. Please pay no attention to Valentina. She is somehow immune to my charm, but —"

"What charm? You're a fifteen-year-old virgin," Valentina interrupted.

"How do you know I'm a virgin?"

"Because there has to at least be someone else participating to make you not a virgin. You can't take your own virginity, even as much as you've tried. Although I am impressed by your vigorous and ongoing effort in the matter."

Taylor was getting less successful in holding her laughter and she choked a little.

"I thought you women liked that. You know, taking a young stud —" Valentina snort-laughed and dramatically rolled her eyes, but he ignored her and continued "— and teaching him what to do. Having me do exactly what you want to bring you the maximum pleasure." He was staring into Taylor's eyes as he spoke and his speech had slowed down, like he was trying to hypnotize her.

"I'm going to have to find a bucket of cold water to throw on you. I thought I told you to be on good behavior."

"You didn't mention that Taylor is so hot! I mean, she could have been a troll. But... wow! Look at her!"

"All right, get in the back seat. Alone. Keep your hands to yourself. And I mean, not *on* yourself. *To* yourself." She looked at Taylor and sighed again. "Tomorrow I'm going to bring Sally Q as a runner instead of him. I can't put up with Mr. Future Sex Offender two days in a row."

Taylor was laughing and fanning her face to cool it. She'd had guys trying to get into her pants for a long time, and she was very experienced at fending them off. She'd never consider Horn Dog as a sexual partner, but she didn't want to laugh in his face and hurt his feelings, either. Valentina's comments and attitude made it difficult to keep a straight face, however. Impossible, actually, but he seemed unaffected.

"Especially around the train station, it's a good idea to keep an eye on your valuables. People get kind of used to seeing something they need and just taking it. You know, that's perfectly reasonable when you're talking about abandoned property. If someone died in Hexen, their stuff is up for grabs. Everybody did it. Does it. But how do you know that something belongs to someone? So, it's a good idea to take a stray kid and have him stay with the car. That way you can leave the windows down in this heat and not have to lock it up. And I didn't know how much stuff you were bringing. We might have needed him as a beast of burden."

That was the local slang, 'stray kid', or just "stray". It wasn't used in a mean way, just as a means of identifying a child who did not have a family. At the ranch, they used 'nodopt' for 'not adopted'. But 'stray' wasn't exactly the right term for the little group of kids that hung around Tony's and Valentina's operation.

Tony had lived in a townhouse, and after Hexen, found that he was the only soul remaining in his little row. Most of the occupants had died onsite or disappeared, and a couple had survived but decided to go somewhere else, either to lay claim to a bigger, grander house or to find a relative in another state. By default, then, he took over the entire row of townhouses.

He gathered a little group of kids around him in a symbiotic relationship. He could walk with the aid of a prosthetic leg and forearm crutches, but the leg muscles had been badly damaged and he couldn't walk far. It took a lot out of him and he used a wheelchair when he could. The kids then became his legs. He showed them how to do things, like gain entry to abandoned houses, and they went out and gathered food and supplies.

Later on, when the canned food ran out, he traded ammunition the strays had found for deer and hog meat from hunters. He quickly went into services that the kids could do, like message-carrying, lookouts, and, for the older kids, armed security. The message-carrying was important. Kids became the new cell phones. If you had to give someone a message, you had to do it in person now. Either that or write a note and have a kid deliver it via bike or on foot. Some enterprising businessmen had a half-dozen kids around, ready to run a message for them.

Security was an even bigger thing. When the police were gone, you had to provide your own security. That even proceeded into some of the kids doing private investigator-type surveillance. On a fairly regular basis, local law enforcement agencies would contract with him for temporary deputies. Valentina had done this several times, being sworn in to serve as a cop for a specified period. But Tony was the face of the company, the point of contact, the trusted ex military adult.

Technically, you could argue that Tony had adopted these kids and they weren't simply strays. He had them living in the townhomes in his block, they ate together, and he home-schooled them. At the same time, they didn't take on his last name and they were free to go as they desired. But lots of things, many normal conventions, had been trashed due to Hexen and it would be for future courts and genealogists to determine who was related to whom and how.

***

Valentina wheeled the Monte Carlo through the streets casually, paying some attention to traffic signs, but not a lot. Taylor remembered a trip her family had taken to the Bahamas when she was a kid. It seemed to her that all the drivers would approach a red light or a stop sign, slow down, tap out a beep-beep on the horn, and drive on through. Valentina was doing pretty much the same thing, but they made it without incident.

"It's still the townhouses," she announced. "Nothing's changed there. Tony's kind of in the middle, with the girls on this side and the boys on the other. This one's mine and I have a room ready for you."

"Cool. Will you allow me to take you and Tony to dinner? On me."

"He was going to set something up for tonight so I'll let you and him fight over the check."

"Okay. And I brought a bottle of some very good tequila for an after-dinner drink."

"Oh, girl, I love you. In the morning, I may wish you hadn't, but tonight it may be good to blow off some steam."

***

Taylor freshened up from her trip and came downstairs to sit with Valentina on the couch.

"You know, earlier when we were talking about Horn Dog, I wasn't trying to dictate who you can have sex with," Valentina stated. "You're an adult, you can do what you want. It's not my decision. You can do the dirty deed with Horn Dog if you want. I mean, it'd be gross, and he's fifteen so that would be creepy, and he'd probably last less than thirty seconds, but it's up to you."

Taylor was laughing by the time she was finished. "No, no," she said, catching her breath. "I didn't take any offense, and I am certainly not letting him touch me. He's kind of cute and he's got some muscles. He'll probably do fine with the girls in a year or two. But no. That's not going to happen. Not with me."

She hesitated, then went on. "As a matter of fact, I just gave up my own virginity last year."

"Really? You were seventeen, then? I had a boyfriend when I was sixteen. Before Hexen. His family took off during the pandemic. They had a cabin in Colorado somewhere. Around Vail or Aspen or one of those places. My parents... you know. And I tried to text him and he wasn't answering. And then all the electricity went out. I'll never know what happened to him."

She took a few deep breaths, trying not to cry over the death of her parents and the very likely death of her boyfriend. Taylor switched seats, to sit beside her and put an arm around her shoulders.

"I'm sorry. I didn't mean to get you started on that track. Or would you feel better talking about it?" she asked.

Valentina cleared her throat. "Not your fault. I was talking about boyfriends and that was kind of a part of it. My first. Anyway, afterwards, I got with a guy. He was older. A lot older than me. But I went with him voluntarily. We holed up in a farmhouse out west of the city for a while, and one time he went out to scrounge for supplies. He was going to go with some guys he had worked with before. And he just never came back. I guess there was a fight over something and he lost. I don't know if any of the guys came back. I didn't really know them. It's not like I could go out and look for them.

"Then there was another guy, for a while, and he just died of something. I don't even know what, an infection or whatever. We buried him out in the field, up near the fence line. His roommate, whatever you want to call him, thought that he had inherited me. He pushed me down on the bed and climbed on top of me and started pulling my clothes off.

"But I had a knife. I stabbed him once in the chest and then we started fighting over the knife. There was a lot of blood and my arm was slippery with it, and it slid it out of his hand. I did a wild swing and it hit him in the neck. Right in an artery. Remember me telling you about the guy that tried to break my arm, when I was doing that extradition for Marten Cattle Company? I stabbed him in that same artery. That's how I knew where it was, 'cause I accidentally hit it with the roommate."

"I got off pretty lucky," Taylor said softly. "I found Eric and Dani quickly and they protected me from all that."

"It's not like I was being raped. The roommate, yeah, he was trying to. But the other two, I was voluntary. Anyway, I cleaned up after I got the roommate off of me, packed up everything I wanted to take, and took off. I had a rifle at that point and I knew how to use it. I'd practiced. And I ran into Tony and he brought me in. He never tried to lay a hand on me or guilt me into having sex with him or anything.

"That's my story. Except for the part about Dani demanding that I help her rebuild the world!" She laughed. "She's a tough negotiator. I'll bet there aren't many people that tell her 'No'."

"Not really. She's negotiated some killer deals for us." Taylor had always been impressed by Dani's skills. She'd learned to barter from her mother, who considered it a tried-and-true South American custom that should be preserved and perfected. Plus, Dani was fearless about asking for something, and able to keep a straight face even when that something was ridiculous. On a surprisingly frequent basis, she got what she asked for.

"What about your first time? It was after Hexen. I guess that presented some interesting challenges," Valentina prompted.

"We have worked a lot with the soldiers from Fort Cavazos, what used to be Fort Hood. The governor wanted to use the troops there and the commander was balking, so he signed a proclamation that all of the military personnel on the post were now members of the Texas Army National Guard. Then he made Eric a four-star general and sent him out to take control of the post.

"Anyway, during this one period, we were on the post for about a month, and there was this one lieutenant. He was tall and lanky and his grandparents had emigrated from Poland. He went by 'Ski', of course. Blond hair, blue eyes. I worked with him for about a week, with us flirting back and forth, and I decided I was tired of the whole virginity thing, so we solved it. I was seventeen and he was twenty-two. It was a good choice, really. He was very gentle and understanding, so it was a good experience. And then we spent the next three weeks perfecting technique.

"At the end of the time, he had to stay there and I went back to the ranch. I wasn't going to just be a military girlfriend, or even wife. I felt like I was making a difference at the ranch. You know, helping to rebuild civilization and all of that. I wouldn't be in that kind of position at Fort Cavazos."

"Did you ever see him again?"

"Yeah, once. I went there again some months later and we spent a weekend together. We wrote letters back and forth for a while, but it just kind of faded out on both sides. If we worked together again, I'd be professional, you know, but our relationship would be reset back to square one. We'd have to start over again from scratch. Or not start it again at all, maybe."

"I guess that's a situation that could have happened with or without Hexen. Military people get transferred and stuff."

"Yeah. After that, was just one other experience with a guy in Austin. We were there dealing with the governor and this little squadron of businessmen that cluster around him all the time. I mean, that's a good thing. We've gotten a lot of business from those people. And, I don't know, I decided to get with this one guy. It was... not satisfying.

"I don't really feel like I can have a relationship at the ranch unless it's a full-on we're-getting-married thing. It's like a small town there, but even worse because everyone lives there and works there and it's just very intensely focused. But on the other hand, if I date someone from outside the ranch, then I'm going to be accused of being a stuck-up bitch, thinking that I'm too good for any of the fine young men there. I'm damned if I do and damned if I don't. And I don't want to jump into bed with some guy I just met every time I'm away from the ranch. That's just not me. So, I'm screwed. Well, actually, I'm not, apparently."

"I'm sorry. I'm kind of in the same situation. I know a lot of guys that I work with, but I can't date any of them because then there'd be accusations of favoritism. And who knows who may come to work for us in the future? 'Gee, sorry, I can't hire you because you were banging my brains out last weekend', you know?"

Chapter Fifteen

THE NEXT DAY WAS a good day. It started slowly, but the hangovers weren't too bad. The two girls had toured a big operation and everything was running smoothly. It also gave Taylor the opportunity to meet the oilfield guys, the clients. It was always good to check up and show the corporate flag, as it were.

They'd had supper in the chow hall with the guys, a couple of whom were visibly disappointed when they learned that Taylor was just there for a brief visit.

"Aww, damn," one grizzled, gray-haired man had exclaimed. "I thought I'd just met my next ex-wife!" That brought a round of laughter. "And she's from Texas, too. You do know that all my exes live in Texas," he followed up, to more laughter.

"Oh, God, Smitty, go away," Valentina sighed, making a shooing gesture with both hands. "You're like six times her age. She doesn't want to look at you." She turned to Taylor. "They're all five years old. This is Valentina's Daycare or something."

Taylor just laughed. She had seen that Valentina had a business side, where she could tell the guys to do something and they immediately did it, but she also had an after work let-our-hair-down-and-be-friends side. She played both sides well. That was a good thing because people generally lived in closer proximity than before Hexen.

With ninety percent of the population gone, that may seem counterintuitive, but the lack of vehicles and expense of gasoline made people live near where they worked. In this case, the security guys and girls lived onsite in dormitories. That was a requirement, since they had to be immediately available if there was an emergency.

The oilfield workers themselves had more flexibility, but they generally lived onsite also, especially for the more remote operations. Or in some cases, the worker dorm was in a centralized location and there was a bus that ran them out to whichever site they worked.

But that all made for a complex operation. It was a lot more than simply issuing weapons to some people and telling them to guard something. Two shifts had to be fed three times a day apiece, supplied with baths and laundry services and a place to sleep, at minimum. The cooks and mechanics had to have all of that, too, plus the food and drink and clean water and grease and repair parts that they used in their jobs. They all had to be paid and evaluated and promoted — or let go, occasionally — and Marten Oilfield Security, MOS for short, had created training classes to certify people to be security guards.

While these employees technically worked for Oklahoma City Security, that company was a subcontractor to MOS, so what MOS said to do was what was going to happen. That meant that MOS sent instructors to Oklahoma to certify people, which required Valentina to find a suitable range for weapons training, a gym for hand-to-hand combat training, and a classroom for instruction. And a doctor and dentist to give people a yearly checkup, both to keep everyone healthy and on the job, and to prevent any fraudulent injury claims.

Tony handled most of the paperwork end of things, but Valentina was the boots on the ground the vast majority of the time. She was the one that made things happen and kept it all running. Taylor was impressed. She had a large part in doing the same things at the ranch, but things there tended to be more stable. In the oilfield, workers and security personnel were rotated in and out and, worst of all, job sites may change.

That meant that everything had to be moved to the new site, and set up again, potentially requiring that an entire new set of suppliers had to be lined up for food and other supplies.

"The good thing about Oklahoma," Valentina had told Taylor, "Is that there is a good variety of food produced here. Cattle, hogs, chickens, dairy products, and wheat are the top agricultural products. Not so much vegetables, but these boys aren't vegans. They eat a ton of barbecue and bread. You probably already know that we're shipping train cars full of wheat to Marten Agricultural Products. We hooked you guys up with the Co-Op here."

"Oh, yeah. Since we had to source food to send out to the oilfield operations anyway, it was a no-brainer to just buy larger quantities and sell other products to our established beef customers. We have a big operation in Troup, Texas now. We actually laid more track and put in some switches so that we can just route train cars off to a side track and deal with them later. We built another ramp, even longer than the first one, for forklifts to unload boxcars, and there is just row after row of warehouses. We're pulling in rice and salted fish and sugar from Louisiana and all kinds of fresh produce from Mexico. And coffee, of course."

Coffee was a huge money-maker, and the Martens were in a good position to import it. The overwhelming majority of coffee is produced in Brazil, with Colombia, Honduras, Peru, and Guatemala also in the top ten. All of that product seemed to come through Mexico and head either to California or straight to the Martens in Texas. California was a mess and the Martens had deep pockets to buy it by the trainload, so they probably handled the majority of it entering the U.S. They sold it wholesale to other companies that packaged and distributed it. There was less profit, but way less work. At some point, one has to realize if there are too many irons in the fire.

***

The next day, Taylor sat with Tony for him to show her his side of things. That also gave Valentina a chance to catch up on anything she had put on hold while showing Taylor the operations.

The following day, the last one of Taylor's visit, the girls were together again to tour some more operations. After a full day of that, they were near home when Valentina saw a group of boys clustered around a house. One of them, seeing her car, stepped out in the street and waved vigorously, making a "come on" signal.

"Damn, what have those little bastards gotten into now?" she muttered under her breath as she accelerated to the scene and braked sharply. Before they were out of the car, the boy was talking.

"Horn Dog's acting crazy! He's up on the roof!" He pointed.

The girls ran up to the building, to find Horn Dog dancing on the roofline, the peak.

"Horn Dog! Come down here right now!" Valentina yelled. "Carefully!"

He didn't acknowledge her, but he did turn and disappear towards the back. Taylor immediately started to run back that way, scrabbling over a broken and mostly-collapsed wooden fence.

"I can fly!" she heard from above, and running steps that abruptly stopped.

She skidded to a stop and turned.

Valentina said "Shit," in a low voice.

There was a quiet moment, utterly silent, like the world paused for a moment, and then Horn Dog's body fell, slamming into the wrecked fence with a sickening thump and a clatter of broken boards.

Both girls ran, reaching him at the same time, and both stopped.

Valentina went pale and muttered "Jesus."

Horn Dog was impaled on a broken fence post, the jagged wood spiked up through his back, sticking out six inches, with him dangling a couple of feet off the ground.

Taylor never remembered if she said anything, but both moved to help him, again in unison. She wrote about it in her journal, but was sure she had the details mixed up. They knew they couldn't lift him off of the fence post because the post itself may have been stopping some of the bleeding. Taylor pulled EMT shears from the first aid kid in her chest rig and cut away his shirt so they could get to the wound.

Valentina ran down to the row of townhouses and got Tony's truck so they could lay him in the bed for the trip to the hospital.

A man from the neighborhood showed up with a saw, and some of the older boys kept Horn Dog from falling while he cut the post.

Taylor was in the scrum of people, trying to use one of the kid's shirts to put pressure on the wound to stem the bleeding. There were eight or nine of them, all crammed together in a tiny space, pressed against one another. And they had to move together as a mass, out of the way of the saw, as the man switched position to cut away at a new section of the post.

During it all, Horn Dog was amazingly quiet and still. She thought he'd died at one point, but he started talking a little. She couldn't understand what he was saying, with the other noise and action and coordination to get out of the way of the saw but still keep him supported.

And then finally they had him in the bed of the truck, with a blanket over him as much as possible to treat for shock. Taylor rode with him, on her knees, pressing a fresh shirt to the front of his wound while another random boy held pressure on his back.

He's not going to make it, she thought. *It might have been iffy even before Hexen. He's got a fucking fence post through his stomach. Probably ripped open the intestines and they're pumping fecal matter throughout his system. That'll cause rampant infection even if he survives the blood loss. We don't have the antibiotics to treat that even if he survives the bleeding. It ran down my arms and is on everything I'm wearing. He's dead, he's dead, but we're going to do everything we can to save him.*

Horn Dog had never screamed or even complained throughout the entire procedure. Now he looked up at her, slowly, dreamily.

"Taylor," he said in the same slow and dreamy way, and smiled. "I love you."

She was taken aback for a moment, before replying "I love you, too, Horn Dog."

"Will you give me a kiss?"

She hesitated again, and then leaned in and pressed her lips against his for a few seconds. She wouldn't have been surprised if he'd pushed his tongue into her mouth, but he didn't. When she pulled back, his eyes were closed.

"I love you," he murmured, faintly.

Ah, Jesus, don't die like this. Don't say you love me and then die!

She spent the rest of the trip with her lips pressed together, tears streaming from her eyes, rolling down her cheeks, and then dripping onto the boy. She couldn't wipe them away because both of her hands were busy pressing down on his wound, trying to stop the bleeding.

Chapter Sixteen

ONCE THEY GOT HIM on the gurney at the emergency room, a nurse's aide came up to Taylor and the guy that had assisted with the first aid.

"Are you injured, or is that his blood?" she asked.

"It's his."

"Please don't touch anything, and let's go outside to get you cleaned up."

She herded them off to a big tent set up in the parking lot.

"I'm going to take you first," the aide said, indicating the guy. "Please place your soiled clothing in the bin."

The next station was a sink that dumped directly into a storm drain, with a gritty, strong soap, the aide pouring water from a pitcher as needed. Then a hand towel, which went into another biohazard bin, a wipe with alcohol, and then a hospital gown to replace his shirt.

The aide showed him out, put a sign outside the tent that said "DO NOT ENTER / NO ENTRAR", and pulled a canvas curtain across the doorway. She smiled at Taylor and said "Let's give you a little more privacy."

Taylor's cleanup was a bit more involved. She washed her hands and forearms first, then was able to use her clean hands to get her rifle and chest rig off without getting them bloody. As she was putting her top in the bin, the aide remarked "I don't know what you want to do with your pants. The gowns don't offer a lot of privacy."

Taylor had been on her knees when Horn Dog was impaled on the post, trying to stem the blood from the entry wound. His blood had run down her arms, to drip off of her elbows onto the tops of her thighs. She considered her options, and ended up cutting the back piece out of her shirt and using that to scrub first her legs and then her pants and simply putting them back on. Then she had to go through the hand wash again.

As she was going through the process, she was thinking of how the conditions had led to scrubbing up in a parking lot. It actually made sense, when the electricity to the hospital was nonexistent or extremely limited. There was none to waste on lighting a bathroom, and plumbing issues may have clogged the drains there. Hence the open-air storm drain, powered by simple gravity. The soap was likely locally-produced, and the alcohol certainly was. The bottle was hand-lettered "DO NOT DRINK!"

The aide helped her on with the gown and tied it in the back for her.

"Ooh, you're a dangerous one, aren't you?" she commented. She had certainly seen the rifle and chest rig full of magazines. Besides that, she got a close-up view of the belt items: pistol, two magazines for it in a double pouch, multitool in a pouch, thirty-round magazine in a single carrier, and fighting knife.

She placed a hand on Taylor's shoulder and stepped closer. "My name is Charlotte," she said, looking into her eyes and smiling. Their faces were close, only a foot apart. "If you need to talk, or just have a few drinks, I live here in the hospital. I have a private room upstairs. Just ask for me at the front desk. Anytime."

Girls had hit on Taylor before. One young lady at the ranch had told her she'd drop anything she had going on if Taylor ever wanted to give it a try. It was really nothing new, but the circumstances were. They'd just brought in a bloody, dying boy, for God's sake!

"Thanks. I need to go check on how he's doing," she blurted out.

***

Badly, it turned out. He didn't make it. He didn't even last long at all after they got him to the hospital.

"It was a massive amount of damage," the doctor told them. "It was unsurvivable, with all of the internal bleeding. You did everything right, with your first aid. There was just no hope with our limited capabilities, now. I'm sorry."

"What... do we do... with his body?" Valentina asked. She looked shell-shocked.

"I'll write up a death certificate and we can turn the body over. To you? Would you be the next of kin?"

"Merle. His name was Merle Harbach. His dad named him after Merle Haggard, the country singer. He hated the name." She wiped tears from her eyes. "He wanted to be a pilot. He wanted to fly military jets."

When the doctor left to do his paperwork, she turned to Taylor and said in a low voice "He was high. He took something. I'm gonna kill somebody."

Taylor hugged her. "I'll help. Any idea who?"

"When we get back, we're going to ask the strays. Somebody knows something."

Chapter Seventeen

THAT SOMEONE WAS WAITING for them when they got back. Maybe not entirely voluntarily, but waiting nonetheless.

Taylor had paid the hospital and included some extra as a donation when Valentina went to get the truck. Horn Dog's body had been wrapped in a dark cloth and then in a plastic painter's drop cloth. The plastic was transparent, hence the reason for the dark cloth. The plastic was to contain the blood that was seeping out of the wound, pulled down by gravity.

Valentina drove to the Catholic church that she attended infrequently. She'd definitely gone when she'd gotten back from extraditing the prisoner that she'd taken to the Martens. She'd gotten away with her life against bad odds. Lately, her attendance had been sporty. Sure, she went on holy days of obligation, like All Saints' Day and the Assumption. Other than that, not so much.

But she knew the priest and they left the body with him. He'd conduct a funeral mass the next day. With no embalming available, bodies were buried quickly.

"He's probably not Catholic," Valentina said, once they were back in the truck. "But the only other option is to pick a church at random, and I don't know any of those priests. Or preachers or whatever the correct term is."

"It'll be fine." In Taylor's experience, the Catholic Church was fairly welcoming and tolerant, unlike some of the strident and judgmental Protestant ones that thought anything that smacked of fun just had to be a sin.

On the way back, they retrieved her car and drove both back home. Tony had been stuck there, since they had his truck, so they filled him in on the details.

"You think he was high on something?"

"Yeah, the strays said he was acting crazy. He was dancing on the roof. And then he shouted 'I can fly' and ran full-speed off the roof."

"I guess the doctor didn't run any tests? But then, they probably used to do that by putting a blood sample in a machine and pressing 'Start'. They can't do that now."

"He didn't indicate that he detected anything, or that he was going to do any further tests. But I'm going to find out. I'm going over there to talk to the strays in a minute."

"Talk to Cody K. He's sitting over there waiting on you. Then we'll compare notes, what he told you versus what he told me."

***

Valentina got Cody K in her car for a little privacy, while Taylor changed clothes.

"Tell me what you know. Tell me everything."

"Horn Dog said that he had tried something called zipper. I dunno what it is, but he was going to get some more of it."

"Who was he getting it from?"

"Some guy called Little Cut, in the apartments by the park. Three or four miles from here."

"How do you know? Did you go with him?"

"Yeah," said grudgingly. "But I stayed back, out near the street. I didn't talk to the guy or anything."

"Did you use any of that shit?"

"No," said more emphatically.

"Okay, you're going to show us where it is. Tomorrow, in the daylight. You're not in any trouble. You're good. I appreciate you helping us."

Tony's questioning of the boy hadn't produced anything substantially different. "Our options are to call the cops, and while we may know them and have worked with them, I wouldn't claim that we have any pull. They're not going to arrest someone just on our claim that a kid said a drug deal took place. And even if they did, I'm certain no prosecution would ever take place.

"The other route is what you seem to be indicating, Valentina. I think that, officially, I don't know anything about that. Unofficially, you have my full support, but CYA. Cover Your Ass. Do some work, see and be seen, don't just drop out of sight."

"Thank you. Right now, I think I need a few drinks. I can't think about it anymore today."

***

Later on, after more than a little tequila, Tony was asleep in the lounge chair and Valentina stopped talking for a moment, looking at Taylor drunk-serious.

"You know, this is technically murder I'm talking about. We could get in trouble. The cops may turn a blind eye, but I can't guarantee it. They may figure, ehh, known drug dealer, who cares? But they may not. And we certainly don't have the pull with the governor here that Eric and Dani do with the governor in Texas. Plus, we may get shot, doing what we're talking about."

"I'm in. We just need to not get caught. Or shot."

"Thank you. I do appreciate it. You have more experience at this kind of thing than I do."

"Maybe, but this is your territory, and you have more experience with surveillance. That's the first thing we need to do, gather intelligence. Make a plan. We don't need to go in there guns a-blazin' without any idea of the situation. We need to check that place out from all angles, plan our attack, and plan an escape route. And a couple of alternate routes."

Taylor was analyzing the problem, considering all the angles. That way, she might be able to fill up her mind and not think about the fifteen-year-old boy she'd kissed right before he died.

His last kiss, certainly. Maybe his first.

Tears came to her eyes again and she wiped them away. She decided to tell Valentina about the kiss, which left them both sobbing.

Chapter Eighteen

THE APARTMENTS WERE A few buildings arranged in an arc around a little strip center. They cruised by the place on the four-lane boulevard that ran by it. None of the businesses seemed to be open, with that quick glance. Maybe a barber shop. That didn't require electricity, to use scissors and comb and razor. The boutique, the insurance agent, the rival insurance agent, and the other shops all seemed to be closed. But they were way too close to the apartments to be used for surveillance.

The best option was the park on the other side of the street. It was a big expanse of open, grassy field, with no trees until the far end, some five hundred yards from the apartments. But they had Cody K in the car with them, and they weren't going to talk about things like that where he could hear.

Instead, they dropped him off at the townhouses, swapped vehicles, and cruised the place again.

"It's a straight shot from those trees to the front door of the apartments," Valentina pointed out afterwards. "We have some really nice spotting scopes. Money-is-no-object quality. We found a guy that was a long-range shooter and got all of his stuff. Well, you know, Hexen got him. We found the stuff in his house while scrounging. But I'm not going to do it that way. I want up close and personal, because this is personal."

"Here's my suggestion," Taylor said. "Put me with a guy, one who knows weapons. Me and the guy will set up in that tree line and surveil. You go to work and act normal, like Tony said. People will notice if you aren't around, but no one is keeping track of me.

"I want the guy to watch my back while I'm concentrating on the target. Or vice versa, if the guy can do the surveillance. I notice that there are some people playing soccer in the field. If they see us and wonder what we're doing, it's just a couple having a picnic or something."

"That sounds good. Let me grab a scope for you, and if there's anything else you need, just take it. Tony can get you together with the guy. I guess I'll see you this evening, then."

When Tony was locating a suitable partner for Taylor, she mentioned two things. "I'm going to tell this guy that I'm engaged so he doesn't try to get into my pants all day. I want him focused on the job. And as far as Cody K goes, it may not be a good idea for him to remain around here. You don't want him putting two and two together and running his mouth when the drug dealer he pointed out turns up missing or deceased."

"I don't really have the ability to send him too far away. All of our operations are in-state. Do you have something in mind?"

"If you don't have somewhere, then ship him off to Texas. Tell him he's on a special assignment, throw his ass on the train, and send him to the ranch. I'll write a note for them to put him to work in Corpus or Houston. He can hand-carry the note to Dani. There's no reason for him to come back here, is there?"

"Not that I know of. Obviously, he doesn't have any family here. That sounds like a pretty nice solution if you can do that. He doesn't lose anything, you know?"

"Give me a sheet of paper and an envelope and consider it done."

***

A couple of hours later, they were in the tree line and set up. They even had a blanket and a little ice chest full of beer bottles, some full, some empty. They'd each taken a couple of swigs to get the smell of it on their breaths before dumping the rest out.

The bag that they carried had the spotting scope, a towel, and a partial box of condoms, just in case anyone wondered what this young couple was up to and looked inside. Even the dumbest person should be able to figure out what they were planning on doing in the woods.

The scope was the only odd item out, but they could always say they liked to look at the stars at night, or they planned to sell it. People found all kinds of things in abandoned properties and tried to sell or trade them. And, if needed, they both had pistols concealed under their clothing.

Taylor was happy with the setup. And her partner wasn't too bad, either. Jason was a couple of years older than her, blue eyes and dark hair, worn a bit long. He seemed to be quiet and laid-back, which was good. She didn't need to be fighting a grabby guy off all day long. This was business.

But she could also imagine a scenario, on their own time, in which they might need those condoms.

***

Late that afternoon was the funeral. Taylor and Jason were there, and of course Tony and Valentina loaded up the strays and attended. Taylor had only known Horn Dog briefly, but she was saddened by his loss. She tried to be tough about such things, but his death was so useless that she was frustrated. And there was that last kiss thing.

Afterwards, the four adults talked strategy over supper.

"Not much activity so far," Taylor reported. "But what there is, is what I would expect from a drug dealer. A few people coming by, but no one before noon. They come in and three minutes later they're out the door. That's not visiting a friend, or spending time with a prostitute, for example. That's dropping ten dollars and picking up a dime bag or whatever.

"I'm betting the real action is at night. You know, people work during the day and come by in the evening to get something to party with that night.

"Also, he has his own little gang of strays. As soon as we start something, those strays are going to scatter. The big question is whether they're going to just run, or if they're going to bring back some reinforcements."

"That means we need to be in and out quickly." Valentina looked at Jason. "Are you on board? Fully? For anything we might do?"

He nodded in his laid-back way. "Horn Dog was a good kid. I liked him. Tony knows I'm good."

"Because I'm talking about an eye for an eye kind of action."

"You know, the funny thing is, if there were more cops, the criminals would get off lighter," he mused. "You'd think it would be the other way around, but it's not. When there are more cops, they arrest the criminals and put them through the court system. With only a few cops, the civilians have to take matters into their own hands. We can't take them through the courts, so the answer is to shoot the criminals. A crime that would put a bad guy in prison for three-to-five becomes a death sentence instead. I think there's a kind of poetic justice in that."

"Okay, I just wanted to make sure everything was clear. I think we three —" she indicated everyone except Tony "— should go back and do a couple of hours. Let's see what the activity looks like tonight. Then we ought to be able to come up with a plan and do something tomorrow."

***

As they drove down the side street to get to their observation point, Valentina remarked "This neighborhood looks kind of sketchy. I wouldn't want to park the truck on the street here. Can we drive up there by the tree line?"

"It looks better in the daytime, but yeah, kind of sketchy in the dark," Taylor agreed. "There is a dirt road that goes right there. We can make it, no problem."

Once they were parked in the right position, Valentina had another suggestion. "I could stay in the back seat here and set the tripod up on the floorboard. Why don't you two do your lovebird impression and sit in the bed of the truck with the blanket and beer and all? Keep an eye out for someone coming up on us."

"It depends on how hungry the mosquitoes are," Taylor joked.

"Just don't go too far with that lovebird impression. I'm not going to be able to see anything if y'all have the truck bouncing up and down." Valentina was obviously starting to get back to normal.

Taylor laughed, but once they were situated in the bed, she held onto the side and rocked her body back and forth a few times, making the truck bounce on the springs. Then she looked back at the cab and laughed even more when she saw Valentina staring out the back window at her with a "what the hell?" look on her face.

She and Jason then spent another couple of hours in conversation or just stargazing. You could occasionally spot a satellite still sailing along in orbit, either dead from the EMP or just useless because the devices that once communicated with it were dead.

"You know," she said, "at some point, their orbits will degrade and they'll come crashing back down to earth. How unlucky would someone have to be to survive Hexen and then have space junk fall out of orbit onto their head?" She laughed.

He laughed along with her and then ran his hand across her back, high to low, a move that would end up with his arm around her waist. About midway across, he remembered that she was engaged and pulled his hand away abruptly. Taylor knew exactly what had happened.

Damn it. Relationships suck. And I can't really do the long-distance thing with no phones or texts or anything.

"I'm sorry," he said. "I just got caught up in the moment. I'm sitting here chatting with a beautiful young lady. We've been together for hours today and talked a lot, and I like you. It just seemed like the natural thing to do."

"It's fine. Things have just been difficult, lately." *And he's a nice guy, too. Arrrgh!*

Finally, Valentina had seen enough and they packed it in for the night.

"It's obvious they're selling drugs of some type. I thought we might make a buy to confirm, or have someone do it, but we don't need that. There are three guys, the dealer and two others, bodyguards, I'd guess. I'm sure they're all armed. They're outside now, sitting on lawn chairs. They have a little fire going in a hibachi or small grill. They're cooking something and it gives off a little light. People come up, they make an exchange, and the people walk away. There's nothing else they could be doing."

"The only question, then," Taylor chimed in, "Is how to do it. You have long range options from the tree line at about five hundred yards, or a parking lot at about three hundred. Both of those are going to be at night, so there is a possibility of a miss, and then the dealer hides out or moves or something and we can't find him.

"Closer options are a SWAT-type raid, which would be a lot easier and safer if we had flash-bangs. Or we could just stagger up to them, like a couple of party girls looking for a high, and take them down."

"Jason, would you be in for the party-girl thing?" Valentina asked. "You could go as you are, I wouldn't make you wear a wig and a skirt."

That brought a laugh.

"I'm in. I still can't believe Horn Dog is gone. That sucks."

Chapter Nineteen

THERE WAS MORE PLANNING the next day, walking the area to map out ingress and egress points, escape routes, areas or obstacles to avoid. Then Taylor and Jason unloaded their magazines, wiped all of the ammo down to remove fingerprints, and reloaded them while wearing gloves. Then the magazines were wiped down. It may have been paranoia, but there was no sense in leaving evidence behind when it could be prevented. It may be damned difficult to compare fingerprints now, on file cards, but that may not always be the case. It may take twenty years to get computers up and running again, but it would happen.

Taylor didn't carry ID and didn't write her name or initials or anything on her equipment. She carried any papers she needed either in a planner or, if there were a lot, in a briefcase. They were all together in one location. That meant that she could be clean and anonymous with minimal effort. She suggested Valentina and Jason also make sure they were unidentifiable.

Valentina was the one that had the highest risk of being recognized, either now or in the future, since she lived only a few miles away. Therefore, they had taken the most trouble to disguise her. In fact, they'd gone overboard on the makeup, on the theory that the darkness would render any subtle makeup unseen, anyway.

She had raccoon eyes with garish light blue eye shadow, fire engine red lipstick drawn outside the lines to make her lips look bigger, and most of her hair was pinned up under a fedora. A final touch was glasses. They could have gotten her clear glass ones from an optometrist, but had gone with the quick option that didn't leave any trail by knocking the lenses out of a pair of sunglasses. There wouldn't be much opportunity for someone to notice that there were no lenses, and no consequence if they did. She could just say it was part of her style.

"Oh, God," she'd said, looking at her reflection in her mirror. "I look like an old barfly. Some old drunk cougar who's looking for a young stud. Or some guy under fifty, if it's after midnight." She pulled her lips in to cover her teeth and then mimed a toothless woman with a cigarette- and alcohol-scratchy voice.

"Hey, there, sonny, you won't believe the things I can do when I take my false teeth out! We goin' to do it granny style!" She slapped herself on the butt a couple of times as she cried "Ride 'em, cowboy!" Then she and Taylor both fell out, laughing.

Taylor had the thought afterwards that she was kind of a prude, compared to Valentina. But then, for all of Valentina's talk, there hadn't been any mention of a man in her life.

***

They waited for darkness.

"Everybody still good? Are we doing this?" Valentina asked once they had parked the truck a couple of blocks down from the dealer's apartment.

"Let's go, *chica*. Or is it *abuela*? *Abuelita*?" Taylor teased her, going from 'girl' to 'grandmother' to 'granny'.

"Waiting on you," Jason smiled tightly. The girls had pinned his hair up as much as they could, and covered his head with a wool cap, pulled down to cover his eyebrows. He had come up with a fake tattoo somewhere, and they had slapped it on his neck, where it would be readily visible. Or maybe the only people who would see it wouldn't survive the night.

The three staggered down the sidewalk, talking and laughing. They passed around a Jack Daniels bottle half full of tea, mixed so that it duplicated the color of the missing bourbon.

All of them had their shirttails out to cover their pistols. Not that carrying a pistol was uncommon now, just the opposite, in fact. But there was no need to give anyone the thought that they may represent a danger.

They turned once they saw the dealer on his lawn chair and headed towards him.

"Y'all need something?" he called out when they were close enough.

Taylor acted as spokesperson, as they'd planned, to put the attention on her and not Valentina. She wasn't wearing any makeup or disguise, but she planned to be in another state the next day.

"Maybe. What's this zipper stuff we've been hearing about?"

"That is the good shit. Smoke some of that and all your troubles go away."

"How do you smoke it? Like in a meth pipe? I got a meth pipe here somewhere." She ran her hand down her pants, feeling her pocket for the pipe, but with her fingers extended so they stroked her crotch. The average male would watch her do that, and these guys were no exception. She was keeping their attention, all right.

"Uh, yeah, that'd be perfect. You know, if you ladies wanted to stay, we could definitely party. No charge with appropriate consideration, if you know what I mean."

Taylor looked shocked. "We couldn't leave Honeyboo!" she exclaimed, throwing her arms around Jason and looking up at him with adoring eyes.

That brought a round of laughter.

"Honeyboo," Little Cut repeated, and he and his guys laughed some more.

"All right, so three hits is thirty Okie dollars. What money are you going to use? There's a discount for precious metal."

Taylor dug in her pocket, put two coins in her left hand, and held it out for him to see.

"I got twenty-five in Texas gold and silver."

"That'll do the trick, pretty girl." Little Cut reached down into the bag by his side and dug out three little twists of paper.

"Are you good with everything?" Valentina asked Taylor. That was their agreed-upon go signal.

Taylor tossed the coins to Little Cut to make him catch them and occupy his hands and mind. At the same time, her other hand was pulling her pistol. Jason and Valentina were doing the same.

"Don't move! Hands up!" they all yelled, repeatedly, at whichever man they were facing.

Little Cut froze, drugs in one hand and coins in the other. The guard in front of Taylor put his hands up. The one Valentina was covering turned and ran.

He didn't get far. Three steps, in fact, but only two of those without a bullet in him. She put two into his back, saw him going down, then swung her pistol to make sure the other two were in compliance. Things looked okay for the moment, so she pivoted back to the guy on the ground.

He was trying to get back up, pushing with his arms. She took a breath, let half out and held the rest, and fired once more into the back of his head. The man collapsed to the ground, completely limp. Lights out for him.

The guard that Taylor was watching was only too glad to get on the ground, once he saw what happened when someone tried to run.

"J-Jimmy, can you check inside?" It sounded like Valentina stuttered, but what she really did was almost call Jason by his real name. She saved it at the last second and threw in the first 'J' name she could think of.

"You, Little Cut, on the ground with your hands out to the sides," she ordered. He assumed the position just as she said, cowed by the unhesitating manner in which she'd just shot his bodyguard, and then coldly finished him off. This wasn't some rodeo where the cops would chase them around and then let them go later on. It wasn't just some stupid bitches with guns that only thought they knew how to use them, either.

Just when things seemed to be going smoothly, Jason walked into the open doorway to the apartment. There was a meaty thump and a breathy grunt as he bent at the waist. Then he disappeared inside, snatched into the darkness.

Valentina swung her pistol towards the doorway, then back to Little Cut, trying to cover both and see what was going on in the apartment.

"Go ahead! I have them both!" Taylor called out.

She stepped off to the side and behind them, so they couldn't see exactly where she was looking. That impaired their ability to make any moves.

Valentina took some steps towards the apartment and jerked to a halt when Jason suddenly appeared in the doorway. Then she saw a man behind him, his arm around Jason's neck and a pistol to his head.

"Honeyboo got hisself in trouble," the man snarled.

Taylor glanced over to see what the problem was, quickly calculated the moves she would have to make to get into position, and then flicked a glance back at the guys she was supposed to be watching on the ground. She had checked out their pistols beforehand. Jason had been sporting a Ruger 9mm with a black frame and silver slide, the same thing that this guy was holding. Sure, a lot of Rugers like that were on the street, but what were the odds of him having the same pistol as Jason?

"Ha!" she called out. "That's his pistol. He never jacked the slide. There's no round in the chamber!" Her voice dripped with disdain, like she thought the guy was a complete moron. Anyone could hear the unspoken "Idiot" in that sentence.

The man looked confused, trying to figure out how to run the slide with one of his hands occupied with his hostage. Then he had an idea. He brought the pistol down to his waist level and pushed down, trying to get the rear sight hooked on his pants, and rack the slide that way.

The important thing was that it took the muzzle away from pointing at Jason's head. And Taylor could see one of his legs from where she stood. It was close to Jason's legs, so this was going to be a game of inches. And not a game at all.

The guy was moving as quickly as he could, gambling that he could get the gun operational and back in position before anyone could do anything. But

Taylor did this sort of thing for fun, starting with her pistol pointed at one target and switching it as quickly as possible to another one. You had to know the weight of the pistol, the feel of it, the way you held it and sighted it, and repeat that, thousands of times, until it just became an extension of your body.

She swung and fired twice, long experience keeping the muzzle under control and the shots close together, both in time and in impact. She was afraid to fire more than that because she knew things would start to move at the first shot and she didn't want Jason's leg in the way. But she knew she could get two shots off before anyone could even twitch.

Both of her bullets slammed into the man's calf, that big, beefy gastrocnemius muscle, and the leg immediately collapsed under him.

For a few seconds, things happened like a dance under a strobe light. You have a glimpse of action here, and then some there, like a jerky stop-motion cartoon.

The man let go of Jason, one hand going for the wound and the other to try to grab the door frame to stay on his feet.

Jason flinched back from the shots, ducking, and then ran when he realized he was free.

The man sank to the floor, the pistol swinging wildly around now, but trending in Valentina's direction.

The Latina responded by unloading her whole magazine on him until the slide locked back.

Jason didn't know who was shooting at whom, so he hooked a sharp turn to get out of the way of any incoming fire, until he looked back and realized he was safe.

Taylor figured Valentina was in control of that particular situation at that point and she needed to make sure she was still in control of the other one. She swung back to the two men on the ground.

The bodyguard had rolled over and sat up a little and was digging in his pants for something. Considering the situation, there was only one thing he was after.

She shot him twice in the chest and then once in the face. He fell back to the ground and threw both hands up to the wound on his face. That gave her a great shot at his throat, so she shot him there, too. If someone is trying to shoot at you, it's always good to make sure they are very thoroughly dead before turning your attention to something else. He curled up in a fetal position and gagged and twitched a little before going still.

She scanned back and forth, searching for threats while keeping an eye on Little Cut. She was the only one that had a functioning weapon at this point, so it would all be up to her to keep their little band safe.

The drug dealer wasn't running. He had his hands on the back of his head, trying to protect it and scrunch his body down into the parking lot as deeply as he could go.

"Shit!" came from Valentina. She dropped the empty magazine and reloaded, still peering at the body in the apartment doorway to make sure he didn't move.

Jason walked by her, slowly, with his hands up so she wouldn't perceive him as a threat. He eased into the apartment and retrieved his pistol.

"Grab your magazine and the bottle," Taylor called to her, when she had stopped fixating on that guy. As soon as she had done that, Taylor added "Too much drama. We need to go. Now."

Valentina walked over to Little Cut. "You son of a bitch, you're getting off easy."

She tried to shoot him but nothing happened. Looking at her pistol, she realized the slide was still locked back. She shook her head in frustration, hit the slide release to run it forward and chamber a round, and shot him three times in the head. He still had his hands on his head and the bullets severed one of his fingers, causing it to pop up and bounce away.

"Let's go!" Taylor turned and ran.

Their route was through the back of the apartments, and then they were faced with a creek and a fenced business. They crossed the boulevard there, into some more businesses, unfenced, and to their truck. They hadn't bothered to disguise it because it was a white Ford F-150 and there were only about a million trucks that fit that description on the road.

Before Hexen, the police would have been all over them. There would have been witnesses every step of the way, cell phone video, security camera footage, people calling 911, radio communication between squad cars, the whole nine yards. Maybe even a helicopter.

Now, their only risk was a random squad car in the area with the windows down, close enough to hear the shots. Even assuming he had a radio to call for backup, he'd have to wait a while for any support to arrive, and it would have to be a bold cop indeed who would charge alone into an ongoing gunfight. It was much better to wait until the morning to let things work themselves out and write a report on what happened, instead of becoming one of the casualties. Especially now, the old saying about pilots went for cops, too: *There are old cops and there are bold cops, but there are no old, bold cops.* Probably not any young, bold ones left, either.

Once they were on the road, Taylor looked at Jason. "You okay, Honeyboo?"

"Yeah. I walked into that apartment and the guy punched me in the stomach. He was waiting back there in the dark."

"I'm just glad he wasn't sitting there with an AK or an AR. He could have hosed us all down and been done with it. I really don't know why he wasn't."

"They had the two guards. Maybe he was just some random asshole, spending the night or something," Valentina suggested.

"And I did rack the slide." Jason said that in a kind of little-boy voice, like he was offended that his abilities would be questioned.

"Oh, yeah, that was complete bullshit. But it did get him to take the barrel away from pointing at your head, didn't it?"

He was in the front passenger seat of the tuck. Taylor was in the back of the crew cab. He turned around to look at her. "But what if he'd pulled the trigger to see? While it *was* pointed at my head?"

"Then he'd have lost his hostage. Where's the logic in that?"

"I don't think those guys were too strong on logic." He ramped the volume up a little, and had a little heat in his voice.

Taylor was cruising on the adrenaline rush. It was her drug of choice, and one of the things it did was make her horny. That was actually kind of a common feeling, of euphoria from surviving a fight. A desire for sex is a natural component of that. She had known that going in, and definitely thought about Jason and her finding a use for that partial box of condoms. Using them for something more than a cover story, like they'd done earlier.

But now he was blowing it.

They'd spent a lot of time together and she'd enjoyed his company. She'd saved his life just now, both with distracting the guy and with a couple of shots to the man's leg. Which neatly missed Jason's leg, thank you very much. He ought to be appreciative of that instead of second-guessing her.

"It worked," she said shortly. He didn't catch the unspoken part: *you aren't going to be getting laid tonight.*

I guess his fragile manhood is in jeopardy, she thought. *Valentina shot three. I shot one. He shot zero. And only one person got their weapon taken away from them, and it wasn't us girls!*

The rest of the trip was spent in silence. Fortunately, it only took a little while, even with the circular route that they had planned.

***

Tony had a light in the window, a candle, so they headed to his place and reported in.

His first reaction was to freeze and stare at Valentina for a second. Then he tilted his head, still staring, like a dog that has seen something weird and thinks that the view from a 45-degree angle will make it more obvious.

Taylor cracked up laughing. The Latina looked confused until she figured it out.

"It's a disguise!" she hastily explained.

"Okay, whatever. What you do in your spare time is your business. But don't give me too many details," he instructed. "I don't want to know too much. Plausible deniability and all that, you know."

"It was actually pretty straightforward, I guess," Valentina related. "We went in like clients and got the drop on them. The problem came in with an extra guy that was in the apartment itself. But it was resolved. We just, uh, made too much noise. I wanted to talk to the dealer and burn his product but I had to... end our discussion rather abruptly. We vacated the premises at that point."

"Sounds like a win to me. And with that, I am going to head to bed. Good night, everyone".

Outside, Valentina announced drinks at her place. Jason had one and then made his goodbyes.

As soon as he was out the door, Valentina looked at Taylor. "If you've leaving tomorrow, that was your last chance to slip between the sheets with him."

"I'll admit I've considered it, but no. I'm good. But if I'm ever feeling horny, apparently OK City is the place to go. Or the place to go to come, I guess I should say. I've had a guy, a teen, and a girl hit on me."

"And Smitty wanted to make you an ex-wife, so that implies a marriage first."

"Oh, my God."

They talked relationships for a while, and went through the gunfight again for about the third time.

"You were the one that had your shit together," Valentina noted. "How do you do that? I'm not that calm."

"I don't know. I had to have been born with it because there was no training that I went through. I don't have much of a startle reflex. Even when I was a little girl, if a boy jumped out and said 'boo!' I wouldn't scream. I'd just look at them. One time I backhanded a boy that did it and almost got in trouble. He kept trying to scare me and I was just tired of it, so I swatted him. Of course, I acted like I was just scared and threw my arms out.

"So, while normal people go through a few seconds of... panic, maybe? I don't know what it is since I don't experience it. Anyway, I have a clear head and can make decisions, so that gives me those few seconds free to do something where other people would be floundering around."

Valentina shook her head in amazement. "I thought I fired about four rounds at that guy in the apartment and my slide was locked back, so I must have just dumped the whole magazine on him."

"You pretty much shot him to rags. But you were hitting him, not just spraying shots all over the countryside, so good job."

She took that as a compliment, since she'd heard about Taylor's adventures.

Chapter Twenty

In the morning, the light coming through the blinds woke Taylor up. She turned over and pulled the cover over her head. But that made it hot, and she had to pee, so she reluctantly rolled out of bed. As she walked downstairs, she smelled coffee.

"Oh, thank God," she mumbled as she walked into the kitchen. Valentina was leaning against the counter, sipping from a cup.

"You're a bad influence, *chica*. I don't usually drink that much."

"Neither do I, but I think you're the bad influence." She poured a cup of coffee.

"Maybe it's not a good idea to put us two together." Valentina sat down at the little dinette table when there was a knock at the door. "Are you kidding me? I *just* sat down."

"I'll get it." Taylor looked out the peephole, turned, and announced "It's Jason."

Valentina shrugged. "Let him in. You have time for a quickie."

She hesitated a moment and then opened the door, wearing nothing more than a t-shirt and panties.

Jason's eyes went wide. "Uh... uh... well, that just blew any concentration I had. I... have no idea what I was going to say, now."

"Well, come on in and get your thoughts together." Taylor turned away from the door and walked back to the kitchen and dining area.

"Are you checking out her ass as she's walking?" Valentina asked. "Because she has a cute little ass. Oh my God, that thing is tight. I told her y'all have time for a quickie."

Taylor retrieved her coffee cup and turned to look at Jason with raised eyebrows. "There is not going to be a quickie."

"Okay, so, changing the subject drastically, I wanted to apologize first to you, Valentina. I screwed up last night. I should have been more careful going into that apartment and I screwed up your operation. I know you didn't get to do everything you wanted to do. I'm sorry."

"It's fine, Jason. You might have saved us from staying there too long. We might have gotten trapped inside the apartment if some of his friends had shown up. And we only had pistols on us, so we weren't armed for anything other than a close-up battle anyway. But thank you."

He nodded. "And Taylor, I wanted to apologize to you and to thank you. I was pretty hyped-up last night. I felt kind of caught in the crossfire with you and her both shooting at that guy. But once I calmed down and slept on it, I realized that you probably saved my life twice. Once was having the quick thought to say my gun was not chambered, and then you shot him and he let go of me. And not only did I fail to thank you last night, I was jacked up on the excitement and I probably acted like an asshole to you. I'm sorry and I want to thank you."

"Apology accepted."

He looked at her for a moment, smiled slowly, and asked "Still no quickie, huh?"

"Still no quickie. She's just being a bad influence, putting ideas in your head."

"I'm glad, actually. I would rather have a deep, long-term relationship with you instead of just sex. But I understand you're engaged. I enjoyed working with you. Goodbye and good luck with everything. Valentina, I'll see you at work sometime. Whenever the schedule works out."

Both young ladies said their goodbyes as he walked out the door, and then there was a period of silence when the door closed.

Am I screwing up? Taylor thought. *Am I letting a really, really good guy walk out the door? Do I even* want *a relationship? It's been my admittedly rather limited experience that boyfriends are generally more trouble than they're worth. Or am I missing something? Like, the right guy?*

She turned to look at Valentina, who was being uncharacteristically quiet. She seemed to have been reading Taylor's mind. She shrugged.

"I don't know. I can't tell you if he's the right guy for you. He's going to be a catch for some girl. Like I said a few nights ago, I'm not trying to dictate who you should or should not go to bed with."

Taylor drew in a deep breath, slowly, and let it out the same way, deep in thought.

"There's been a lot of stuff going on in a short amount of time. I'm not going to make any big decisions right now."

Now it was Valentina's turn for a deep breath. "Before Hexen, I was okay. Life was good. After Hexen, I didn't care if I died. I hated the world. Then, with the great support I got from Dani and you and Tony, things turned good again. And they're still good. Horn Dog's death sucks and it's going to take me a while to get over it. But it is something that could just as easily have happened either way, in that world or in this one. I hate that he died, but it could have happened no matter what else is going on. The one good thing about this world is that we got to... um, 'discuss' the matter with the drug dealer. In the old world, nothing would have happened to him."

Taylor smiled over the rim of her coffee cup. She made a quote sign in the air with her other hand and repeated "Discuss."

"That's the way a conversation with a man should be. Tell him what he did wrong and then shoot him in the head. Am I right?"

Taylor almost choked on her coffee, but recovered enough to reply "That certainly keeps them from doing it again."

***

They hugged at the train station, then Valentina clutched her close in a bigger hug and kissed her on the cheek. She had tears in her eyes when she pulled back.

"Thank you for everything," she said, her voice tight with emotion.

"I'm glad I could help. We need to get together more often. Why don't you come down to the ranch in a few months?"

"I'd like that. But not too often, because these hangovers are killing me!"

Chapter Twenty-One

It was late before Taylor made it back to the house. Eric and Dani were just about to go to bed, but they delayed a bit to greet her.

"We had an incident that just came up," he informed her. "Two of our guys in Oilfield Security in the Midland area managed to get hold of a quantity of high-quality cocaine and were planning to turn it into crack and sell it."

Taylor's eyebrows went up. That was a very serious incident. These things weren't plea-bargained down any more, either. Those boys were going to spend long years at hard labor in prison. No sitting around watching cartoons in air-conditioned facilities while other people worked. Prison wasn't like that now.

"Where I thought it might interest you is if you wanted to look into it. The guys rolled over and gave out the name of the guy they got it from, apparently a mid-level dealer, and where they met up with him. If you wanted to just verify that there is a guy there and make a small buy from him, that would prove he's the one. Something like that shouldn't be dangerous. Just act like a customer. You wouldn't need to arrest him or anything. Once we have information, I can get the state police in on it. Because the word is that the local police are dirty. Obviously, this needs to be undercover from them, too.

"This shouldn't take but a couple of days. Then you can go on and work for a month or whatever at Oilfield Security."

"Sure, I can do that," she replied. "Marten. Taylor Marten." She did an imitation of James Bond's signature introduction, complete with a finger gun.

***

In the morning, she went to see Brennan to get the full details. Brennan was a big woman, big as in tall and muscular, a dark-skinned Amazon warrior. She was retired Air Force Security Forces, which are the military police of the Air Force. She had hired on very early after Hexen, and Eric put her in charge of all of the security here at the ranch. That expanded to authority over their other security operations as they were created, Oilfield, Rail, and Bank.

"If the local cops are corrupt, then why don't the state cops investigate?" Taylor asked the question that had been bothering her.

"Too much to do and too few police to do it. You wouldn't believe how wide-open things are out there. We're insulated here because of the strong leadership that Eric and Dani provide. Other places don't have that. They don't have funds for police and law enforcement. If we just give the state police a name to investigate, they may never get around to it. There's no real weight behind that. But if we have one of our investigators actually make a buy, now we have undeniable evidence."

"So, this isn't some little bullshit assignment to keep me busy?"

"No, it's an important thing. We're viewing this little idea of cooking up crack very seriously. Eric damned near wanted to shoot those guys on the spot. We do need to know where it's coming from and see if we can get those guys taken out of business."

"Is anything going to happen with the police even if I do verify the guy?" Taylor asked skeptically. "I mean, I know Eric has influence with the governor but if things are wide open like you said..."

"It's going to be very important to us and the governor both. Nobody wants someone to get high and then screw something up at any oil and gas operation. One little mistake in the wrong place can cause huge expenses and even loss of life. I'm no expert, but think about this: they are refining gasoline. You know

109

how explosive that stuff is. Those guys are sitting on a bomb. A very large bomb. If somebody switches a valve wrong, or misses a danger sign, or doesn't read a gauge, the whole place could blow up. You really don't want someone that's responsible for something like that stoned off their ass."

"I can see that."

"Eric is concerned enough about it that he wants me to look into setting up a program to train drug-sniffing dogs. You don't recall anyone that listed 'dog trainer' as a job skill, do you?"

***

Since the mission had become an undercover one, the parameters and necessary equipment changed. Taylor dug a baby Glock, the model 26, out of the armory. The model 17 is considered the standard size in 9mm. The model 19 that she always carried is the compact, and the 26 is the subcompact. It drops an inch and a half from the overall length of the full-sized and, more importantly, an inch and a half in height. When attempting to conceal a weapon, height is more difficult to hide than length.

The penalty with the smaller weapon is that magazine capacity is reduced as the height is shortened. The seventeen rounds of the standard model drop to fifteen in the compact and ten in the subcompact. She figured to carry an extra ten-round magazine in her boot when undercover and carry the pistol inside the waistband. She already had an inside-the-waistband holster that would work with all models.

While she was in the armory, she grabbed an M67 hand grenade and a flash bang. That was one of the perks of a close relationship with the Army, ready access to weapons that civilians usually didn't have. Taylor didn't really like the M67. She wasn't able to throw it far enough away to feel comfortable. When it exploded it sent steel fragments out in every direction, including hers. She had used them once as booby traps, which was fine since she could be a long way away when they went off. She opened the little cardboard can with metal ends that the grenade came in and dropped in a length of heavyweight fishing line in case she needed it for a trip wire.

For other tools, she selected a flat twelve-inch wrecking bar, which was almost always a useful tool post-Hexen. Eric had nicknamed these pry bars 'master keys' since there were plenty of abandoned houses and buildings that they needed to get into. The bar could pry open a door or smash a window with ease and also made a pretty good hammer, digging tool, or general-purpose blunt instrument.

Taylor had learned the basics of lock picking but was certainly no pro at it. She dug out her tension wrench and rake pick and practiced with them. Whether she got any better or not was debatable, but they didn't weigh anything so they went in her kit. Zip ties got the nod for the same reason, light weight.

In Brennan's office, they discussed issuing Taylor a fake ID. Marten Cattle Company had the authority to issue Texas ID cards and had a supply in stock. They were really driver's licenses but no one was too concerned about people actually having driver's licenses, so they issued them to everyone. Thirteen-year-old kids had them. They didn't have photos and they weren't laminated, so their usefulness was perhaps minimal, but it might help to at least have something with Taylor's alias on it.

Brennan typed one up on the manual typewriter they had found in an antique shop and got all of the physical information in but paused on the name.

"We'll want something that has some similarity to your real name. There's something called the 'cocktail party effect'. It means you can walk through a cocktail party where there are dozens of conversations going on, but if someone says your name, you'll pick it out of all the noise. More obviously, if you're walking down the street and someone calls your name, you'll react. Any ideas?"

She'd never thought about a name that was similar to her own. They both sat there thinking for a moment.

"Maybelle," Brennan suggested.

Taylor choked on that and laughed. "Oh, God, no. Absolutely not. That sounds like the dairy cow". She switched to an exaggerated backwoods country accent. "Got to go do them chores. Got to go milk Maybelle."

Brennan laughed, then folded her arms and thought.

"Taymeeka," she suggested.

Taylor looked at her, wide-eyed. Brennan was black, and Taylor didn't want to offend her. The silence drew out for a few seconds until Brennan laughed.

"Girl, we're not going to give you a black girl's name," she scoffed, chuckling. "You couldn't pull that off!"

"Okay, you got me with that one," Taylor laughed.

Further thought produced "Kayla", which became the winner by default. Then they started on the last name.

"Isn't there a name like 'Hartbein' or something like that?"

Brennan got a good laugh out of that one.

"If you reverse it, 'beinhart' is German for 'hard as bone'. Where did you say you heard that?" She raised her eyebrows and leered at Taylor.

Taylor almost blushed. "I don't know. Okay, bad choice. Never mind that one."

They eventually settled on 'Kayla Carlson'. It had enough parts that were similar to her own name to allow her to pick up on it, yet was a completely different name if someone was reading it. Brennan completed the ID and then they aged it so it didn't look so fresh and new. A little light scraping with a knife and a coffee stain across a quarter of it made it look like it had been around for a while.

They made a run into Tyler to find some wigs. That was one of the few stores that hadn't been cleaned out. Food and ammunition, followed by alcohol and tobacco, had been at the top of almost everyone's list. Wigs, not so much, so they had an adequate selection. They chose a brunette and a red, both long enough to hang past her shoulders, just like her natural blonde locks. That and some makeup could do wonders in changing her appearance.

Chapter Twenty-Two

THE NEXT ITEM THAT Taylor wanted was a little more problematic.

Liz Mitchell was their medical and education officer and had been the one who rescued Taylor and brought her to where they met up with the Martens. Before that, she had been a neighbor of Taylor and her family.

She found Liz in her office and asked if she had a minute.

"Sure, come on in. How are things?"

"Can I close the door?"

"Of course. Is this medical? Is everything okay?"

"First off, this is secret. I am going to go out somewhere and do something undercover, you might say. With that in mind, I am gathering together anything I might possibly need. What can you tell me about date rape drugs? Specifically, can you make some?"

"Wow, okay. I had the idea that maybe you were going to ask for a pregnancy test or something. It's always an adventure talking to you, Taylor."

"Are you saying I bring some excitement into your life?"

She snorted. "I could actually do with a little less excitement. I think I'm full up for this lifetime. So, this undercover thing, you think you might need to knock someone out?"

"I have no idea. I think there might be a possibility. It would be better for me to have the capability and not need it, than need it and not have it."

"You do realize there is a question of safety? An overdose could be fatal, or cause damage to the brain or kidneys or other organs? I mean, I have no idea what dosage would be appropriate. The person's health and body weight, if they have any other things in their system like alcohol, all of that plays a part in determining dosage."

"Figure an average male, good health, maybe late twenties or early thirties. And if you give me two or three doses, I can estimate if I need to give them some extra."

"Something like GHB immediately comes to mind. It's a liquid. You introduce it into someone's drink and it'll hit them in fifteen or twenty minutes. It's a depressant that will cause the victim to become drowsy or pass out."

"That's perfect."

Liz looked off at the wall, not seeing it, and thought about the request. Then she looked at Taylor for a moment.

"You know, there are four people on this ranch that I would say 'let me see what I can do'. Everybody else, it would be a 'no'. But I've known you since you were a little girl and I trust you, so you're one of the four. I know you won't do something stupid with it. That's provided I can get some or make some. I'm going to have to do some research."

"I appreciate that, Liz. I honestly do. Thank you for having that trust in me." Taylor was eighteen now and she thought it was more appropriate to call her by her first name instead of "Mrs. Mitchell".

"Don't kill someone with this stuff." She gave Taylor a stern look.

"If I use it on someone, I am willing for them to take that risk."

"That's not really the answer I was looking for, but I guess it will have to do. When do you need it?"

"I'd like to leave in about four days."

"Let's see what I find out."

***

They decided she should take a truck with her instead of buying one when she got there. That was too uncertain. There may not be any available, or the prices may be ridiculous, or what she got might be unreliable. It was much better to simply grab a known good truck and throw it on a flatcar to travel with her. She could bring it back or leave it for Oilfield Security to use.

In keeping with her undercover role, the truck was a white Ford F150. That is as generic as generic can be. There were probably only eight or ten million white F150s in Texas. It didn't have any special equipment like roll bars or extra lights or anything. No pop-up machineguns or ejection seats, either, just a reliable truck.

The Marten Cattle Company standard truck was thoroughly rebuilt from the old junker that it had been. Since the EMP had fried all of the fancy computers and electronics of more modern vehicles, these trucks were all pre-1990 or so. There were some exceptions where newer ones had been rebuilt, but that took more work. The newest cars and trucks with computer-controlled transmissions and brakes and other components obviously took an even greater amount of labor.

The usual was an older model that had been completely refurbished — rebuilt engine, transmission, brakes, differential, everything. The interiors sported new leather seats. Leather, for a cattle company, was a cheap and easy material to acquire, and there was in fact an active industry on the ranch of small shops that produced boots, belts, packs, coats, and many other goods from the plentiful leather.

After that rebuild, some were painted in an olive drab and some in a flat black primer and some were simply touched up with something close to their original color. Rumor had it that Dani had mentioned that she was bored with all of the trucks being green or black so that came to a stop. Happy wife, happy life!

Following paint, the vehicles were finished off with brush buster bumpers, winches, extra off-roading lights, and rollbars. The trucks used by Security had rollbars that went the whole length of the bed so that people could run a strap from their belt to the bar and stand in the bed while underway without worrying about falling out of the truck.

The other type of truck was the 'stealth' model. The stealths were not stealthy because they were painted in flat colors and had quiet mufflers; just the opposite, in fact. They were stealthy because they didn't have the distinctive look of the other MCC vehicles. They wore their factory colors, whatever paint they had when they rolled off of the assembly line. They didn't have any of the extra equipment or lights or anything. Mechanically they were perfect, with everything rebuilt, but the mufflers might be a bit loud. The standard trucks had quiet exhaust systems because Eric thought that sneaking up on an enemy may be necessary. It had come in handy more than once before. The stealth trucks didn't have that restriction. They were just trucks.

***

Taylor trolled around the ranch, looking for anything else she might need on this little adventure. She wanted to be prepared for anything, so she included a lot of unusual items. One was a Bernzomatic torch that she spotted in the motor pool. This is the little handheld torch that is used in plumbing to solder pipe joints, by mechanics to loosen stuck bolts, and other small tasks. It is simply a small propane tank, about the size of a one-liter bottle of Coca-Cola, small enough to hold in the hand. It has an angled brass tube and tip screwed onto the end of the cylinder with a valve to regulate the flow of the gas.

Taylor spotted the pretty blue cylinder and asked what it was, which led to requesting a demonstration. The mechanic was only too glad to show her how to light it with a spark igniter and adjust the gas flow to get the flame optimally intense. When she left, the torch and the igniter went with her.

Chapter Twenty-Three

TAYLOR SLIPPED ONTO THE morning train as discreetly as she could without obviously looking like she was hiding. She had the thought that a quiet start with no fanfare was best, so she had said her goodbyes at the house. Dani had hugged her with tears in her eyes, and maybe Eric had had a little dust in his eyes. There had been no going-away party and not much mention. Actually, the girls in the dorm had done a little party, but nothing out in public in the E Club.

The occasional beauty pageant contestant preferred to have the spotlight off of her, now. She liked working in the shadows, behind Dani. She wanted to display substance, not flash.

This morning, she had on a cowboy hat and sunglasses, with her hair tied in a loose ponytail and tucked down the back of her shirt. No one could claim that was a disguise, yet it changed her appearance quite a bit. She strolled in and got on the train directly, without rushing. Her ticket called for a private compartment so once she was in, she was hidden.

Quietly, then, her new adventure began.

***

The train stopped in Dallas, then Fort Worth. The cities may have been depleted but they weren't dead. There were some businesses going, mainly clustered in the downtown where there was some electrical power coming back. Further out were the forted-up communities, the *barricadas,* and other areas where people were just too poor to rob or hassle.

And there was the sin industry.

The neighborhoods around the typical train station looked like the Zona Norte in Tijuana if you turned the bad parts up to eleven: full-contact strip clubs, prostitutes, bars, drugs, gambling and various fighting competitions that bettors could risk money on, and pretty much anything else people would pay for.

Farm boys and cowboys and roughnecks rode in on the trains or busses, got drunk, got laid, and rode back out. Or sometimes ended up with a knife between their ribs. It was tolerated because no one could do anything about it. If the governor wanted it cleaned out, he could send troops in, but it all came back as soon as they left. He had tried it before, twice. The state couldn't afford to keep enough troops there to keep it clean. He'd tried that once. The pimps and drug dealers just moved their operations back a few more blocks. If the troops expanded their perimeter, the sleaze just moved back further and sent vans in to bring partiers from the station to their new locations. When the troops left, they moved back closer to the station.

It was a no-win situation for the state. They had to settle for keeping the station and the immediate vicinity safe and leave it at that. Coldly put, there were no critical operations threatened, like with the oil industry. Even then, they didn't have the resources to investigate and keep a handle on everything, hence Taylor's mission.

She stayed in her compartment. There was no reason for her to go out in that mess, and she had a little work to do.

***

During the trip, the blonde that had gotten on the train became a brunette. Taylor braided her hair, then wrapped it around her head and held it in place

118

with bobby pins. A wig cap went over that, just a thin cotton covering, and then the wig. She had bangs now, and long, dark, silky hair that spilled over her shoulders. Her eyebrows were naturally dark enough that they didn't look odd with the change in hair color. She used eyeliner around her eyes and applied eye shadow, blush, and lipstick. As she did it, she smiled at the memory of her and Dani pranking Eric.

They were playing with the wigs, a couple of them, and did Taylor up with the dark one she wore now, plus full makeup. It felt weird. She'd really never put on this much makeup before. Her norm was none, and if she 'did' makeup, it was just eyeliner. This was the whole works.

When Eric got home, they introduced Taylor as the Kayla alias. He shook her hand but he was giving her a strange look the whole time. He knew something was wrong, he just couldn't figure out what. Dani couldn't hold it in. She snapped like a cheap number two pencil. She burst out laughing, followed by Taylor.

They counted that as a success. He had known Taylor for four years. She lived at his house the entire time, so he was tough to fool. Other people, not so much.

That was who they were worried about. They didn't want someone recognizing Taylor and knowing instantly who she worked for, which may not match up with who she was claiming she worked for. Many of the guys and girls they employed at Oilfield Security had met or seen her. She wasn't hard to look at, so lots of them would remember her.

On the train, in her private compartment, she completed the makeup and put on what she thought of as her escape kit. It consisted of two items. The first was a handcuff key. They're all the same; one key works with any handcuffs. The other item was a small knife, a Spyderco Ladybug. Closed, the knife is less than two and a half inches long, with a two-inch blade, fully serrated. The two items were connected by a strong trotline string. She duct-taped it to her back, low enough that she could reach it if her hands were bound together but high enough that a frisk along her waistline should miss it.

"I hope I never need you guys," she mused as she stuck the items to the tape before sticking it to her back. That was as close as she got to praying.

Taylor, now Kayla, got off the train in Midland and walked back to where they were unloading her truck. The workmen got the chains released and drove it off the flatbed, onto the dock, and then down the ramp. They didn't even shut the engine off because she was right there with her claim ticket. She threw her gear in the vehicle and drove off.

It was late afternoon but she didn't see any reason not to start now. The original plan had been for her to get a room, survey the situation, and make the buy, all under the Kayla alias. Then she could ditch the disguise and check in with Oilfield Security as Taylor and go to work for them. MOS, Marten Oilfield Security, had purposely not been given a head's up that she was coming. There was no reason to put pressure on her with an artificial deadline. Of course, she would report back to headquarters regarding the success or failure of the undercover part of her job, and that situation would work its way through the appropriate channels of police and prosecutors and defense attorneys and whatever.

Yeah, she wasn't going to do that.

Her thought was that a little more direct action would be a lot more fun. And more justified. The kiss with Horn Dog hadn't been romantic, *per se*, hadn't been skillfully done, wasn't her first — in fact, there would be nothing memorable about it, except that it was his last one. That meant that she would remember it forever. It also put her in a rage, simmering at a low intensity right now, but ready to boil over into a murderous fury once she had an outlet.

No, she wasn't out here to set up a situation where she sat in a witness box and testified that, on such and such a date, she had purchased exhibit number one from the defendant. Not quite. That sounded extremely dull and boring. Besides, she wasn't going to risk her life for one lone asshole to be sentenced to a few years of incarceration, if that. Because that's really what she was doing, risking her life. Life was cheap and there were few witnesses and none of the clever ways that police had found to locate and track people's movements and do forensics and reconstruct crimes. Not that those had ever done any good for the dead victim, anyway.

No, the reality was that if someone thought they were going to go to prison because of her, they'd kill her and dump her body somewhere and not worry too much about ever having to answer for the crime. Or maybe they'd keep her alive and sell her to a pimp in Mexico after having their fun with her. She wasn't risking all that to try to send one easily replaced guy to prison. She had bigger things in mind, a blood debt that she was going to collect.

She thought that Eric was underestimating the danger. Or maybe she was overestimating it. Whatever, she was the one doing the risking, and Eric always said that the boots on the ground should make the call, not some fat-assed officer in a nice, warm, safe office a thousand miles from the action. It was her boots on the ground, her ass on the line, so she was making the call.

Her call was that she was going to put a lot of guys down, hard.

Chapter Twenty-Four

SHE DROVE AROUND SOME, just getting a feel for the city. Midland could have been in the Middle East as far as the terrain went. There was a little bit of greenery, grass and weeds, and there had probably been more before the end of civilization, but almost everything seemed brown to her. Sand, dirt, rocks, and low, scrubby brush dominated. And oil wells.

Lots and lots of oil wells. She had read that there were over thirty-thousand oil wells between Midland, Odessa, and West Odessa. And more in just about any direction one cared to go. As a number on a page, that didn't mean a whole lot. She'd always known Midland was an oil town, but the reality of seeing it in person was amazing. The city seemed to display an intense focus on the oil and gas industry, a single-minded devotion that allowed no other intrusion. Travel in any direction led to metal buildings housing some type of oilfield-related business, pipe yards, trucks, trailers, and industrial equipment.

It was like seeing her first horse race close up. You know that horses are big, and that a group of them running by will be loud and impressive. In person, however, right up in the front row, the hooves thundering on the ground, the massive amount of horseflesh racing by, the rush of air as they swept past, was almost overwhelming.

When it started getting dark, she focused on looking for a place to eat. She wanted something substantial because she didn't know when she'd eat again. Also, she was going to a bar and may have to drink some alcohol. It would be much better to do that on a full stomach so the effects were lessened. On the other hand, she didn't need to eat too much and feel sluggish.

The top two choices that appealed to her were steak or Italian, and she hadn't had good Italian in some time. She got plenty of steak on the ranch. While it got good and dark she filled up on garlic bread and lasagna with a glass of wine, the wine more to have something safe to drink. It wasn't wise to simply trust that any water would be safe.

Out in the parking lot she brushed her teeth to get rid of the garlic breath, using her own known good water. She didn't intend to kiss anyone but she didn't want to drive anyone away, either. The most powerful weapon she was going to take into that bar tonight was herself. Oh, she'd be armed with firearms and blades, but the big gun she was bringing was sex appeal; her face and body and the possibility of getting her into bed.

It shouldn't be that difficult. She'd had to turn down a couple of offers already, just trying to get a meal.

She upper the ante by unbuttoning her shirt a bit. When she'd dressed this morning, she'd worn a cute, lacy black bra. Now she made it a little easier to see, not out there on display, but if she leaned forward, or someone taller than her was standing close enough, they could see some cleavage.

She had a hand-drawn map which wasn't too bad. Of course, there were no street lights, so finding the names of some of the streets was a chore. She was backing the truck around to get the headlights on one sign when another truck pulled up beside her. The older gentleman driving it gave her directions and she made it the remainder of the way without problems.

To the bar named The Pumping Unit. She was a little dismissive of the name for its double entendre.

"Sounds like a whorehouse," she muttered to herself.

Pumping units were not hard to find around Midland. Just the opposite. They were as thick as flies. A pumping unit is the metal structure common in oilfields that looks somewhat like a bird dipping its head down and then back up, over and over. It was hard to get away from them in the area. An old one, or a good facsimile of one, was front and center of the bar. Again, there were no lights, but a pair of fires in steel drums flanked the device and shed some degree of light on the sign.

She backed into a parking place and shut it down. It wasn't a random choice. She selected a spot that would allow her to run out the door and around the truck to get to the driver's side, shielding her somewhat from any incoming fire. The truck was sideways to the front door, which meant that she could pull the AK up from behind the seat and it would already be pointed at the door. Or more precisely, straight at anyone coming out the door and heading towards her. And it was backed in so she could just put it in drive and hit the gas if she needed to get down the road in a hurry.

She was on her operation now, her mind in top gear, running hot, scanning, evaluating, assessing, planning. Anything and everything she did tonight, including nothing, could get her killed. She needed to be aware of everything going on around her, needed to be on top of her every action, needed to perform at the highest level.

Around her were other trucks, motorcycles, and horses. There was a section just like she had seen in Western movies, a rail to tie horses up and a water trough below for the animals to quench their thirst. Maybe it had been for show at one time but now it was in real use.

She took a deep breath, a little apprehensive, and checked her gear. First, the wig, to make sure it was straight. Next were the little vials in a pocket. Then a Glock 26 in a holster inside her waistband at the five o'clock position, hidden under her shirttail. A spare magazine was in her boot, in the sock. She didn't intend to do much walking and no running, so it shouldn't chafe her leg or fall out. She had a lockblade knife, a Cold Steel Recon I clip point. The company included both right- and left-handed pocket clips with the knife, and the thumb stud was reversible. She preferred to carry it in her left front pocket, set up for left-handed use. Not that she was left-handed; if anything, she was ambidextrous, but she had had an encounter once that almost ended badly.

Fighting two-to-one odds, she had been trapped in a corner with her right arm pinned. One person had her in a clinch and was punching her in the face. The other was trying to jerk her slung rifle off of her shoulder. She had managed, barely, to get her knife out and open left-handed and stab one of her attackers and take control of the situation, but it had been a close-run thing. The knife she had then was not intended to be opened left-handed and she almost dropped it, which would have meant her death. She had immediately searched for a knife that was left-hand friendly after that.

This one was now well-used and opened easily, and was honed to a literal razor sharpness. That was kind of a thing with Eric, sharp knives. They were simple tools, meant to cut, and they didn't cut well when dull. Walking around with a dull knife was like building a fire and then putting a pot of stew far enough away from the fire that it barely warmed your meal. It just didn't make any sense to deliberately do it.

The knife and the pistol were the only weapons she was carrying inside. The rest of her gear was staying in the truck. That included the AK behind the seat with the seventy-five-round drum magazine locked in and a round in the chamber. If she had to come running out of the bar with someone in pursuit, she wanted to be able to lay down some substantial firepower.

The next most important thing she carried was under the AK, an assault vest. This was also called a chest rig, which allowed her to put it on and immediately have everything she needed for battle. The pouches in front carried six thirty-round magazines. Other pouches held a first aid kit, canteens, an M67 grenade and M84 flash bang, and a big knife. This one was an Ek Model 5 with a seven-inch bowie-style blade.

It also held a small survival kit, which she knew how to use. She knew because she'd had to use it in training. Eric didn't believe in theory. He believed in practice. That meant that you went out in the woods and *used* your survival kit.

Nothing else, just your kit, while moving from point A to point B and carrying your rifle and a full load of ammunition. He tried really hard to run that training when it was raining. She learned what worked and what didn't, both equipment and practice. She learned from spending some nights cold and wet and miserable out in the woods. She discarded gear, added new, modified existing, and then went out to test the new stuff. And did it again to test the next set of changes.

Throughout all of the training, he'd been hard on her and Dani. He threw water and dirt on them when they were trying to hit targets at hundreds of yards. He'd made them run down to the targets to check their shots, run back, and then shoot again. He'd made them suffer, because it's better to sweat in training than to bleed in battle. Taylor smiled a little, thinking of how many times she'd called him a son of a bitch, and even a few when she'd really gotten mad and called him a motherfucker. But he'd always laughed at her, and a couple of times when she'd been ready to cry and give up, he'd encouraged her. He looked her in the eye and said "You can do this. You *can* do this. I know you can. I believe in you. You're strong. You just have to believe in yourself. Now dig your heels in and do it, *chica*." And she had.

She was strong. She could do this, too. Butterflies flitted through her stomach, but there was the anticipation there, too.

The hunt was beginning. It had been a long time since she'd hunted men. Deer and hogs and coyotes just weren't anywhere near as exciting. Smarter, in some cases, but not as exciting.

Chapter Twenty-Five

TAYLOR WALKED THROUGH THE door and stopped, giving her eyes a chance to adjust and surveying the layout. It was dark, of course. There were candles on the tables and on shelves along the walls. There was some type of electrical generation somewhere in the area but the output was being used for oil and gas operations, to run those pumping units that were everywhere around the city. People can do lots of things in the dark, like light rooms up with candles, but it's a lot easier to pump crude oil with electric pumps. Priorities.

She walked to the bar, a little amused by the fact that she wouldn't be old enough to drink legally in Texas for another two and a half years. The bartender saw her coming early on, moved to an open area, and watched her come up. He smiled at her and she returned it. It looked a whole lot better on her than it did on him.

"Do you have a light beer?" she asked.

"Sure do. The brewery calls it Lite Sweet Crude. After, you know."

"The oilfield, I'll bet," she played along as he opened a bottle for her. Light sweet crude is the most sought-after petroleum, as it is low in sulfur and delivers a higher yield when processed into gasoline, kerosene, and diesel. It's also known as West Texas Intermediate and is a standard benchmark traded on the New York Mercantile Exchange. Or was, before the world ended.

The beer was almost cool. A step above lukewarm, anyway. Ice was more important than lights in a bar. Priorities, again. The bartender pulled a wet cloth from out of a bucket and wrapped it around the bottle. As the water evaporated, it would help to cool the beer. As he worked, he talked.

"I haven't seen you in here before."

"Is it that obvious that I'm new in town? Do I have a neon light flashing over my head?" she laughed, holding up a hand just above her head and opening and closing it to simulate a flashing neon sign.

"You're beautiful. I'd remember if I had ever seen you."

"Oh, well, aren't you the charmer? I'm actually on a mission. I'm supposed to talk to a guy named Dennis."

The bartender looked disappointed at that. "If you're going to buy something from him, I might be able to hook you up for free. After I get off work, you know. Depending on what you want."

Yeah, right, she thought. *Get the girl high and then it's straight off to bed. It's free if I let you get into my pants.* Aloud she replied "I promised someone that I'd talk to Dennis. But —" she gave him a look and purred "I'll be back."

He didn't look convinced, but was hopeful. He nodded towards a group off to his left. "I would say Dennis is the guy with the ball cap and tattoos and beard, but that wouldn't narrow it down none."

She looked in the same direction and laughed. That description fit all of the dozen or so guys there. Shaving was something else that had gone by the wayside to a large extent. There were no factories pumping out millions of razors, so for a lot of men, a shave became something they did whenever they got a haircut. Or maybe not even then.

One of the guys in the group saw them looking in their direction, or needed a fresh beer, so he started walking towards the bar. Taylor started in his direction, her beer in her left hand, to keep her right free. They met somewhere in the middle and she asked "Are you Dennis?"

"Darlin', I'll be anyone you want me to be."

"Except truthful?"

He shrugged dramatically, arms out and admitted "Busted. You can't blame me for tryin', darlin'."

She walked up to the rest of the guys, who stopped whatever they were doing to watch her as she came closer. *Like a pack of wolves looking over a tasty morsel,* she thought. *You bastards have no idea that* I'm *the one with fangs in this room.* She got a little thrill, just a hint. Something began to come awake inside her. "Dennis?" she asked the crowd in general.

Five or six of the guys groaned or made some muttered comment. One stepped forward, smiling broadly. "At your service, little lady."

"My name is Kayla. A friend of mine wanted me to talk to you."

"Really? Why don't we —" whatever he was going to say was cut off by the house band tuning up. The drummer decided to go through a little solo as a test or something. Dennis looked at him in annoyance, then pointed to a far corner that was empty.

Once seated at a table in the back, Dennis asked what she would like.

"Some friends and I managed to come into some cash. We'd like to invest it in some products and move it and distribute it. Small loads at first, and work our way up to bigger things."

"How do I know you're not a cop?"

Taylor's face fell and darkened. "Fuck the cops." There was heat in her voice. "They didn't do shit for me when I needed help, when I was fifteen. I'm not going to fucking help them now."

"Hey, I understand. I'm sorry to bring up bad memories. I got a lot of those myself." He did look contrite. "What did you and your friends do to come into this cash?" Dennis asked.

She looked off into the far distance and her jaw clenched, then unclenched and she turned her gaze to look into Dennis's eyes. "After Hexen, there was a man named Larry, who gathered young, pretty girls around him. And he fed them and gave them a place to stay. As long as we were nice to him. And nice to his friends. He had a lot of friends, every night. But recently Larry died, and we took our inheritance."

The story wasn't true, not for her, but it could very easily have been. Unfortunately, it was very true for far too many young girls and boys who had suddenly been orphaned and cut adrift in a lawless world.

"Y'all didn't kill him, did you?"

"No, he had a heart attack or something. Aneurysm, stroke, whatever. I'm not a doctor. He was an older guy. He just collapsed and died." She shrugged.

"How'd you know to come looking for me?"

"There were some oilfield guys that were customers. They mentioned your name and this place."

"Oh? Who was that?"

She gave a little snort that meant she thought he was an idiot and gave him a hard look. Aloud she said "I never bothered to ask any of the guys their names. Not after the first thirty or forty."

Dennis seemed to be dredging up bad memories for the girl with every question, so he held off. He figured if this girl had spent the last four years as a whore, then she shouldn't have any problem spreading her legs for him tonight. They could work out any business details later. Pleasure first, then business. He dropped the questions and turned on the charm. He needed to get her in a better mood.

They flirted, with Taylor becoming less pissed and more friendly. Hexen and the EMP had kind of killed small talk to a large extent. No one wanted to talk about their family (all dead, most likely), their career (ruined, unless they were a farmer or rancher), or sports (nonexistent other than local leagues). Even with those restrictions, Dennis did a good job. He asked if she was a Texas girl, then segued that into horseback riding. He had a partnership in a ranch nearby and floated the possibility of them doing some riding. That gave them some common ground to chat about, since she had taken riding lessons, both English and Western.

At one point she actually found herself enjoying it. They had the E Club at the ranch, and a couple of other places that served alcohol. Dive bars, more or less, or private clubs. She could walk in and would be served whatever she ordered, no issues with her being underage, but this was different. This wasn't some place that she had helped build. She hadn't been in on the plans and meetings about this place. The bartender and the band and the patrons weren't people that she had known since they straggled into the ranch as refugees, hungry, dirty, and shell-shocked. That was the same condition she had been in when she got there. The difference was that she had arrived at the beginning, when Dani and Eric were just starting their ranch. She was part of the establishment when everyone else came in.

Here, she was new and unknown. It gave her an unusual feeling of freedom. At the ranch, she had to watch herself and show some restraint. She couldn't get sloppy drunk and leave with some random guy. Not that she wanted to do that in the first place, but just the fact that she couldn't tended to lurk there in the back of her mind as a restraint. She didn't have that here.

Of course, she had another restraint keeping her from doing that. She was here on a mission, not to party. She had a responsibility. She was hunting, and she had her trophy buck in her sights. Despite that, she had a momentary pang of regret for that other world, the one that had died. She would have liked to have gone out to a club with her friends and partied. Once. Just once, without the heavy weight of responsibility on her shoulders. Just once, to be a silly, carefree young girl.

It was something that would never happen.

Tears came to her eyes and she turned away from Dennis and wiped them away. He noticed but quickly turned his attention to pulling up his socks or something. That was one of the new customs since 'The Loss', as some people called it. Everyone had lost family, frequently their entire family, and the grief came in like a spear sometimes, sharp and deadly, out of nowhere. The person would then turn away from or turn to the people around them, depending on whether they needed a moment alone or needed some comfort in the form of human contact. If they turned away, then they should be given space.

He was doing that for her and on the one hand, it made her mad that he was being nice to her. It didn't mean that she was going to be nice to him, though. She had her plans for him. Maybe she was more mad at herself for being weak in the middle of an operation. She composed her face and turned back, taking a swallow of her beer. She didn't apologize for taking a moment and he didn't ask if she was okay. That was the other part of the custom. If the person wanted a private moment, then nothing was said about it afterwards. The moment didn't exist. Turn away, take your time, then come back and things went on as if there had been no interruption. The work or conversation or whatever picked right back up where it had stopped.

"I'm gonna head to the men's room. Back in a minute," he said.

She nodded, looking down like she was still upset. He had half a beer left, which was perfect. The place was dark but the candle on the table might still show too much. She blew it out as discreetly as she could, and then swapped their beers. She figured if someone saw her putting something in her own beer, that was vastly different than leaning across the table and obviously dosing up his drink. The GHB was in a plastic straw that had one end heated, flattened, and allowed to cool. The top was sealed with plastic wrap, so she could quickly dump it in the beer and get rid of the straw. Then she simply swapped beers again and relit the candle.

She waited for someone to come up and grab her, demand to know what she was doing, tell Dennis about what they caught her doing. Then they'd probably make her drink his beer and, well, the rest of the night wouldn't be good. The rest of her life, either.

No, she resolved that if someone did grab her, he was going to jam her knife in between his ribs. If that didn't discourage him, then she'd pull it out and jam it in somewhere new, and repeat that until he lost interest in her. Then she would make a break for the door, and once she got to her truck, any pursuers could catch some AK rounds. But knife first, rather than pistol, because if you start shooting, then there's no telling who's going to pull their pistol and spray the general area.

The little thrill inside her came up in power, like turning up the volume on a stereo. Not music, just the hum of white noise. Intensity.

A hand seemed to come out of nowhere to clamp down on her wrist, and a voice triumphantly cried "Gotcha!"

Chapter Twenty-Six

TAYLOR ABOUT CAME OUT of her seat. A shock ran through her body and she turned to look up into Dennis's smiling face. He was clamped onto her gun hand so she jammed her other hand in behind her back, going for her pistol. Screw all of her plans to try to quietly knife an attacker!

But then he let go, laughing, and walked around the table to take his seat. Innocent. Normal. Nothing out of place. No buddies of his crowding around to see him take her down, this obvious cop or informant or whatever she was. She'd been deep in thought and he'd sneaked up to scare her. That was it.

She closed her eyes for a moment and breathed deeply.

"Goddammit, you scared the shit out of me. You damned sure owe me a beer after that."

He laughed some more, then drained his beer. "I'll grab us a refill."

She watched him like a hawk and didn't see him put anything into her glass. Hopefully he didn't have a code word or something with the bartender that would have him dose her mug up before he even put it on the bar. But then, he didn't seem to be a fan of Dennis, so maybe she'd be fine. She wasn't going to drink much, anyway.

It didn't take long at all before Dennis shook his head a bit in amazement. "Damn, this is hitting me pretty hard."

"Ah, you wimp. Bottoms up!" Taylor taunted with a smile to take the sting out of it. He was a big, studly guy. He couldn't let the challenge go unanswered and chugged his beer. She tipped her own beer up but kept her lips closed and didn't allow any into her mouth, simulating drinking without actually doing so. Her intake over the last hour was probably four ounces.

She looked impressed when he chugged the last of his bottle. "So, why don't we go to your place and I can sample those items we were talking about? And I assume I can spend the night?"

A foolish question, if it had actually been a question. Drunk or not, he wasn't about to turn down the chance to get this sweet young thing in bed. He wobbled out, a bit unsteady on his feet, and she herded him to her truck. "You may not want to drive and I have my things in my truck. I'll drive."

He opened the window to get some fresh air on his face on the drive but was really staggering by the time they tried to walk inside. She got him into the bedroom and he fell onto the bed. She started to take his clothes off and he helped at the beginning, for a few seconds, until he passed out. Taylor had timed it perfectly.

Well, almost. She wanted him naked. Not for sex, for questioning. She had read something in one of Eric's books about interrogation techniques. He had a lot of books on some very... interesting topics. But the point was that a naked person feels vulnerable and it is an added stressor for interrogation. If the person is a woman, then they should be screamed at and ordered to take off her clothes. If they do it themselves, then they will have a sense of guilt that they contributed to their nakedness. Conversely, if it is a male, it is best to forcibly strip his clothes from him. That way he is ashamed that he is not even man enough to keep his clothes on.

She didn't have the option here of ripping his clothes off against his will, and she thought at one point that she wasn't going to be able to do it at all unless she cut them off. But some effort and cursing and pulling and she had managed the trick.

No time to celebrate, though. She carried her pack in and made sure the doors were locked. The first thing was to secure Dennis, so she spent some time with paracord and duct tape. She tied him spread-eagle on the bed, with three separate ropes on each arm and leg. Each rope had its own knots and she covered the knots with tape so that he couldn't get to them even if his hands had been tied together.

Then she made a little patrol around the house, checking it and the neighborhood out, her pistol at the ready. It was a nice house, middle to upper middle class, in a neighborhood that was apparently deserted. He didn't have a roommate, so it seemed like the perfect place for an interrogation.

She did have a bad moment in one of the upstairs bedrooms. She spotted movement and light in her peripheral vision and jumped in surprise, before realizing it was a full-length mirror. Hot wax from the candle she was using for light splashed on her hand and it almost went out. Taking a moment to catch her breath, Taylor looked around the room.

It was neat and tidy, done in pink pastel tones, obviously a young girl's room. She felt a pang of regret: sadness for their lost civilization, for her losses, and for the probable loss of this poor young girl and her family. Her body, and those of the rest of her family, was likely out there in the desert, unburied. They wouldn't have fled towards the Dallas-Fort-Worth area or south towards Mexico. They'd have headed east into the Hill Country or west into the desert, or north into the Panhandle.

And died there, more than likely. Or maybe the girl had survived and was living out the cover story that Taylor had used, forced into prostitution to survive. Maybe addicted to some of the very drugs that were being run by these bastards right here. Tears almost came to Taylor's eyes, thinking of the girl's fate. As many times as she had seen abandoned houses and possessions, she always felt the loss. Now that emotion channeled itself into anger. It wasn't a fiery rage that forced her into immediate action, but a slow-burning, expanding weight of fury.

These people smuggling drugs were killing people, torturing and degrading them and making their lives miserable, and they were going to pay for that. She was going to kill them. There would be no hesitation from her, no sympathy, no slack. Things were beyond that point already.

Raking the wax off with her fingernails, she continued her patrol.

***

If someone did come up tonight, or if Dennis got loose somehow, then her excuse for tying him up was that he had been thrashing around, apparently having some kind of seizure, and she was trying to keep him from hurting himself. If that didn't work, she would say she liked sex that way, with the guy tied up and helpless, but that he had been too drunk to perform.

Like peeling an onion, always have a couple of layers of excuses. The excuses should go from innocent to something that was embarrassing or even slightly illegal, which is why you didn't mention them first.

She had brought a device that was an adjustable steel tube with a Y-shaped piece to go under the doorknob and a rubber footpad that went against the floor. Anyone trying to open the door would have their force transferred to the floor through the tube. It wouldn't hold forever, but long enough to wake Taylor up and get her launching bullets through the door.

She had to do something else for the back door since she only had one of the security bars. Using what was on hand, she dragged the breakfast table over against the door and stacked it with pots and pans. If someone forced the door they would make a hellacious noise.

Relatively secure, she stretched out on the couch, fully clothed even down to her boots, with her AK within arm's reach, and went to sleep. Dennis would be out for some time, six or eight hours. Or maybe in a coma or dead, if the GHB had been too potent.

The little adrenaline that she'd gotten into her system, excited by the impending action, kept her wired awake for a while but then dropped off and she fell asleep. Nothing was going to happen until tomorrow.

Chapter Twenty-Seven

DAWN WOKE HER AND she scrounged up a breakfast for herself of cheese and bread, something like a bolillo. She brushed her teeth, washed her face, made sure her wig was in place, and fixed her makeup. She decided she really didn't like wearing makeup about then, but today was, hopefully, the big day. This is when she really needed it as a disguise.

Dennis was still out like a light, so she searched the place more carefully, finding his stash. He had quantities that were obviously far more than personal use, but nothing huge. There were a couple of pounds of marijuana, some bags of off-white chunks, and three varieties of pills. Except for the weed, it all fit in a couple of boot boxes, which are like big shoeboxes that cowboy boots come in. Not much, in other words. She figured there had to be more somewhere. Maybe this is what was being sold to the local guys, but what was the next step up in the chain? Who was he getting this stuff from?

She dug into her bag and came out with the Bernzomatic torch and spark lighter, which she set on the dresser in the bedroom, right where he could see it.

***

He finally came to a couple of hours later. She was trying every fifteen minutes, shaking and slapping him and calling his name, until his eyelids fluttered. It was starting to get hot and stuffy in the house. She had closed all of the windows in anticipation of him screaming at some point.

The first thing he did was try to move. He woke up much faster when he found out he couldn't.

"What — what the hell? Why am I tied up? Untie me!"

"Oh, I'm disappointed," Taylor cooed. "You don't remember last night? I was riding you like a bucking bronco." She moved her hips in and out a couple of times. "Ride 'em, cowgirl." She slapped herself on the butt and laughed, remembering how Valentina had done that exact thing a few days ago.

"Really?" Now he was interested to hear if he had scored with this beauty.

"Right. And you were going to tell me where you get your supply from, because this little stash you have here ain't shit." The laughter was gone and she had suddenly turned colder.

"I can't really tell you that. Why don't you untie me and we can discuss it?"

Taylor's face changed. The laughter, the fun, the good-time party girl was absolutely gone now. She sent a laser-like stare at Dennis and reached into her pocket, pulling the knife out. Left-handed, she swung the blade out until it locked into the open position with an audible click. She paused, murmured "I guess I need gloves," set the knife down beside the torch, and disappeared into the living room.

Dennis certainly saw the torch now that she had drawn his attention to it. It wasn't his, so she had brought it in. And the only reason he could think of for her to tie him up and bring a torch into his bedroom...

'HELP!" he screamed. "HELP! HELP!" He jerked at the bindings until it looked like he really was having a fit of some sort. Not that it did him any good. Nothing came loose.

Taylor came back into the room, not hurrying, and backhanded him in the balls. That shut him up.

"You know, you're an idiot. You live alone on a cul-de-sac with no neighbors. Who are you screaming for? There's no one around to hear you."

He was still gasping from the backhand to the jewels and didn't answer.

She smiled and ran the knife up his leg, not cutting but pressing the back of the blade against his leg so he felt the steel. He tried to turn away, but stopped when he realized that any movements he could make might cause a meeting between the edge and his flesh. When the blade got close to his crotch he went rock-still.

"Stop, stop, stop," he begged. "I'll tell you anything. Don't cut me. What do you want to know?"

"Everything. Tell me everything." She was breathing hard, almost panting. "Don't leave anything out or I may have to slice something off."

***

They had barely gotten started when there was the sound of a truck with loud mufflers coming up the street. Taylor stopped, waiting, listening. If no one else lived on this cul-de-sac, then any traffic had to be coming here.

Then it turned into the driveway. Taylor cursed under her breath and swapped the knife for the duct tape. Dennis got frisky then, moving his head abruptly away from her, trying to stop her from getting tape over his mouth.

"HELP! HELP!" he started screaming again.

After a few tries, Taylor stopped and gave him a dirty look. Then she took a step towards the foot of the bed and gave him a right hook straight into the gonads. This was a hard punch this time, not a casual tap to get his attention.

He gasped and his whole body spasmed. He tried to curl up into a fetal position but the ropes kept him where he was. But it did occupy his attention long enough for her to get some tape over his mouth, and then some more. She threw the pillows over his face, stripped the gloves off, and closed the bedroom door on her way out. Her pistol came out.

Someone was beating on the door and calling Dennis's name.

Her adrenaline ramped up. She might have a little gunfight on her hands in a minute.

Chapter Twenty-Eight

SHE LOOKED OUT THE peephole, silently thanking the previous owners for not being gadget freaks and having a camera, and saw two guys. Just guys, not all decked out in SWAT gear, ready to breach the door. Just guys.

But now that they were here, she couldn't let them leave or they might see something and come back with that SWAT team. Her adrenaline ramped up quickly and she licked her suddenly-dry lips.

Be a dumb party girl, she thought. *Slutty. Get them inside and close the door before you do anything. The neighborhood is deserted but you don't want to end up chasing someone down the street, shooting at them. I need more time here.*

After pulling the security bar away, she set her boot firmly on the floor six inches in front of the door and opened it that far, peering around the corner with a smile on her face. The pistol was in her hand, aimed at the guys but hidden behind the door. She could shoot through it if necessary.

"Oh, wow, I see why Dennis hasn't been around," the first guy exclaimed. "I wouldn't be around either if I was, um, entertaining a beautiful young lady. My name is Mike." He put out a hand to shake. Taylor didn't want to put her hand out like that but didn't see a good way to refuse. She quickly holstered the Glock, hiding the movement behind the door, before opening it wider and reaching out to shake.

"I'm Kayla."

Mike took her hand gently in his and brought it up to his lips to kiss.

"Oh, you're a real charmer, aren't you?" she purred, deliberately putting a twang into her accent, doing her cowgirl act. Her normal upper-class Dallas accent was not twangy and not Southern, not really much of an accent at all.

She looked him up head to toe, slowly, and followed that with an abbreviated one at his friend. "Dennis is asleep. I guess I wore him out." A pause for her to giggle with a hand over her mouth and then have a thought. "Why don't y'all come in? I'll take both of you studs on at the same time. If you think you can handle me, that is."

Mike's mouth dropped open at the unexpected offer, then he grinned and slapped his buddy on the arm. Taylor left the door where it was and danced back from it to give herself some maneuver room. She didn't want them right up against her, but she needed them inside the house, so she stood there with the big smile until they got the door closed and a couple of steps into the foyer.

Come into my parlor...

In the blink of an eye, the slutty party girl disappeared and Taylor the Terminator stood there with a pistol held easily in her hands. "Hands up. Get down on the floor. *Now!*"

They both gaped at her in surprise for a second before Mike complied. The other guy put his hands up and slowly started to go down to the floor before he panicked and bolted. He turned and ran for the door. Taylor blew off four shots into his legs and then was annoyed with herself.

I should have just shot his dumb ass. Why did I go for the legs?

She swung the 9mm to cover Mike and saw he was flat on the floor, trying to be very quiet and still and nonthreatening. Looking back, she saw that the guy she'd shot was bleeding badly.

"Oh, God, oh, Jesus! You shot me! Oh, God, I'm bleeding! Get me to a hospital! Please! Help me!" he went on without stopping.

Arterial blood doesn't shoot out in an uninterrupted stream. The heart beats, refills with blood, and pumps again. That's what the man's thigh was doing. He had his hands on the sides of the wound but was afraid to touch it any closer.

It bled in the squirt — pause — squirt — pause that indicated a fatal wound in this world. Especially in these circumstances: not only the fact that medical personnel were few and far between but Taylor didn't need him around. Didn't want him around. Couldn't afford to have him out of her control, alive and talking.

"Okay, just calm down. Get your heart rate down and you'll bleed less," Taylor said in a soothing yet commanding voice. "Take a breath and hold it. And another. Now take a deep breath and hold it for ten seconds. Deep breath. One." She aimed at the back of his head.

"Two." She started a slow and steady trigger squeeze.

"Three." The trigger broke and sent a 9mm hollow point bullet into the back of the man's skull. His body shivered at the impact and then fell back and seemed to melt into the floor as all of his muscles relaxed.

As soon as Taylor fired the shot, she turned to make sure Mike wasn't up to anything. He was. He was low-crawling away from her, deeper into the house.

What the fuck? She thought. *He thinks if he runs, he gets shot, so he crawls away?*

She shook her head, then walked past him and dropped into the couch in the great room. Now he was crawling directly towards her.

He stopped and stared at her as if he couldn't figure out the magic that had enabled her to levitate across the house so quickly. If the air had shimmered with colored lights and she had beamed down from an orbiting spaceship, he would have been no less amazed.

"Listen to me," she commanded. "I could maybe use some help today, and if you cooperate, I'll let you go. Or I can do it all myself, after shooting you in the head. I think you just saw I don't have any problem with shooting people in the head." She held her pistol casually, pointed down and off to the side for now.

"How many people have you shot in the head?" tumbled from his mouth.

She considered the question. "You know, it's enough that it actually could be a separate category, now that you mention it." She started holding up fingers.

"The second guy I killed. The first woman. That guy just now. Some others. Yeah, that could be a thing. But the important part for you is that you be a good boy today and not go on that list. Right?"

"Yes, ma'am."

"I need you to focus here. I know you're kind of dazed right now. You were thinking you were going to have wild sex and all of a sudden, things changed, but you need to get your shit together. First off, do you have any weapons on you?"

"I have a knife clipped to my belt."

"Slowly, emphasis on slowly, take it off and set it on the floor. Now put your hand flat down on the floor and just skid that knife off a couple yards. That's good. Now take off your clothes."

"What?"

"No, you're still not going to get laid. Take off your clothes and toss them over here to me. This is better than frisking you. I get a show out of it." She smiled for him at her joke but he didn't seem to get the humor. He was still dazed, but he had enough of his senses about him that he could see she was deadly serious. Forget the smile; she had just shot a man. It could have been him just as easily. It still could be. He started undressing.

Chapter Twenty-Nine

ONCE HE WAS DRESSED again, Taylor had him open the door to the bedroom where Dennis was tied up. If he had gotten loose somehow and was waiting to attack the first person through the door, it wouldn't be her. But he was still securely trussed up.

"Mike, rip that tape off his mouth."

That was easier said than done. In the movies, duct tape just flies off of someone's face with no effort. In real life, that stuff sticks just as hard as it's supposed to. It took a couple of minutes of tugging and pulling and trying it from a different direction, with Dennis starting in on Mike as soon as enough of it was away from his lips to allow him to speak.

"Are you working for her? You back-stabbing bastard! You filthy piece of shit! You —"

"I'm not working for her! She's got a gun on me! She just shot Jim out there in the living room!"

Maybe Mike got a little irritated at the accusations, but he snatched the last section of tape off. Dennis groaned loudly and closed his eyes for a moment. His beard was kind of ragged now since the tape had pulled some of the hair out. A lot, actually.

But after getting a breath, he started back on cussing Taylor out. She leaned in and backhanded him in the balls, just enough to make him gasp and get his attention.

"Mike, go stand in the corner over there and don't touch anything."

She smiled at the captive in the bed. "Now, Dennis, do I need to remind you of what happened before we were interrupted? You were telling me who's involved in the drugs here."

"God damn it, everyone's involved, you stupid bitch. The mayor. The police chief. Both deputies. People that drive trucks and stand guard duty and sell it. Everyone. Your best hope of staying alive is to run. Right now. Just turn around and run. Leave Mike here and he can untie me, but you'll get a good head start."

"The amount of drugs you have here isn't jack shit. Where's the warehouse? The stash house? Where do they keep the quantity?"

"Fuck you."

"Did you suddenly grow a set of balls? Are you putting up a brave front because Mike is here? Because you were crying like a little girl two minutes ago."

"Fuck you. I was not."

Taylor turned and picked up the Bernzomatic torch, lit it off with the spark lighter, and adjusted the flame to a nice light blue. The blue extended a couple of inches and came to a fine point, like a little spear. It gave off a low, deep hissing sound.

"Get away from me with that!" Dennis yelled. "You burn me and you're just going to make it harder on your —" and then his words degenerated into a scream as she ran the torch up the inside of his leg. There was a little crackle and the stench of burning hair. Dennis screamed and thrashed violently, as far as he could with the bindings. He couldn't get far.

Then Taylor became aware of someone else screaming, and caught motion from the other side of the bed. Mike had his arms out and was imploring her to stop. Tears streamed down his face.

She looked up at him and growled "Step. Back," through gritted teeth.

He looked into her eyes and saw his death, no question about it, if he didn't obey her. He also thought he saw a vision of Hell itself. A few minutes ago, when she was playing the party girl, her big green eyes were dancing with fun and excitement and mischief. Now, he might have been looking into the eyes of Satan. Maybe it was the lighting. The day was a rare overcast one, the room unlit except what weak glow came in through the partially open blinds. The only light was from the torch, an eerie blue accompanied by the hairs on Dennis's leg which flared briefly with a yellow flame before they burned down to nothing.

Dennis flailed on the bed, screaming at the top of his lungs, the bedsprings squeaking with the motion and the headboard thumping against the wall. Smoke or steam or something arose from his once-hairy leg. And the smell —

Presiding over this scene from Dante's Inferno was the beautiful young lady, something foul crawling in her eyes that no human being should have. The scene had it all: Satan, fire, and the screaming, tortured soul of the damned. Mike truly would not have been surprised if the girl in front of him had physically transformed into a horned and winged demon with scales, or her head spun completely around, or a plague of locusts issued from her mouth.

He didn't even notice he lost control of his bladder. He turned to face the wall, dropped to his knees, and prayed. Satan must have gone back to work because Dennis's screams ramped up again. The louder he screamed, the louder Mike prayed, eyes closed, tears streaming from them.

***

At some point it ended.

Mike couldn't say how long it took, seconds or minutes or hours. It just gradually dawned on him that it was quieter. Not quiet, just quieter than it had been. Dennis was moaning and cursing loudly but no longer screaming.

Something hit Mike in the back of the head and he wondered if this was death, if this was what it felt like to be shot, if a bullet had smashed its way through his skull. Maybe she had decided to shoot him after all. Perhaps these milliseconds were the last ones he had, his last thoughts, before the darkness of death embraced him.

Then he realized someone was calling his name, and had called him several times before.

The girl. Kayla. Satan.

He turned his head and a pillow fell from where it had draped over his shoulder. He realized that she had thrown a pillow at his head to get his attention.

The Devil throws pillows, he thought. *The* Devil *throws* pillows. The incongruity of it was mind bending. Astounding. A world turned upside down. It was like Santa Claus chopping the heads off of good little children with an axe.

But he saw that Kayla was back. The girl. The Devil was gone. Perhaps. Maybe this was just another ploy. *A trick. A pillow. Making you comfortable for a moment so the pitchfork hurts that much more when it comes.*

He stood, shakily, putting a hand against the wall to steady himself. His eyes, seemingly with a mind of their own, travelled down Dennis's naked body, looking for what she had done to him. But his imagination got the better of him and he looked away, afraid that he would see something that would haunt his dreams forever. A cold chill went down his spine and he shivered as if someone had poured ice water down his back.

He felt like he'd been asleep, or drunk, or stoned, or all three. Really, really fucked up. He couldn't hear well. Everything seemed weird. He certainly couldn't think. Maybe he had tried acid or something. Maybe this was all some bad trip. This couldn't really be happening, could it? His buddy Jim shot to death out there in the foyer and Dennis all burned and —

"Mike!" Kayla barked. "Focus, here. Do you know where this address is? Can you take me there?"

"Where?"

"Say it again," she ordered, prodding Dennis with the brass tip of the torch, now shut off. He didn't jump at the touch, meaning the tip was cool. Mike wondered how long he had been praying if the hot tip had had time to cool. Or maybe it had cooled more quickly when pressed into Dennis's flesh previously. Dennis croaked out an address and added a nearby intersection that was north of the location. His screaming had damaged his vocal cords and his voice sounded like something being dragged over gravel and broken glass. His eyes were unfocussed and vacant. A little bloody foam flecked his lips and around his mouth and ran down one cheek.

"Yeah, I can drive right to it."

"Did you piss your pants?"

He looked down and his cheeks flared red. He turned his face away in shame. But she was not humiliating him. She was asking a legitimate question.

"Put those on. They're too big for you but use your belt to cinch them up. Throw your underwear away," she ordered. "Just in the corner or something. It doesn't matter."

He swallowed his pride yet again and undressed in front of her, turning away so he wasn't fully exposed to her, and put Dennis's blue jeans on.

"Are you good now? Stand right there for a second." She sounded like a mother getting her five-year old squared away for a day at school.

She put a pillow over Dennis's face and shot him twice through it.

Casually.

Casually, like you might put a dirty dish in the sink or decide to clip your fingernails. It was nothing more than a routine decision. There was no drama, no lead in, no deep breath to steel her nerves before the deed.

Just the deed itself.

Put the pillow here to reduce the blood spatter. There's no need to soil one's clothes while committing a murder, now is there? And then the draw, the presentation of the pistol, and the shots. Two to make sure, since she was aiming at a pillow where she thought Dennis's head was. He might have moved.

"Oh, God! Oh, my God. Please, please stop doing that!" he burst out.

The shots were still echoing through the house and the smell of burned gunpowder and primer filled the room, mixing with the stench of other burned things. Fire and brimstone. This was undoubtedly Hell.

The girl smiled at Mike and he saw that Satan had suddenly appeared again. She was breathing in little pants through her mouth and licking her lips. She laughed a little, husky-voiced, deep in her throat. He prayed for the Devil to release his hold on this poor child of God. Surely this lovely creature couldn't be responsible for these horrible actions. She had to be possessed.

"We have work to do. First thing we need to do is get him into the closet. And your buddy, too. Mop up the blood in the foyer. Stack furniture."

Chapter Thirty

TAYLOR KNEW HOW TO set fire to a house. It was like a campfire, requiring airflow, fuel, and a source of ignition. She had Mike move the furniture in the bedrooms together against an inner wall, with the dresser drawers piled on top. She directed him to the garage where they found cans of gasoline. Everyone had cans of gasoline and maybe diesel. The regular supply of fuel was sporadic and not guaranteed, so everyone stocked up whenever they found some.

She didn't want either of them to get their clothing soaked in fuel so she had Mike open the cans and throw them up on the furniture so that they would land on their sides and spill their contents. They used four cans, twenty gallons, in four locations around the house that Dennis had taken over.

They opened all of the doors and windows and pulled blinds and curtains out of the way for maximum airflow. If they'd had the time she would have kicked out some of the sheetrock to expose the wooden studs, but she just needed a visible fire. She wasn't that concerned about burning this whole house down. The bedroom furniture would make several nice bonfires, one in each bedroom.

She pulled her Zippo out. The old-style lighters had made a comeback, like so many things that were once thought obsolete. When all of the plastic butane lighters ran dry, people figured out how to work the old Zippo-type ones: fluid, flint, cotton, and wick.

It made the distinctive genuine Zippo click when she opened it, and the wheel spun freely to spark off the flint so they could set the house on fire.

***

A half hour later, Mike was tied up with zip-ties in the passenger seat of the truck, bent over with his wrists secured through the seat frame. After lighting the fire, Taylor had driven to the next street over and then down it until she was in line with Dennis's house. It was easy to see which houses were occupied, since those were the ones that weren't deteriorating back into the earth from which their components had come. All of them seemed to be abandoned on this street, which suited her perfectly. She parked in one driveway and walked into the back yard and kicked boards out of the fence until she could pass through to the next yard. Now she was in the dining room of the house across the street from Dennis's house.

With her AK rifle.

She had a lot more experience with the AR platform, and had a very nice one that they had assembled from a selection of components from both commercial and military sources. The end result was a weapon capable of single shots or three-round bursts, with a 10.5-inch barrel and a suppressor. It was smooth and she had run literally thousands of rounds through it.

The AK she was using today was not as nice a weapon. She had selected the one that shot well and then spent time with the armorer to help her fluff and buff it. That is not slang for a sex act. That means she used emery cloth and very fine sandpaper to smooth out all of the contact points between moving parts. The action, the trigger, and the safety were now much slicker than a standard-issue rifle. She had also opted for convenience and gone with an underfolder. That is a folding stock version, where the stock folds up under the rest of the action. It's convenient to carry but less comfortable to shoot, with the shooter's cheek pressed against stamped steel rather than a wooden stock.

Today she had extended the stock and wore eye and ear protection, seated at the table as if ready for her dinner to be served. She was geared up, with her chest carrier full of loaded magazines.

152

She played out scenarios in her mind as she waited.

Everybody was corrupt, Dennis had said, and we already knew the cops were dirty. Police chief. Both deputies. Mayor. Plus his buddies at the stash house.

Basic tactics: take out the biggest threat first. The guys at the stash house are staying at the stash house. They guard it. That's their job. The mayor is one guy and he's not coming after me. That leaves the police. They have guns, mobility, and authority. That makes them the highest priority target.

And I think I hear them coming now.

She figured they would see the smoke or get an alert from someone who did, and being in partnership with Dennis, they would come in hot to see what was up. Or maybe Dennis was exaggerating his importance and they wouldn't care. If so, no harm, no foul. She'd just have to find them elsewhere. And then there they were. One of them, anyway.

He screeched to a stop and ran up to the front door. The blood on the floor in the foyer had come up nicely with a little mopping and Mr. Clean so she hadn't been concerned about leaving the door open. He ran in, calling out, but was back outside quickly. The flames were too much for him to go too far.

The bodies were in the closet of the master bedroom on the first floor. Taylor had made sure that furniture was piled in the doorway of that bedroom and thoroughly soaked with gasoline and diesel and motor oil. No one was going in there. She wanted to keep Dennis's demise hidden for a bit. At least she didn't want the cops to see his body, with evidence of being tied up and tortured. That would put them on high alert instantly and she didn't need that.

The cop was out quickly and ran around the back of the house, doing a good job of protecting his community, actually. If you were willing to overlook the part about being in collusion with drug dealers, that is.

Taylor the hunter sat and waited. If there had been anyone observing her, they might have thought that she was patient. She was not. The volume, that white noise, was ramped up inside her like a rock concert and she wanted very much to move, to strike, to do something. It felt like her whole body was vibrating. It took a force of will to sit there motionless.

In a few minutes another police vehicle pulled up and two men jumped out. Taylor watched them intently, only her eyes moving. A chief and two deputies, that was the entire force, according to what Dennis had said, and here were three cops. One of them was obviously older and had some more insignia on his uniform. That made him target number one. The next oldest was probably more experienced, or would the younger have quicker reflexes? Target two, target two, which one are you?

They were standing in the street right in front of Taylor. It was a ridiculously easy shot. She just needed them all to stand still for a moment... and there it was. The chief was facing in her direction, might even spot her if she moved. But she knew how to snipe from a building. You sat back from the window. You didn't stick your barrel out the opening and let everyone in a hundred-and-eighty-degree arc see it. You remained still or moved very, very slowly. Your eyes moved but not your head unless absolutely necessary.

She had the chair pushed back and the table pushed forward so that she could lean over and rest the forearm of the rifle on her hand on the table. That made for a steady rest and kept her profile low at the same time.

They were probably fifteen yards away. Twenty, maybe, no more. Her hundred-yard zero would run the shots high so she aimed an inch lower than she wanted them to strike. She wanted bullet placement in the high chest area, right in the heart, lungs, and artery area. It didn't matter if they were wearing Kevlar. That only protected against pistol rounds. She planned her shot sequence out, there, there, then there. Breathed in. Breathed half out and held it. Squeezed the trigger slowly and steadily.

The shot blasted off and the rifle recoiled up off of the table, gravity pulling it back down to pinch a bit of skin between the forearm and the table. A little painful, but expected. She took the pain and kept going, not bringing her hand off and rubbing it like most people would. The bullet slammed into the chief and he went back and down, no drama. The other two ducked and went for their weapons, looking for the shooter.

She swung to target number two, the older cop, and put a bullet into his chest as he was turning towards the sound of the shot. His legs went out from under him and he fell heavily back against one of the cars. She was already going for target number three. That was the long swing. The chief had been in the middle, so she had to shoot center, a short swing to left, and then the long one to right. Starting at the left target and simply moving in short swings left to right may have been quicker, but she wanted the chief down first. He was the boss so she wanted him down hard.

The third guy was fast. He took off like a sprinter and her shot missed and then he was on the other side of the first police cruiser. She stood up to change position and bullets started coming through the window and the walls at her. SHIT!

She dropped to the floor, cradled the AK in her arms, and low-crawled laterally away from the target area. Bullets, glass, wood splinters, and dry-wall dust filled the air above her. The tile in the foyer hurt her elbows but adrenaline was roaring through her system now and what little pain she felt was almost a stimulant. She made it to the room across from the dining room, a study, and came up for a scan. She had already opened the blinds there to the right angle in preparation for changing her firing position if needed.

The chief was still down, had never moved once he hit the ground. A blood pool was expanding out from beneath him. Target number two was sitting, leaned up against the car door, but had dumped his whole magazine at the dining room and was fumbling to reload. He was bleeding to death, she was confident of that, but he was going to fight until the end.

The young cop's head popped up over the fender of the other car and she swung her rifle up and fired. The head went down. Hit or miss, she couldn't tell, but wasn't hopeful with the snap shot. She put four more rounds into the fender, trying to either hit him through the sheet metal or at least keep his head down for a few seconds while she shot out the tires.

She ran back to the dining room as a wild half-laugh escaped her lips. She felt a thrill like an electric shock run through her body and the thought flashed through her mind that maybe Mike the Charmer was going to get laid today after all. Zip-tied and helpless... her on top... hmmm... maybe that was an idea to consider... Having someone shoot at you and miss is *so* energizing!

Then she was at the dining room window and someone was putting rounds into the study window. The wounded cop had reloaded and was launching bullets again. She put two shots into him and put a stop to that, then shot out the tires on that vehicle, turned, and ran. She was done for this ambush.

Bullets punched into the walls behind her and beside her and she laughed again as she ran.

Chapter Thirty-One

TAYLOR CAME UP ON the truck, popping her head up and then back to see if Mike was still in there. He was, but was he still zip-tied? She opened the driver's door with the AK up, safety off, her finger on the trigger.

"Are you still tied up? Prove it to me," she commanded.

He looked up at her dully, eyes gaunt, haunted by the gunshots he had heard. The fresh murders that he was sure had occurred. How many men had she killed this time? How much blood was on her hands? At least someone was left alive; there was still shooting going on. But he pulled his hands back and forth a couple of times, showing that they were still secured to the seat frame. Satisfied, she flipped the safety on and slid the rifle behind the seat. The Glock went into her left hand to hold while she drove, just in case he was fooling her somehow.

She drove fast, but well. Eric had set that as part of her and Dani's training, willing to burn the increasingly rare gasoline in order for them to have the skills. And he wanted them to know how to do things like J-turns and PIT maneuvers and similar techniques. Then once the oil companies, plural, that they were partnered with began to churn out petroleum products again, they were right at the head of the line to receive them and they got even more practice in.

She had rolled a truck once on a practice run, pushing too much speed in a turn. She came up with a handful of minor cuts and bruises but wasn't seriously injured since she'd been wearing a crash helmet and had been belted in. Eric asked her what she'd learned instead of bitching that she'd wrecked a vehicle.

He knew that you had to go over the line sometimes just so you knew where the line was. She'd never rolled another one but she'd frequently pushed the line.

A firetruck went rolling past as she got out of the immediate neighborhood but the only police presence was back there with disabled vehicles, and only one man remaining. Maybe wounded, but she doubted it, and that was all right. She had gotten the chief and the other deputy, so that was good. She wasn't going to shoot everyone that had any involvement. Winning didn't necessarily mean total annihilation.

***

She got a few miles down the road and found a quiet place to pull over.

"Okay, here's what's going to happen," she said. "I'm going to hand your knife to you. You're going to cut yourself loose and then fold the knife back up and gently toss it onto the floor on the driver's side. You need to pee? Just open the door and step out and do it right there. No need to go hide. I've seen you naked twice today already. And here's a bottle of water."

As Mike stood there relieving himself, he thought *I'm a dog. She left me in the truck while she did her errand. Now she's let me out to pee and she's giving me some water.*

He had a vision of her throwing a stick and him bringing it back in his mouth, bouncing up and down, happy that his master was playing with him. He almost laughed, but it came out more as a gasp. If Taylor heard it, she didn't comment. He was in Hell, and the Devil was literally and figuratively in the driver's seat.

When he sat back down in the truck, she pointed at some more zip-ties that she had put on the dashboard. "I want you to put that one around your thigh. Not too tight. Don't cut off the circulation. Now tie your wrists to that one. See? Isn't that much more comfortable? You can sit up with your hands in your lap."

And put my head out the window and snuffle at all of the new and exciting scents Mike thought. *I can bark at any other dogs I see.*

"I want to drive by the mayor's house. Just check it out. Then we go by the stash house. What do you know about that place?"

He opened his mouth to answer but he was stopped by a cold spike of fear that she already knew the answers and was trying to catch him in a lie. He hadn't heard what Dennis had told her. He had been praying loudly specifically to drown out the screams, but there had also been periods of speech, answers, gasped out through gritted teeth, as Dennis reached the end of his endurance to pain.

Unbidden, his brain flashed up what he imagined Dennis's manhood looked like after she had run that torch over it. He hadn't actually looked at it, but he could estimate. He shuddered and turned his head aside as if that would shield him from the sight. The smell of burning pubic hair and seared flesh seemed to fill his nostrils and his stomach heaved. He threw up a little water and bile in his mouth and spit it out the window.

Taylor looked at him appraisingly for a few seconds. She had an insight, that he was upset about the Bernzomatic thing. The fact was, she had barely singed the hairs on Dennis's leg. Okay, and maybe a few in his crotch. And yeah, she'd had to do it a few times because he didn't just spill everything all at once, but she hadn't done any real damage to him. Until she'd shot him, that is. She actually opened her mouth to tell Mike that before she thought better of it. Maybe it would be more to her advantage to keep that under wraps and intimidate him with it.

"Keep it together," she said instead. "I know this is more exciting shit than you thought you were signing on for, but you need to maintain."

He spat again and awkwardly wiped his mouth on his sleeve since he couldn't raise his hands. He knew if he fell apart, he was going to end up dumped somewhere with a bullet in his head. She wasn't keeping him alive for his charming company. That appraising look was her evaluating whether he was going to live or die. That almost made him wet his pants again. Maybe he would have if he hadn't just emptied his bladder.

Here was a girl sitting beside him, coolly making the decision on whether to kill him or not. Or maybe just not yet. That was something else that was pretty astounding. The thought, the very idea that someone could sit and make the decision on whether to coldly kill you in the next few seconds or not was absolutely terrifying. His knees knocked together until he pressed them against one another.

After a deep breath, he confessed. "I work there, in the stash house. I pull guard duty, move the product in and out, load and unload trucks. Whatever they need done."

"Really? That's interesting. How many guards are there now?"

"There would be two right now. And Big Tim will be there this early. He lives there. He stays up late and sleeps late. When they're loading or unloading a truck there are the extra guys there to do that."

"What guns?"

"The guards carry AR rifles or whatever they want. Whatever they own."

"How about Big Tim? Does he carry?"

"No, he doesn't. I don't know if his fat fingers would even fit through a trigger guard."

"When's the next truck scheduled?"

"Saturdays. The truck comes in and some of the load stays here. Most goes on an outgoing truck that rolls out that night. As soon as we make the load."

Today was Friday so that was a nonstarter. She had already fired off a chain of events that had to take place today, pretty much now, or not at all.

"Tell me all about it. Details."

He shrugged. "It's a simple operation. There's no code words or meetings at night under a bridge and testing the load or anything like that. The trucks come in the same afternoon, one from Dallas and one from Mexico or wherever. Big Tim says this package goes and this one stays. The Dallas truck gets loaded with the product and he goes back to Dallas. The cops escort them in and out. The incoming driver from Mexico spends the night in the guest house, out in back of the main house. With his truck locked up in the garage. Fully fueled, with the gold already loaded. In the morning, he goes back to Mexico."

She caught her breath and her eyes widened. She hadn't even thought about the profits from the drug sales going back to the druglord.

"So, two trucks. Drugs to Midland, then transferred to another truck to go on to Dallas. The truck coming from Dallas brings in the gold, which then goes on the truck back to Mexico."

"That's it."

"What kind of truck? Just a pickup truck or what?"

"They're white box trucks. You know, a single axle in the back with dualies — two wheels on either side. There's a million of them on the road. No business logo or anything."

"What route does the Dallas truck take coming in? The one bringing the gold?"

He shrugged again. "I-20. There aren't many alternate routes. Like I said, it's simple."

"What time does that truck arrive?"

"Both trucks are supposed to arrive around four o'clock in the afternoon, but it's variable. One wasn't in until maybe four forty-five once when there was a wreck or something that blocked the road. We unload the cash, load the product, fuel him up, and he's gone."

"Is the stuff concealed in the trucks? Like, a couple of boxes hidden under a load of tomatoes or something?"

Mike snorted. "Not a damn bit. The gold is pretty compact but the stuff coming in is bulky. Lots of weed. Maybe half a truckload."

Taylor looked at him for another few seconds, but he couldn't meet her eyes. His were downcast. "I am a sinner. But I am renouncing my sinful ways and devoting my life to Jesus. If, by the grace of God, I survive this day —"

"By the grace of *me*," she interrupted.

"— then I will forever be indebted to Him, and will —"

"Save it!" she snapped.

He stopped. Pissing her off would not be conducive to a long life.

"I don't have any objection to your religion but I am not going to have you spouting that... sort of thing in front of those guys. We don't need any sudden personality changes from you, got it? If you want to say you're hungover or something, let's do that. Your best chance... Look at me. Pay attention. I can get into that house without you. I can charm my way in. Do you seriously think that they won't let me in? I do my slutty cowgirl act, show some cleavage, and I'm through the door in a heartbeat. Or have you forgotten how we met earlier this morning? Guys have been trying to fuck me since I was about twelve years old. I know how to use that against them if I want."

That meeting, when he met her earlier this morning, seemed lifetimes ago to Mike. And she was right. Those guys would invite her in immediately. Happily. Without hesitation. Just like he had rushed into Dennis's house when he thought he was going to go to bed with her. He looked down in shame and his cheeks burned.

"Now, my thought is that I can use you to get into that house on a different basis. I want to pose as a buyer, sent there by Dennis. The story is Dennis said he would be busy with something but he sent you along with me, to show me the house and to carry product for me. Got that? Because if I go in alone, I don't need you. And if I don't need you, I don't want you running around warning people. What do you think my options are to stop you from warning people?"

Mike was still looking down. "You would shoot me in the head," he said in a small voice.

"No shit." She sat there for a count of ten to let him stew.

"The best chance for you to live through the day and devote the rest of your life to Jesus is to help me. What's going to happen between me and the boys at the stash house is going to happen, with or without you. We've already

162

established that. You're not going to carry any guilt for that. The only question is whether you're alive or not when it happens. Option one: you try to escape, you get shot. Option two: you refuse to help, you get shot. Option three: you fight against me, you get shot. Do you see a trend here? Or option four: you work with me, willingly, and — guess what? You stay alive. I would take option four. You don't want to disappoint Jesus, now do you?"

He looked up, met her eyes. "Please don't kill me. I'll do anything you want. Please, Kayla. I know I haven't made much of my life but I'm going to change that."

She stared at him for a few seconds. "Where's the mayor live? You're my GPS."

Bark once for a left turn, Mike thought. *Bark twice for a right. Lord Jesus, please guide my actions today. Help me to do the right thing. I really am a changed man. I swear it!*

Chapter Thirty-Two

TAYLOR PICKED OUT SOME landmarks and was sure she could get back to the mayor's place without assistance. That was more training, navigation in this case. Not only how to read a map and use a compass, but simply paying attention to details, landmarks, that would allow you to get back to a location.

This one was easy to find. It was a big house in an expensive subdivision, and most of the houses there were well kept. No flaking paint and broken windows and yards gone back to the wild allowed here. When ninety percent of the population died, all of that real estate came up for grabs, and no government was left to impose a property tax on the squatters. Just move in.

Sure, there were a lot of situations where the new owners had to dispose of the bodies of the previous owners, but a short, distasteful job was a small price to pay to live in the lap of luxury. Of course, that luxury came without electricity, which meant the gigantic flat screen TVs didn't work, the lights didn't work, the air conditioning didn't work, little things like that. No heat or bubbles for the hot tub. The Ferrari in the garage didn't run. The toilets worked until the sewage plant backed up or something. But four years in, things were getting better.

None of that was a shock to Taylor, though. This was her world. She'd grown up in it. The first time the spoiled little rich girl had had to go to an outhouse, now *that* had been a shock to her. It was old hat now. This was nothing other than real life.

Once they were out of the subdivision and a few blocks down the road, she stopped again.

"Decision time." She stared at Mike. "What are you going to do with the rest of your life?"

You're not really making a deal with the devil, he told himself. *You're not getting anything out of it. Not riches or power or fame or anything. Just a chance to preach The Word for the rest of your life.*

"Op, option four," he stuttered. "I will help you get into the house. I'll vouch for you. I won't interfere with anything you're going to do anyway. I imagine you're going to burn this place, too?"

"Oh, of course. I need to burn up any product they have. So, you carry cans of gasoline."

"I'll carry cans of gasoline," he parroted. "And you won't shoot me. Or hurt me in any way."

"I won't hurt you in any way," she promised. She pulled his knife out of her pocket and handed it to him to cut the zip-ties. "But I am taking that knife back when you're done with it."

God, please don't let that be a pillow. Her promising not to kill me. Because then the pitchfork would be... Mike didn't want to think about that. He prayed.

While she drove, Mike sat silently for a few minutes before asking "What are you doing here? What's the purpose?"

She looked at him curiously. "What does it look like? I'm putting a crimp in this drug operation."

"You're not going to stop it."

"Yeah, I'm not going to stop world hunger, either. That doesn't mean I'm not going to try. Look, nobody cares about weed any more. No one goes to jail for marijuana even if you have a truckload of it. But narcotics, now, that's a different story. When you start talking about pills and crack and shooting shit into your veins — no. No. Absolutely not. That's where people become addicted and ruin their lives. Or they do something and accidentally kill themselves." Her mind's eye provided a little video of Horn Dog spiking himself on that fence post, whether she wanted to see it again or not. And that lead her to think about that Goddamned kiss again.

"Okay, but it's not a death penalty thing. If the cops had busted Dennis, they might have sent him to prison but they wouldn't have tortured and shot him like that."

"The cops? You mean the corrupt cops here? The ones that are part of the drug gang? *Those* cops?"

"I'll admit that they're some good ole boys that decided to profit from their positions. I meant the state police." He stopped as a thought came to mind. "You're not a cop, are you? You can't be, not with..." He made a little hand gesture that was meant to encompass everything she'd done that morning. "Unless you're some kind of government agent. A hitman. Um, hitwoman."

"Let's just say I'm a concerned citizen."

"So, you're not some kind of highly trained, professional assassin or something? Working for some agency that no one's ever heard of?"

"No, this is my thing. No one told me or assigned me. It's all on me."

"But you still can't go around killing people like that."

"I can't?" Taylor asked with fake, exaggerated amazement. "Wrong answer, but thanks for playing. We have some nice parting gifts. You remember how they used to have Black Friday sales, back before the world ended? The big day was the Friday after Thanksgiving. They had huge sales with deep discounts. Well, this is kind of like that, only instead of deep discounts on merchandise, there are extra penalties for crimes. Like, deal narcotics and I'll blow your fucking head off. You? You're lucky. You have a coupon. That coupon says that you get to walk away if you cooperate with me. Don't fuck it up."

She let the silence go on for a few seconds before she spoke again.

"A big part of it is deterrence. If you see a couple of your friends dealing drugs and living the high life and getting away with it, then you start to think that you ought to do it, too. Even if they get caught and only get a slap on the wrist, you might figure the odds are still in your favor. It's worth the risk. Well, I'm making it not worth the risk. I'm making it so guys are terrified to have anything to do with dealing drugs for fear that I'll show up and put them down. No courts, no plea bargains to lesser charges, no fucking attorneys trying to pull every trick to get them off, no nothing. Just finding themselves on the wrong end of a firearm.

"With all the people that died in Hexen and the EMP, with everyone's life shattered, with all of the misery that brought, I just can't understand why some people have to make a profit off of the suffering of others. No one is happy being an addict. They may be numb when they're high, but reality is always going to come back to them. I'll admit that alcohol may not be the best thing, but it's legal. Marijuana may as well be. Isn't that enough to drown your sorrows?

"And those cops, those fucking scumbags. They're supposed to be protecting the community. Fuck them. They deserve everything I gave them. In fact, they got off easy."

There was heat in her voice and Mike wisely kept his mouth shut.

Chapter Thirty-Three

GETTING INTO THE STASH house was a piece of cake. The guys on guard duty knew Mike and they wanted to get to know the hot girl with him. They were all smiles, and 'let me introduce myself', and 'wouldn't you really rather be with me'? Although they hadn't actually said that last part yet, not in their out loud voices.

The commotion rousted Big Tim. He came down the sweeping grand staircase in cowboy boots, jeans, a guayabera shirt, and a cowboy hat. And he was big. Taylor could have used the shirt for a tent, although the thought almost made her gag, thinking of what it would smell like. He was maybe six foot two, not overly tall, but round. Being fat in this world was definitely unusual, and pretty much a deliberate act. An accomplishment, even.

When the EMP hit, while the Hexen flu was killing by the hundreds of millions, everything stopped. Food processing and deliveries, for example. The grocery stores contained three days' worth of food for the full population, which meant thirty days for the Hexen survivors. But either number really meant nothing in the long run. Farmers and ranchers couldn't deliver product to anyone beyond walking distance, all of a sudden.

There was a desperate outflow of people from the cities trying to get to that food. City dwellers, who had possibly never seen a cow in person, or up close, now had to figure out how to kill one and butcher it and preserve the meat. And potentially fight off their former neighbors who were desperate enough to kill them for a steak. Probably another high percentage of the survivors of Hexen starved to death due to ignorance. They simply didn't know how to hunt or fish or farm or raise animals or pretty much do anything from the eighteenth century, which is what the world had suddenly become, in many ways.

But apparently Big Tim knew how to find food. He had found a lot. That was his skill set.

After introductions, Taylor started her spiel. "I met Dennis and he sent me here, to you. I am with a small group that wants to up our game. We want to buy in quantity and distribute to some of the smaller towns. I don't think we would be in competition with your guys, doing that."

"Why didn't Dennis bring you here himself?"

"I don't know. He said he had some pressing business, but he got Mike to bring me."

Big Tim looked past her at Mike. Mike held his hands up. "Dennis didn't tell me. I guess it was none of my business."

Taylor almost laughed when she realized that Mike had actually told the truth.

Big Tim paused for a second and it was plain that he was mentally making a note, maybe to chew Dennis out for not bringing the girl himself. But that was only for a second, and he turned back to Taylor and favored her with a smile as if she were a German Chocolate cake.

"Let's go back in my office and discuss things. Maybe you can stay a while and we can mix a little business and pleasure. You could sample a little of this and that and party tonight."

"You bastard!" suddenly came from above. Everyone looked up. There was a girl standing at the top of the stairs, pretty, maybe early twenties, a brunette. The thing Taylor noticed most, though, was that she was virtually naked. She had on skimpy lacy panties and a see-through negligee that left nothing at all to the imagination. That was it. You could have folded the entire outfit up and put it in a jeans pocket with room left over for a wallet. Apparently, Miss Nakedness

169

had heard Big Tim hitting on Taylor and was pissed. She dramatically flounced off down the hall and slammed the door.

Big Tim looked at Taylor, shrugged, and said "My office is right this way."

***

"What product do you want and what kind of quantities were you thinking about?" he asked once he had eased into a groaning chair.

"A variety. We can get weed anywhere, and meth, so we're looking for anything else. Coke is at the top of the list, but we'll consider anything. Uppers, downers, whatever. Small loads, for the first few runs, but we'll ramp that up as soon as possible. No more than enough to cover the bed of a truck a few inches deep and allow us to put something on top. Peppers, onions, cow shit. Something no cop wants to dig through."

He laughed. "Right now, today, we're not set up to sell you truckloads. We have a small quantity here to serve local needs, which go out through Dennis. Mainly we are a transshipment point. But I can make arrangements to bring bigger loads in for you. It'll take about two or three weeks to get that set up. Communications, you know. If cell phones worked, I could hook you up in one week. I have a straight-line connection.

"In the meantime, why don't you stay here? On the house. Everything, all the alcohol and party favors you want. It'll give you a chance to sample everything we can offer, something different every night. There's a swimming pool and hot tub out back. Clothing optional, of course."

Taylor's stomach turned at the thought of this pig putting his hands on her, or even worse... no, she wouldn't even let that thought cross her mind. If she imagined him naked there was no way the revulsion would not show on her face.

"Business before pleasure." She smiled at him. "Why don't you show me around the place? It looks very impressive."

He was glad to do that, happily showing off the house and grounds, none of which he'd paid for, but at least he kept it clean and maintained as much as he could. But it also gave her the opportunity to learn more about the operation, too, and what they did have on hand.

***

As soon as they were out of earshot the guards turned to Mike for the scoop.

"Damn, that's the girl that came looking for Dennis at the bar last night. I guess she spent the night with him, huh?" Paul asked. He was visibly disappointed.

Mike's mind raced. Should he alert them or not? He knew these guys. They were his friends. Not childhood friends that he's known all his life, but he'd known them for a couple of years. What did that say about him if he just left them to their fate? But then, isn't everyone going to meet their fate? Isn't that the definition of fate? Would saying something to them alter anything? That girl, Kayla, was the Devil, or possessed by him. She'd know if he said anything, and then she'd simply kill him, too. It meant nothing to her to add another name to her list. As if there was even a list in the first place. It was like swatting flies to her. No one kept a list of the flies they'd smashed.

He felt sick to his stomach.

"I'll be back," he got out before trotting to the front door and outside. He choked and spit up some into the overgrown bushes in front.

Back inside, he poured some clean water to wash his mouth out. Then he splashed some of it into his hand and then into his face.

"You all right, man?" Paul asked.

"My stomach. I got a bug or something. If I had anything in it, I'd blow it all over the floor here." His brain insisted on replaying the mental image of Dennis's burned crotch but he tried to turn away from that thought as fast as he could.

If I told them, would they even be able to kill her? he thought. *I'd have to convince them that she'd tortured and killed Dennis and shot Jim. They'd think I was joking. Could I convince them before she got back? And if they did believe me and got the drop on her, would it do any good? Could she still kill them anyway? And me, too? If she's really the Devil, they can't kill her. Even if I just ran away, ran out the door right now, I'd spend the rest of my life looking over my shoulder, expecting her to show up at any moment. Lord, please, please guide me. Tell me what to do.*

Chapter Thirty-Four

THE TOUR WOUND BACK around from the pool and spa, Big Tim mentioning that it was clothing optional again, to the house. Always the grandiose gentleman, he held the door open for her with a small bow.

Taylor's adrenaline ramped up as they approached the door. She had taken a big risk, leaving Mike in there with the guards, but she couldn't really demand that he go along with them. There had been no good reason to insist on that and Tim wouldn't have wanted him to come along. She couldn't have made a scene to demand that he follow without raising suspicion.

The result was that she could be walking into an ambush. There was no telling what Mike had done. Had he alerted the guards? Would they be pointing their rifles at her as soon as she walked through the door?

Her mind raced, planning her moves. If they drew down on her, they also had Big Tim in the line of fire right behind her, so they couldn't shoot. Any missed shots might go into him. Hell, any hits would likely go right through her body and into him. Hopefully they were smart enough to realize that.

She would have to get around behind Tim, use him as a shield. Get him on his knees to reduce his mobility, with a shot to the leg or foot if needed. If she could do that, she was probably safe. She could pop out from behind him, shoot at the guards, and they couldn't return fire. Again, assuming that they wanted to keep ole Timmy alive. This would be a prime opportunity for a little 'accident' if they wanted some payback or had ambitions to take his job over. If not, then she had a free fire zone, with nothing and no one around that she didn't mind shooting.

At across-the-room distances, she was more than confident of her ability to put rounds on target. She was actually more worried about the guys turning and running before she could hit them. That would give them the ability to go outside and loop around the house on different sides, allowing them to flank her. She'd rather not play hide and seek with two men with rifles. That would just be a deadly crap shoot. She wanted to put them off guard and strike with complete surprise. She was outnumbered and outgunned right now.

She had a pistol, a short-range weapon but still not a hand-to-hand piece like a knife. If she could get close to them but not too close, that would be better. She needed to be charming and control what they were thinking about. Flirt. She knew how to do that. She needed to set up the shoot, plan it out. Take the guards down hard and disable Timmy where she could question him.

Mike was a question. If he had been a good boy, he was safe. If she had some indication that he had not been good, then he was done. Hopefully they hadn't provided him with a firearm if that was the case. The fewer guns she was up against, the better.

When Big Tim opened the door for her, she paused, not wanting to just blindly go walking into a bad situation. She turned to look at him, smiled, and thanked him. Turning back, she had a second to survey the situation, perhaps the most important second in her life. Possibly one of the last seconds in her life. Right now, she had to decide to go in or to run, but things seemed to be fine. The guards were just standing there casually. Mike looked kind of hangdog but more sick than guilty. But then, she didn't know him that well, either. Go inside or bolt now? This was the decision point. Well, no guts, no glory.

She walked inside.

Chapter Thirty-Five

"YOU HAVE TWO GUYS dedicated to security at all times?" she asked. "That's impressive. Most places just have some assholes sitting around smoking weed and playing cards. They might have some filthy old guns in their bedroom or something, which generally look like pigsties. Not this place. Your guys look squared away and this place is exceptionally clean."

That made Big Tim's chest swell with pride. She was willing to bet that ole Timmy hadn't had too many girls compliment him on anything, ever.

"Boys, show her your guns," he ordered. They were happy to talk to the hot girl again.

Taylor was paying attention to everything, every second. She had to be on her game. It was literally life or death for her. That's why she knew instantly what to do. Big Tim was on her left so she wanted to admire the rifle of the guard to her left. Then she would go to her right. That would move her away from being in the center of the group, out to the edge. It would also put her holster as far out of sight as possible from the group.

Following that plan, she admired Paul's rifle first. Ever better was the fact that she knew as much about firearms as he did and was able to make intelligent comments. It was much more meaningful than her making inane comments like "Oh, that's pretty!" when he was talking about how something functioned. Function is not really pretty. It may be elegant, but it is not pretty.

Next, she stepped over and looked at Cody's rifle. He was very proud of it. He had built it up from parts, massaging each and every one, researching and saving up and getting exactly what he wanted, all of which he lovingly described to her.

"Here, put it up to your shoulder and see what you think," he offered.

Taylor had been smiling the entire time and looking more at him than at his weapon. "Maybe when you're off-duty we could do some shooting," she said, her voice husky. "See how many rounds we could go through." She handed the rifle back to him while looking up at him.

That has to be a sexual reference, he thought, surprised. He didn't have any witty comment to come back with. He couldn't believe this gorgeous girl was actually hitting on him. She seemed to be panting, and then her little pink tongue came out and wet her lips, running across the top one, then reversing course to go along the bottom.

She had to be flirting with him. She was smiling and staring him dead in the eye. He hadn't gotten that a lot in his life. The apocalypse had hit when he was a high school sophomore, sixteen years old, and he hadn't been getting much action. Then or now, to tell the truth.

Hexen had drastically cut down the number of available females. Males, too, of course, but those who could provide became the kings and those who were just getting by were lesser mortals. The girls swarmed to the kings, who took their pick. Back in the old world, when everyone had food readily available, there was less of a divide. Other factors were more important, but now everyone knew that they couldn't eat coolness. The jock that could pass a football with expertise now found himself working in the fields for the farmer that was sleeping with — and feeding — the prom queen.

"It looks like you have it all together, Cody." She was staring deeply into his eyes. She was undoubtedly breathing heavily. He felt himself getting excited.

Big Tim cleared his throat loudly. He was pissed. He saw what was happening and he wanted any action that Taylor was going to put out. She turned to him, still smiling. "Sorry. Let's go to your office and get down to some details about how we can help each other out. Pricing, quantities, things like that. Maybe I can stay for a few days after all."

Big Tim smiled at that and started to turn away. Taylor's hand eased back around behind her, under her shirttail, and to the holster inside her waistband unnoticed. Her body shielded the movement from anyone but Cody and he was so wrapped up in a mental picture of them having steaming hot, passionate sex that he didn't notice a thing.

Mike had been expecting Taylor to make a move and had been hanging back, out at the edge of the little conversation group. Maybe he subconsciously thought that if he was standing with the other guys, she'd just put bullets into all of them. He intended to drop to the floor at the first sign that she was going to start shooting.

Even as closely as he was watching her, and as much as he knew she was going to do something, it still happened too fast for him to follow. Too fast for him to react to in time.

Chapter Thirty-Six

TAYLOR MOVED, VERY QUICKLY, very precisely. She knew exactly what she was going to do and exactly how to do it.

The two guards were obviously the primary threat and Taylor had one of them thinking about sex, the other maybe jealous but still not envisioning her as anything he should guard against. Her hands rested casually on her hips when she was looking at Cody, and then, all of a sudden, they were moving, her hands coming in to meet, up and then out and there was a gun and a shot and a bullet went through Cody's eye and into his brain and he was dead.

She didn't wait to see what affect her shot had. As soon as she fired, she spun to the other guard, the muzzle coming down some, and fired two bullets at his chest. One of them hit the rifle he was holding and sent a piece of something winging off to the side before entering his body on a shallow angle. A third shot went into his face.

Her muzzle covered Mike briefly as she continued to swing around to her left and down, before shooting Big Tim in the foot. She took two shots there. The first one just cut a groove in his boot. She wasn't satisfied with that, so she aimed a little more precisely and put a bullet through the top of his foot.

Then she danced backwards, three steps, so that Big Tim didn't fall on her when he came crashing down. Which he did, like a massive pine tree cut down and thundering to earth.

The whole thing was almost a ballet. A sudden, dramatic thrust with the arms, a precise pivot, a second precise pivot and downward drop of the arms, exactly three steps back, and a sweep of the arms back the way she had come as four men thumped down to the floor like a drum roll. The shots at the end of each of her movements accented them like drumbeats, like a musical accompaniment, a *sonatina* with multiple fatalities, perhaps.

Mike couldn't say what she did, but he dropped at the first shot, headed to the floor. He didn't make it to the floor before the last shot was in. The shots came so quickly it seemed Taylor had a machine gun, and the bodies of the three other men in the room hit the floor fractions of a second after him.

And then the Devil that threw pillows stalked around the scene, her pitchfork out now, making sure that those she wanted dead were dead.

Cody had been gone before he hit the floor, as soon as the hollowpoint bullet had gone in through the eye socket and hammered through his brain. He never even knew there was danger. He died imagining what Taylor looked like naked, him kissing her neck and working his way down to her cleavage. His body served a last duty as a cushion for his beloved rifle. The muzzle brake rapped the tile floor once but wasn't even marked.

Paul had ended up with only one solid hit to the chest and the face shot hadn't entered the brain. It had broken his jaw and ripped a lot of face off below the cheekbone but nothing fatal. He was rolling around on the floor, back and forth, moaning and clutching his face and the sucking chest wound that would be fatal soon. Taylor took aim, timing his roll, once, twice, thr — BANG. The rolling and the moaning stopped. His feet kicked a couple of times and went still.

She took both rifles and seated herself in a chair near where Big Tim was cursing and moaning. She reloaded the Glock with a spare magazine from her boot, then field stripped Paul's rifle. She pushed the pins out and separated the upper from the lower receiver, pulled the bolt carrier group out, and dug out the firing pin retaining pin. Once that was out, the BCG — Bolt Carrier Group — came apart into the carrier, bolt, cam pin, and firing pin, which she casually tossed around the room in different directions. Cody's rifle was a keeper. She liked it and was taking it with her.

Mike, meanwhile, had gotten up, slowly, grabbed five bottles of beer from the big ice chest that was in place of the refrigerator, and sat down at the counter between the kitchen and the great room. He started slamming the beer down as fast as he could. He felt guilty. All of the thoughts were screaming through his mind again, just now in past tense: should he have warned them? Would they have believed him? Could they have killed her? And on and on. He drank the beer to quiet the racing thoughts. To drown the sorrows that she had mentioned earlier.

No, the Devil would have shot them all, just like she did anyway, but with me included, he thought. *Either way, they were dead men walking. There was nothing I could have done to stop it.*

His hands trembled so badly he had to prop his elbows on the bar and use both hands to keep the bottleneck at his mouth. Even so, he rapped the bottle against his teeth painfully a couple of times.

He'd never seen anyone shot to death before and he'd had a front row seat today to four. Plus, the results of a Bernzomatic torch on a man's — NO, No, no, no, no, no, don't go there! Don't think of that, don't bring that mental picture up, ever. For a moment he thought he was going to throw the beer up but it strangely seemed to settle his stomach, having something in it. The heavy, dark beer diluted the roiling stomach acid.

Big Tim was holding his leg just below the knee because that was as far down as he could bend. People probably wondered how he put his socks and boots on in the morning. Or took them off, for that matter.

"So, what the fuck is going on?" he demanded, teeth clenched against the pain. "You're not a cop. Are you a freelancer? You thought you'd knock over a stash house? Well, you fucked up. We don't really stash much here. Just enough for local use. I told you that. Stuff comes in here and gets loaded that day on another truck and out of here. And that's not for — Well, I guess that traitorous bastard told you all about it." He glared at Mike. Mike was in the middle of chugging a beer and ignored him.

"Who's involved?" Taylor asked. "The police chief and both deputies, right?"

Big Tim transferred his glare to her.

"The mayor? Judge? Some other officials? Who?"

No answer.

"I guess I'll just have to kill them all, then. You know, let God sort them out."

"The judge doesn't have anything to do with it. There's no need. If the police don't arrest someone, then the judge never has to be involved."

"All right, I'll buy that. How do you know the cops are bad?"

"They escort the trucks here. They take the money that I give them, that's how."

"Where's the stuff coming from? Mexico?"

"Yeah, Mexico. Some bad honchos down there. You'll meet them. They'll come looking for you."

"What gang? What's their name?"

"*La Compañia*. The Company, is all they call it. Mike, you backstabbing fuck, can you get me a clean towel from the kitchen?"

Mike heard that and looked at Taylor before he moved a muscle. There were knives in the kitchen and he didn't want her to think he was going to grab one and come after her.

"Bring him one," she commanded, eyes still on Big Tim.

Mike pulled Tim's boot and sock off for him and applied pressure with the towel. Tim moaned and cussed some more before he took a few deep breaths and focused on Taylor again.

"What's your plan here? Am I wasting my time trying to stop the bleeding?" he asked.

She ignored the question. "Going north, then. The drugs get loaded on the truck and go to Dallas. Where, specifically?"

"I honestly don't know. They compartmentalize." He was starting to really feel the pain now. People frequently tend to not feel the pain of a wound initially. He had just felt a thump like he'd been punched in the foot and it collapsed under him. Then it was hot. Then all of the pain in the world seemed to descend on him, crushing him, twisting his body in unnatural ways, washing through his body in waves of fire. He gritted his teeth and started breathing like he was pumping iron, through his mouth in short explosive bursts. Not that he ever pumped iron.

"But you have a contact. A boss. Someone you report to."

Tim gasped a couple of times but didn't say anything more.

The girl he knew as Kayla laughed, a short, little trill of amusement.

"I think you'll want to answer my questions," she stated. "Or do I need to tell you how Dennis spent his morning? I tied him to his bed. Naked. And then I slowly and carefully ran a Bernzomatic torch up his leg and back and forth across his genitals a few times."

Mike choked and turned his head to the side to spit up a little of the beer in his stomach, followed by a little dry heaving and coughing.

Taylor pointed with her chin in Mike's direction. "He saw. He was there. But not to worry. After Dennis told me about you and this place, I put him out of his misery." She stood. "Do I need to go get my torch? Because I have it in the truck, and it still has fuel in it. Shall I do another weenie roast? I think it hurts *really* badly."

"No. No. No. We run messages. Hand-carry them on the train to Fort Worth. In code. Top of my desk. Black leather notebook. Addresses. Codes. Shit, you gotta give me something for this pain!"

Taylor slung the rifle and kept the pistol out. The rifle was more powerful but she'd never fired it and wouldn't trust it until she had. She found the notebook and flipped through it. There were nicely tabbed sections for addresses and codes, just like he'd said. If nothing else, Tim was detail-oriented.

She sat back down with the address section open. "What am I looking at here?"

"You gotta give me something for the pain first."

"How about I shoot you in the other fucking foot? That'll make you forget about the first foot."

"No, no, don't do that." Big Tim, gasping and cursing, went through the list: a primary contact address, which was just a house where messengers dropped off the coded communiques that he created, a secondary address if the first one went down, a mailbox if that one went down, a couple of locations where he could get black market gasoline and diesel, several sites with numbers spread across town for meetings, and a house of prostitution.

"How many girls at this house?" she asked.

"Three or four. It changes sometimes."

"Are they there voluntarily?"

"Hell, I don't know. I can't think right now. I need something for this —" He stopped abruptly when Taylor swiveled Cody's rifle towards him. It was still lying sideways on the arm of her chair, but no one wants the barrel of a loaded rifle pointed their way. She pulled the charging handle and let it clank back in battery, loading a round in the chamber.

He gritted his teeth and closed his eyes against the pain. "Yeah, I guess. They aren't locked in or chained up or anything. There's one guy. No guards, nothing like that."

Taylor considered that for a minute, obviously considering the situation, before nodding slightly. Next, she took him through the code, asking if it was changed periodically and if there were any key phrases that had to be there to validate the message or that signaled danger or anything. None of that was required.

"Anything you want to say to convince me to spare your life?"

"Look, you don't have to be like that. You missed the big score but I do have some gold saved up. Cash money. Not here, not much. But I have more. I can get it for you but we have to make the transfer someplace public."

"Where's your stash here?"

"In my desk. Bottom drawer, right side."

Taylor turned her head. "Mike, would you please take a look?"

He looked at her suspiciously for a second, wondering why she was being so courteous. But he didn't hesitate too long, not with her itchy and well-used trigger finger.

Fetch, boy, go fetch, he thought.

"Wait," she said abruptly, thinking of something. "I'll go with you. Just open the drawer and step back." She didn't think Mike would use a pistol if he found one in the drawer, but better safe than sorry. He might be panicking about now. She stood, but looked at Big Tim, considering. "I just don't trust you. Or like you."

She brought the Glock up and shot him twice in the chest. He clutched up, made one long, low groan, breathed in deeply three or four times, and then went still.

Chapter Thirty-Seven

MIKE'S SHOULDERS WERE SLUMPED as she trailed him into his office. "How can you do that?" he asked. "Be talking to someone one second, even flirting with Cody, and just shoot them the next second?"

"It's easy. I go into it knowing I'm going to shoot them. I knew I was going to shoot the guards before I ever walked through the door. It's not like I was flirting with him and decided I ought to shoot him all of a sudden. There's a plan. None of this is random."

"How about promises, then? Do you make promises knowing you're going to break them?"

"That's different!" she said with heat. "I didn't promise those guys shit. I promised you I wouldn't kill you and I won't. Well, unless you attack me or something."

He gave her a hangdog look of suspicion and opened the drawer. Nothing blew up and there was no gun.

But Taylor still had her blood up. "Listen, it's none of your business, but I buried a boy less than two weeks ago. He was fifteen. He took some narcotic and thought he could fly. He impaled himself on a fence and bled to death. You might say that I don't have a lot of Goddamned sympathy for drug dealers right about now."

That made Mike do some soul searching over the next half-hour or so.

I've been aiding and abetting things like that, he thought. *I have to own up to it. I could have been working in the oil patch or something, but I accepted this job. I agreed to guard drugs, and load and unload them. I wasn't selling them directly, but I did things that facilitated the sale. I just put it out of my mind. I was just fooling myself that I was merely moving boxes and sitting around with a rifle. I have to repent. Lord God, please forgive me. I will work for your blessing if You'll allow me.*

***

There was a box of gold and silver coins in the desk, six or seven thousand dollars at a quick glance. Taylor took it for operating expenses. She had another plan forming in her mind.

She collected a kilo of uncut cocaine that was in the storeroom, Cody's rifle, and the gold coins and put them in the cab of her truck. The coke was not for recreational purposes. She was going to turn it over to Medical at the ranch, since it is an excellent topical anesthetic and causes vasoconstriction or reduced blood flow.

Here, she wanted to burn the drugs. The easiest way to do that was to stack them on the dining room table, move some more furniture into that room as firewood, and soak it all with fuel. There were multiple 55-gallon drums of diesel in the garage for the delivery trucks, plus the usual cans of gasoline. She intended to use a mix, first a soaking with diesel, topped with gasoline. The gas would light off quickly, bringing the diesel up to its much higher ignition point and then lighting it off. It was like a two-stage burn. If the gas didn't catch the wood furniture on fire, the slower burning diesel would.

While Mike was stacking furniture, she made sandwiches for both of them. It was lunch time and she was hungry. The fact that there were dead bodies leaking blood in the living room was irrelevant.

"Sandwiches are ready," she called out.

He walked into the kitchen as if in a dream. Here was the Devil, this vicious, cold-blooded killer, offering him a sandwich she had made. She was acting like a

186

girlfriend, as if they had made hot, passionate love the previous night and many times before that, then went to sleep in each other's arms. The morning after, here she was fixing her man a sandwich.

But that wasn't the reality at all.

He still couldn't understand how she could switch like that. Were there two personalities in there? This one, the sweet young girl that smiled at him and made him a ham and cheese on a plate, and the other one that unflinchingly ran a blowtorch across a man's genitals and then blew his head off? And if so, what did he need to do to never see the evil side again?

He sat down at the breakfast table, across from her, where she had set his plate. He looked at her, stared at her, as if he could divine who she was. What she was. He recognized power. She literally held the power of life and death in her hands. She could take a life in an instant, with one quick decision. She was a judge, with the power to determine guilt and carry out the punishment instantly.

He remembered a television show he'd seen, one of the talent competitions. A young woman had come onstage and he'd thought she was kind of cute, but only kind of. But when the music was going and she was belting out a song, stalking around the stage and commanding it, she was *hot*. She was beautiful and desirable and powerful. Power is the ultimate aphrodisiac, and those who have it can be irresistible.

That's what he was seeing here. The difference was that Kayla was a beauty to begin with, not just kind of cute. And she wasn't merely commanding a stage, she was that ultimate authority, that instant and permanent fate for the guilty. She was Death, but not the skeleton in a hooded robe. No, the Devil threw a pillow here, too, with the pitchfork hidden behind it, as always. He had put an angelic face on a killer's mind.

Then that 'girlfriend' thought came around again, and he imagined her casually taking off her clothes in front of him, as if she'd done it many times before. And him putting his arms around her from behind, pressing their bodies close together, her skin smooth and soft, and her hair tickling his face as he nuzzled her neck. Maybe running a hand down to her ass, squeezing one cheek a little so she definitely knew his hand was there. Kissing her on the neck, then, and moving the other hand up to cup her breast. And then she would turn to face him, kiss him deeply, and they would move slowly towards the bed and an afternoon of vigorous, passionate —

"Are you not eating?" interrupted his little fantasy and making him jump, the innocent question coming in like an artillery shell even though she used a normal speaking voice.

"Yes, yes. Sorry. I was lost in thought."

She smiled at him a little, as if she knew exactly what he had been thinking. Maybe she did. Maybe she had put the thoughts there. Maybe this was a way of toying with him, of showing him something extremely desirable that he would never have.

His head was swirling with these thoughts when there was a heavy thumping on the front door. He jumped so much he dropped the sandwich he had just picked up.

"Open the door! Open the door!" someone was calling, a deep voice, and slamming a big hand into the door. Mike looked at Taylor, in the kitchen on the other side of the bar, and her eyes were wide.

SHIT! She thought. *Why the fuck did I put Cody's rifle in the truck? And stripped the BCG on that one so it's useless. God damn it, that was stupid! Damn, damn, damn, damn, damn.* She pulled her pistol, put it behind her back, made eye contact with Mike, and head-bobbed at the door.

"Get rid of him. Either that or get him inside and close the door. One or the other. Nothing in between."

Chapter Thirty-Eight

MIKE GOT UP TO answer the door and had intended to stand in the doorway to keep whoever it was from coming in and seeing the bodies on the floor. No such luck. As soon as he unlocked the door and opened it an inch, the guy on the other side bulldozed his way through.

And he was talking as he came in. "Big Tim! Dennis's house is on fi —" He stopped in mid-sentence and mid-stride, seeing the bodies on the floor. His eyes swept the room, taking in everything. "What the fuck?"

Mike looked at Taylor, now standing in the living room, and he could tell that the other side was back. The evil side. Oh, she still looked sweet and innocent but there was something there, or something missing, from the girl that had made them sandwiches a few minutes ago. He closed the door quietly and scurried off to the side, out of her line of fire.

"Wow, you are a big one," Taylor said, giving the man the elevator look; down to the feet and back up to the face. He was a giant. He was probably six-four and three hundred seventy-five pounds, all of it muscle, nine inches taller than her and more than three times her weight. Taylor didn't know if the eleven rounds in her baby Glock were going to be enough. Then she had to revise that number downward to nine since she had shot Big Tim twice from this magazine. She tried to remember how many were in the other mag in her boot. Three or four. Not nearly as many as she wanted. No, actually, she wanted Eric's .308 with a couple of full twenty-round magazines right now. Or anything else that would be suitable for grizzly bear.

"What the fuck?" the giant rumbled again, taking a step and waving an arm across the room at the dead bodies. The bicep on that arm looked as big around as Taylor's waist and rippled with muscles.

Okay, enough small talk, she thought.

She brought the Glock up from behind her back and started with what had always worked, two in the chest, one in the face, known as the Mozambique Drill. The head shot was in case they were wearing body armor or were so hyped up on drugs that they wouldn't go down from the torso shots until they bled to death. She was going to repeat that as necessary until he went down, but hesitated when she saw something she'd never seen before.

The head shot bounced off his skull. Her mouth fell open. *It fucking* bounced off.

The light coming through the window blinds had caught it just right and she saw a flash of copper jacketed bullet carom off his forehead and spin away and out through the window. It carried some blood droplets off with it but it wasn't rattling around inside his skull like she wanted it to do.

Oh. My. God.

He didn't even seem to notice the chest shots. Hell, he didn't notice any of them.

Then things got worse. He charged her.

She almost peed a little. She dumped the magazine, firing the whole thing into his chest as quickly as she could pull the trigger. It took a couple of seconds, no more, for the slide to lock back. He didn't even slow down. No, he was coming at her like a high-speed freight train.

She turned and ran for her life.

A lateral movement was really the only option, into the kitchen, then through it and into the dining room. The drugs were stacked on the table there, with other furniture piled on and around it, but Taylor dove through a gap between two chairs. She whacked her elbow on one of the chairs, skidded under the table on hands and knees, shoved another chair out of the way with her shoulder, and made it to the foyer.

She paused for a second there, weighing the option of running upstairs versus running down the hallway back into the living room. She didn't know what was upstairs but thought it probably dead-ended into bedrooms. At least there was a roundabout here.

She was trying to locate the giant, and heard him behind her crashing into the dining room furniture. He slammed into the table and things tumbled to the floor. Then more things flew around the room, rattling against the walls and the windows. He must have swung an arm in frustration or anger and swept some of the product off the table. Taylor thought she heard him wheeze and hoped it was a sucking chest wound. Or eight sucking chest wounds. That would be even better!

Running back to the living room, she ejected the empty magazine but didn't have time to bend down and grab the one in her boot. Looking over her shoulder she saw the hulk coming around the corner and pounding down the hall after her. The good thing was he was slowing down. His steps were thumping down heavily and his knees were flexing more and more. His body was getting closer to the floor with every step. He poured blood. It ran down his face in a cascade from his forehead wound and the front of his shirt was a sopping wet, red mess. He left a trail of blood drops behind him.

She sprinted into the kitchen, but it was an open concept plan and she could still see him. The only thing that separated the living room from the kitchen was a counter with a bar top.

He stomped around the curve of the bar, moving slower and sinking deeper by the second. He ground to a stop, one of his paws on the bar holding him up, wheezing and bleeding. He used the other paw to wipe the blood out of his eyes but it was instantly replaced. Head wounds bleed profusely and his face was a red mask.

He saw her. They were no more than eight feet apart but with the cabinets and dishwasher and a slab of granite or quartz or something between them. He lumbered towards her again, one more step, and she almost turned to run, but saw him slowly sink down out of her sight.

She breathed a sigh of relief, a big gust of air that she directed upwards to blow her hair away from her face. She knelt down to get the magazine out of her boot and froze.

A hand had come slowly around the counter, just above the floor. It gripped the edge and pulled. The giant's face popped around the corner, sideways. He was lying on the floor, on his side, but he was still coming after her, slithering towards her like some primordial swamp monster.

He had a huge head, to go along with the huge body, with big eyes glaring at her. The whites of his eyes were in contrast to the blood that covered his face. He looked like he had war paint on, like maybe an oversized totem pole come to life.

He dug his boat-sized rubber-soled work boots in and pushed and the blood he was losing acted as a lubricant on the tiles. He slid forward surprisingly quickly and was suddenly within reach of the girl who had hurt him.

His arm shot out like a giant striking rattlesnake, straight for her ankle.

Taylor screamed, a guttural "AHH!" and launched herself up, over the huge arm that came for her, up onto the island in the middle of the kitchen.

Almost.

Another inch and her hip would be over the edge of the island and she could pull herself up. But she was stretched out, gripping the edge of the countertop with one hand and clutching the Glock in the other. Her legs dangled just over the beast's arms. She had no leverage. She couldn't pull herself up. She couldn't drop down onto the monster. That way meant death. And she couldn't hang there for another second because he was sure to reach for her feet, which dangled mere inches above him.

192

Desperate, she swung her legs away from him and then back, taking the risk of him grabbing a moving target, and using the momentum to swing her legs up onto the island. A shock went through her body when they touched, his hand and her foot, but she was moving too quickly and her foot bounced out of his grip before he could close his fingers.

Up on the island, she rolled over into a sitting position and stood from there. The hand slapped up onto the island, seeking her, seeming to shake the whole house. She moved back a half-step and was out of room. She felt her heel hit open air a fraction of a second before she put her weight on it and dumped her onto the floor. She bent her knees and threw her arms out to the side for balance. If she had gone off the island she would probably have hit her head on the counter and been knocked out. And then the giant would have crawled over and killed her.

But she wasn't safe on the island. It wasn't that big and that arm was pulling the beast back up to his feet.

Her options were rapidly narrowing. She dropped the slide on the pistol and holstered it to give herself two hands to work with. She bailed off of the island and her feet barely hit the kitchen floor before she bounced up onto the countertop, then up the additional few inches to the bar. She squatted there, hesitating, scared but also fascinated that this giant could take that many hits and keep moving. Not only moving, but standing up again.

She wanted to see what would happen. The thought flitted through her mind that she ought to cut him open, do a little field autopsy, to see if the hollowpoint bullets failed to expand or if she missed or something.

Then she remembered the Terminator movies and wondered if this bastard was going to chase her for the rest of her life. *I think he's even bigger than Arnold!*

Reload! Reload! Reload! a voice was screaming in the back of her mind, so she did, without taking her eyes off of the monster. They stayed like that for a few seconds, eye to eye, not ten feet apart. If he moved, she could go off the bar into the living room and have the counter between them again. If he stayed there, he'd bleed to death.

Actually, he'd bleed to death regardless, the only question being whether he took Taylor with him. But his time was limited, and she could keep running for quite a while.

Just when she was starting to feel almost safe, a chilling thought intruded.

All Mike has to do is come up behind me and shove me into that monster's arms! The beast can snap my neck like a chicken's! She looked quickly to her right and left, turning her head as far as it would go, and didn't see him.

But she did hear the giant move towards her. He made a groaning, wheezing sound and tried to take a step in her direction but his bloody hand slipped on the island. It shot out from under him and that was his support. He fell to his hands and knees.

She leaned over and shot him in the top of the head. His head moved but he didn't collapse.

Slowly, slowly, slowly, his head started to sink down towards the floor and his knees started sliding out from under him.

She shot him again in the head. There didn't seem to be any effect. She couldn't tell if the rounds were even penetrating or skidding off like the other one. There was blood, there was skin missing from the scalp, but nothing else. No telling if the bullet penetrated the skull.

She fired again, into the spine this time. No effect.

She aimed again, a kidney shot this time, and tried to squeeze the trigger but the slide was locked back. The Glock was empty.

His head and torso continued their gradual descent until they finally rested on the floor in a lake-sized blood puddle. All of his muscles relaxed and his limbs moved a little as gravity pulled them into resting positions. One leg was straight out but the other was still curled under him.

"Holy fuck. *Holy fuck!*" Taylor was shaking.

Mike peered around the corner a few seconds later, just as she was jumping down from the counter. She looked at him for a couple of seconds, breathing hard like she'd been sprinting.

"Who's the Incredible fucking Hulk?" she asked.

"That's what they call him, Hulk. He's one of the guys here. You know, guard, load and unload, that sort of thing."

Taylor's hands were trembling and she didn't want him to see that, and she wanted to get out of the house, and she needed to fucking reload before —

Calm down, chica, she told herself. *Stop bouncing off the walls.*

She realized that this was the first time that she didn't have a loaded weapon around Mike. She had a lockblade, but would he feel like he was free of her now? What if he just turned and walked out the door?

"I'll be back in two seconds. Can you start pouring diesel in the dining room?" she asked and then she was out the door, moving quickly, scooping up the ejected magazine as she left.

At the truck, she grabbed her Glock 19 and a dual magazine carrier from her pack, leaving the smaller Model 26 and its magazines. That made her feel a little better. She folded the AK stock and slung it over her shoulder, with an extra thirty-round mag in a back pocket. That made her feel even better. She took the time to lean against the truck and take a few deep breaths and tremble for a minute.

Chapter Thirty-Nine

THEY MADE UP A torch with a chair leg wrapped with a kitchen towel and soaked in gasoline, lit it off, and then tossed it into the dining room from the front doorway. As soon as she threw the torch, the instant it left her hands, she remembered the girl.

"Oh, shit!" She clapped a hand to her mouth.

Mike goggled at her. He had never seen her like that. Not that he knew her that well, but she had seemed so firmly in control of any situation that came up that he was amazed to see her not in control. It must be something very bad to make her look like that. She had been confused when Hulk hadn't reacted to being shot, but this was different.

The gasoline fumes had lit off with an explosive whump and sent a blast of heat and dust particles through the door and past them. It was blazing furiously. Taylor thought back to the tour that Big Tim had given her. They hadn't gone upstairs, but she only remembered the one set of stairs.

The stairs that were three or four steps from the dining room.

The dining room that was on fire.

She stared at the steps through the open front door. "Shit," she said again, under her breath. It was resigned, like she knew she had to do something, didn't like it at all, but was about to do it anyway. Then she ran, one hand on the AK to keep it from swinging on the sling and beating the crap out of her.

Through the foyer, the heat from the dining room seemed to sear her face and arm and she worried that the wig would catch on fire. She charged up the stairs two at a time.

Don't trip, don't trip, don't fucking trip!

The top of the stairs was almost as hot, the air rising above the fire and drawing in more air from the open doors and windows, which fanned the flames and sent more, hotter air to the top.

She knew which way the almost-naked girl had headed when she flounced off, so she tried the first door she came to. Locked. She slapped the door.

"Hey! The house is on fire! Come out!"

Not knowing if the girl was in that room or not, she ran to the other door and tried it. It was unlocked and was set up as a bedroom but no one was there.

She ran back to the first room. The doorknob didn't have a lock, so it had to have been locked from the inside. She kicked the door.

"Hey! Open the Goddamned door! The house is on fire!"

"I don't care!" came the muffled reply.

Taylor clenched her teeth and her fists and wanted to hit the girl really, really hard. "Open the motherfucking door, you stupid bitch!" she screamed. "The fucking house is on fire!"

"I don't care!"

Taylor made a guttural sound deep in her throat. She turned around and kicked the door as close to the knob as she could, giving it a mule kick, the best way to kick a door open. It took two shots and popped open. She charged through the door, scanning the room.

Where in the hell is she?

Suddenly there was noise and movement off to her side, and the girl was charging out of a closet, swinging a knife.

The only thing that saved Taylor's life was the amateurish way that she swung it. It must have been something she saw in a movie. She started with her arm all the way over by her left shoulder, swinging the knife in a broad arc horizontally until her arm ended up as far to the side as it could go without her turning her body. Very dramatic.

She was moving forward as she swung. The blade caught Taylor right on the cheekbone and sliced for a couple of inches before angling down towards the earlobe. If she had held the knife out like a spear and just run forward, she could have killed her.

Taylor didn't even feel it as pain, just a scratching. She was hyped up and was reacting to danger. She stepped back and turned to meet the threat, saw the girl's swing take her weapon effectively out of the fight, and stepped in with a right fist. Her foot hit the floor at the same time that her fist hit the girl, a long-practiced move that put her weight behind the punch. The girl took the full brunt of the punch in the nose and fell back into the closet, thumping hard on the floor. Taylor chased her down, going after the knife. The girl let it go, all fight gone out of her. She curled up and held her bloody nose and burst into tears.

Taylor stood, tossing the knife through the open door and down the hall and evaluating the situation. The girl was still nearly naked, so she needed clothes. Taylor grabbed her ankles and dragged her, screaming, out of the closet, then went in herself. She grabbed the first sturdy looking pair of shoes she saw and tied the shoelaces together for easier carrying, then snatched a pair of jeans and a shirt from their hangers.

The girl was still on the floor but sitting up now, her back against the bed. "I don't like those shoes," she pouted.

If Taylor had been mad before, she was *really* mad now. She marched out of the closet, leaned down close to the girl's ear, and screamed as loud as she could: "SHUT THE FUCK UP!" The girl sunk back down to the floor and covered her ears, looking at her wide-eyed.

With the clothes and shoes under her arm, Taylor grabbed the girl's ankle and dragged her down the hall to the other bedroom. They were going to have to go out a window, she could tell from here. Just the air pumping up the stairs was hot enough to make her sweat heavily. Smoke was pouring up and collecting on the ceiling, getting thicker by the second. She didn't think they could go down the stairs past the dining room again. Surely the diesel had caught fire by now and the fire was even more intense.

She opened the window and saw there was a hedge under it. She didn't know how soft that would be so she stripped the pillows and blankets off of the bed and threw them down to try to cushion it. Of course, none of them fell in the right place to offer any assistance. And then Mike came around the corner. Apparently, he was running around outside the house looking for them.

"Hey!" he yelled. He ran up, worked his way behind the hedge, and held his arms up. "I'll catch you as best I can."

Taylor threw the clothes out past the bushes, then stuck her index finger in the girl's face. "I'm going to lower you out the window and he'll catch you. If you fight me, I'm going to knock you out and then throw you out the window headfirst!"

The girl lowered her head and sobbed "Why are you being so mean to me?" Taylor came really close to slugging her but held off.

She managed to get the girl, screaming in terror, out the window and dropped the short distance into Mike's arms. It wasn't easy. The girl had sat on the windowsill and put her legs out the window without too many threats, but there she froze.

"Look, twist around a little and take my hands in both of yours. Okay, now just slide off the windowsill and I'll hold you," Taylor had instructed. As soon as the girl took her hands, Taylor put her shoulder against the girl's back and shoved her out the window.

That started the screaming, and continued with the girl dangling from Taylor's arm out the window, swinging back and forth a little. Taylor waited a couple of seconds for the motion to abate a little and then let go.

Nothing happened. The girl had a death grip on her hands and kept up the screaming nonstop.

This will be a funny story later on, Taylor thought. *Dani will laugh her ass off, but right now I'm about to kill this bitch.*

Then something made a noise downstairs and she felt a wave of hotter air gust through the room.

That means playtime is over!

She grabbed one of the girl's little fingers and pulled it back in a direction that it wasn't built to go. The girl released her grip — it was either that or have the finger broken — and was suddenly dangling from one hand. Still screaming, of course. Mike was standing under her with his arm around her legs, trying to talk to her in a soothing voice. Taylor grabbed the remaining little finger and pulled it back harder than she needed to, but she was rapidly losing patience. The girl dropped.

Then the girl couldn't walk since she was barefoot so Mike had to carry her out from behind the hedge into the yard. Taylor debated just jumping since the smoke was coming into the room quite a bit now, but she waited for Mike to get back in place. She hung off the windowsill to the full extent of her reach and let go. She crashed into him and they both fell back into the shrubbery.

She lay there, unmoving, for a few seconds to catch her breath and make sure that she hadn't twisted an ankle or anything. That was perfectly fine with him. He had the thought that they were in the position that he had fantasized about just a little while ago. He was under her, actually, instead of behind her, but the position was the same. They were virtually cheek-to-cheek, and he could have just turned slightly to nibble on her ear or whisper dirty things into it.

One of his hands was on her stomach, on her bare skin, since her shirt had ridden up in the drop. His other hand was just below a breast, maybe an inch away. Her hair tickled his face. He could smell her. He wanted to remain like that for a while, with her pleasantly lying on him, willingly.

But no, it only lasted a few seconds before she tried to sit up. They were at an awkward angle, almost but not quite flat on their backs, supported by the shrubbery. But not firmly supported because it flexed and bounced when she tried to push against it. She bent forward quickly, trying to use momentum to stand, but the bushes flexed and dropped her back. Mike put his hands on her waist and gave her a push to help. He was happy that she wasn't objecting to him putting his hands on her body. At least she wasn't swatting them away immediately.

She pushed off again, letting the foliage flex down and then spring up. As it came up, she pushed off again, and then twice more, gaining a bit each time, until she could get her feet under her and stand. All of that pushing meant that she was thrusting her ass against his crotch repeatedly, effectively dry humping him. He had felt himself begin to grow hard when she was on top of him. He was pretty worked up by the time she was on her feet.

"Thank you," she said, sincerely. She had turned to face him and reached out a hand to help him up.

"You're bleeding." He stared at her cheek, noticing it for the first time. She put a hand to the wound and came away with bloody fingers. She knew where it was from and gritted her teeth yet again.

"That bitch tried to kill me," she muttered. After wiping the blood on her shirttail, she helped him stand.

"We have to go. Why don't you ride in the back with that stupid bitch and get her dressed?"

She dug her AK out of the hedge where she had dropped it right before she went out the window and left Mike to deal with the girl and her clothes.

As she drove, she considered the fact that Mike had had free access to Cody's AR in the truck. It was loaded and ready to go. And she'd dropped her AK into the hedge before she went out the window. Plus, Big Tim's gold was in the truck. He could have taken off with the loot or shot her as she was trying to escape the burning house, or both.

He hadn't.

He could have been in great shape. There was no one still alive that knew he had helped Taylor. He could have been the hero to the cartel boys. Maybe he wouldn't have saved the other guys, but he would have gotten the *puta* that had killed them and burned their stuff. That could have been very profitable.

Taylor didn't know why he hadn't done it. She'd have to think about that.

Chapter Forty

AT THE TRAIN STATION, she parked and walked back to the truck bed. She waited until Mike helped the girl out, then pulled him aside and handed him the bulk of the gold coins from Big Tim's stash, four or five thousand dollars. He looked at her in amazement.

"My advice would be to get out of town. Someone may have seen you with me and there might be bad things happening to you because of it. Don't go back to your place and get anything. Just go." She nodded towards the station. "Or maybe they didn't see you, if you feel like taking the chance. If anyone asks, feel free to tell them everything you learned about me. You know, before they kill you."

"I don't even know anything about you. I guess your name is fake. Kayla."

She didn't bother to answer that, just tilted her head a little and looked at him.

"What about —" he started to ask, then gestured towards the girl. She was holding his handkerchief to her bloody nose. At least she had clothes on now.

"She pisses me off every time she opens her mouth. I don't care what happens to her."

"But you do care," Mike pointed out softly. "You just risked your life running into a burning building to save her. And you did save her, even after she tried to kill you."

She started to reply, hesitated, closed her mouth, and was silent for a couple of seconds. When she did talk, it was on a different subject. "If you're smart, you'll take a train in one direction and then another in a different direction. Like, go west and then go north. Maybe three trains. Change your appearance in between if you can. End up a couple of states away. But make your own decisions."

As she spoke, she was getting in the truck and putting it in gear. When she finished speaking, she accelerated off. She could see in the rearview mirror that he was watching her go, staring at the truck like he was a puppy that didn't understand why his owner was leaving without him. She wondered what that was all about, until she turned a corner and found another place to stop.

She examined the cut on her cheek in the mirror and decided it didn't need stitches. It wasn't that deep and had already stopped bleeding. But she didn't wipe the blood off of her face. That might come in handy for one more thing she had to do.

***

She didn't do it.

Not that plan, anyway. She cruised past the city hall, in the middle of downtown, and there were a lot more people around than she had imagined. She had had the idea to go in, a girl in distress, bleeding, with news that she had to tell the mayor right now. Interrupt a meeting or whatever, but right now! And then shoot him or knife him or something. Run out afterwards, screaming "he has a gun! He shot the mayor!" or something and play the victim. It would work with just a few witnesses, with Taylor in a bit of disguise.

But not today. Too many people, both inside and outside, that would see both her and her vehicle. And people would have guns. Not everyone would be walking around heavily armed, rifles and extra magazines, like after Hexen. But the world still held many dangers and there would be a lot of weapons close at hand. Police officers were in short supply everywhere since most local governments still had a long way to go to really be called governments. Their tax bases were gone, absolutely zero federal money was coming in, and every person that wasn't growing food somehow still had to eat every day. Like cops. That meant that everyone was their own first responder. Actually, it had always been that way, but now the majority realized it once again.

She drove out of the area until she found some place quiet and cleaned up the cut and put some antibiotic on it. It had expired a couple of years ago but it was all she had. She'd put a bandage on the cut to sleep but didn't want one during the day. Any bandage on the face feels huge.

She decided to get out of Midland for the rest of the day and headed up I-20 for thirty-five or forty miles to Big Spring. In between the two cities, she pulled off for a minute to swap the license plates out. They didn't mean anything now, but if someone had memorized her tag, she wanted a different one, choosing Mississippi plates from the little stack she had under the seat.

It was also time to change her appearance. She pulled off the dark-haired wig and gave her scalp a vigorous scratch as much as she could around her braids. She enjoyed it as much as she could, because the next thing she did was dig out a red wig with hair almost down to her shoulders and put it on.

**

There wasn't much to Big Spring. She bought a couple of items of clothing at a place there and found a little restaurant where she could just rest for a while without looking over her shoulder too much. There were no other customers there in the middle of the afternoon, and she began chatting with the owner, a tiny, wrinkled woman from El Salvador. Taylor was fluent in Spanish, from living with Dani for four years, which the woman appreciated.

"Is there some place where I could get a room?" she asked. "Just for a few hours. I need to take a nap." She figured the woman would see the moneymaking opportunity and try to accommodate her, which is exactly what she did.

"My son's room. He has a good job in the oilfield. Two weeks on, two weeks off."

The son probably wasn't actually a son, maybe a nephew or maybe just a stray. That was the reality now. Hexen had shattered every single family in the world. There wasn't a racial or a geographic or a genetic or familial immunity that they could find. Twins, maybe, but they hadn't encountered any. No one knew why some had been immune but not others that seemed to be similar.

Taylor asked the woman if she had any paint, and was directed to the shed behind the building. There, she found a couple of cans of paint. One was a dried-up paste, but the other was at least fluid, and a dark green. She wanted to disguise her truck more than just changing the license plates. If anyone was cruising around Midland looking for the girl that had whacked their friends and burned their stash house, she didn't want to fit the description. Presumably, that description, if there was one, included a white truck.

She didn't think Mike would go running to his buddies and tell them all about her, but maybe he would. Maybe when the terror that he had felt faded he'd be angry with her and looking to settle the score. Maybe leaving him alive had signed her own death warrant. If so, nothing could be done about it now. She only had a little more exposure and then she'd be done.

She pulled the truck up close to the shed and went at the front end with some rags, since she couldn't find a brush. She smeared the paint all over both front fenders, saw that there was paint left over, and did one door. A little water added in stretched the paint to finish the other door. Now she had a truck that no one would just call "white". The other color covered enough that they would have said it was a white truck with green doors and fenders.

It was a horrible paint job and would never have looked normal pre-Hexen, but this was now. The only vehicles that anyone could get running again were older models that didn't have computers and modern electronics. That meant that all of those old junk trucks up on blocks in the yards of rednecks were suddenly valuable and highly sought-after. Rust, body filler, and primer paint were the norm now.

Where the disguise might fall apart is if someone lifted the hood or opened the doors and saw that the inner parts of the fenders and doors were white. They weren't replacement parts from a green truck. She just couldn't let anyone get that close.

With that in mind, she pulled on gloves from her pack and reloaded the baby Glock magazines and the AK mag that she had fired. When she picked up each round, she scrubbed it on her shirttail to make sure any fingerprints were gone.

The restaurant was in the front of the house, what had been the living room for indoor dining and the front yard for *al fresco*. The living quarters were the bedrooms. Taylor carried all of her stuff inside, to not leave it in the truck, and barred the door. She still had her Y-shaped tube to go under the doorknob and block entry.

Safe, she stripped down and took a sponge bath in the hot water she had gotten from the woman. Still slightly damp, she snuggled down under the sheets which the woman had claimed were clean but still smelled of her son.

I wonder if his mother will tell him there was a naked girl in his bed? Bet he'll be so disappointed he missed it! I wonder if he'll smell me? She chuckled to herself and reached over to locate her AK, by her side like a lover.

The day had been tough. It had actually started last night at Dennis's house, when she could only sleep lightly and woke up four times to check on him and the neighborhood. Then she had had to be completely switched on for most of the day, hyperaware of everything that was going on around her. Her life had depended on it. Multiple shots of adrenaline had boosted her energy for short periods but then left her exhausted as it went out of her system. She really needed to crash all night, but it was not in the cards. She needed to do what she was going to do and then get the hell out of the area. Sticking around and taking her time would not contribute to her longevity.

Chapter Forty-One

THE WOMAN KNOCKED ON the door at dark. Taylor groaned and wanted to curl up and sleep longer, but duty called. Plus, her stomach growled. She could smell good food cooking. She dressed in the same clothing she had been wearing, jeans and a black shirt, but fresh underclothes. She had taken the bobby pins out to give her head a rest and now had to do that all up again to get the red wig on.

She filled up on *pupusas*, the El Salvadoran version of the taco. They have a thicker flour shell and are less spicy than Mexican fare. She appreciated that. One of the last things she needed tonight was to have to take a bathroom break in the middle of something. For the same reason, she had a bottled beer with her food. Not to party, but to have something to drink that was less prone to germs than water that may not have been sterilized properly. Montezuma's Revenge was prevalent in the U.S. now. Your system could get used to the water in your local area but there was no telling what it was like even as close as a quarter mile away.

While enjoying the food, she decided she'd rather sleep in a bed tonight than curled up in the truck.

"How about tonight? Can I come back to sleep in that bedroom tonight?" she inquired. She received a big grin and a nod in reply. She had paid the woman generously for letting her nap in the room, for the food and paint, and now she slipped her another coin. "And another one of these in the morning," she promised. That got an even bigger grin, if that was possible.

***

Taylor gunned up. She had the Glock 19 on her hip with the dual mag carrier and two twenty-one-round Magpul magazines on the other hip. She still had the Cold Steel Recon folding knife. The AK was in her lap as she drove, with extra magazines jammed in between the seats and the seat backs. They were readily available and the fit was tight enough that they wouldn't slide off onto the floor if she went around a corner or jammed on the brakes. Tonight, she didn't intend to shoot anyone, but she was damned sure going to be ready if anyone needed shooting.

She didn't know what kind of hornet's nest she may have stirred up in Midland, and she was driving straight into it.

She didn't drive fast. There were no lights anywhere, just rare vehicle lights, and the danger of animals or tumbleweeds coming across the road did exist. Tumbleweeds were nothing to sneeze at. Some of them were huge, three and four feet in diameter. They are basically rounded, dried bushes, with finger-thick branches that are hard as steel. With a good wind behind them, they can do some damage to a person. It's not something you want to get jammed under your vehicle, either, even if you don't care about the paint job.

The common practice was to at least slow down at stop signs and traffic lights. Besides cross traffic, there could be bikes or ATVs or horses or whatever on the streets. But there seemed to be nothing dangerous. No roadblocks, no bands of armed vigilantes patrolling the streets, nothing. Just some normal civilian traffic, most seemingly headed to the bar she'd been to last night. No disaster stops bars and liquor stores from running, nothing at all. Just the opposite: business increases.

Her Plan A had been to shoot the mayor at his office if she could get in and out quickly enough. A wig and the blood on her cheek should have distracted and confused any witnesses. She had seen some city halls that were virtually deserted. Not this one. That plan was a nonstarter here.

209

Plan B was to wait until dark, knock on his door, and shoot him there. But what if he didn't answer the door? What if it was his wife, or kid, or butler? Or even a security guy? She would take out the bodyguard but would that make enough noise that the mayor would run off where she could never find him? Or would others grab guns and shoot back at her? Even supposing they didn't, she wasn't going to kill a bunch of innocent people because they saw her face. A wife and kids were unquestionably off limits. Or what if he had a little harem of teenaged girls? No, no, no. Shooting drug dealers and gang bangers and drug house guards was one thing. Shooting innocents was something else, something that wasn't going to happen. Plan B was down the tubes.

Plan C was in process.

She found her way to the mayor's house with only one wrong turn, which she immediately recognized and corrected. She parked a few blocks away and considered her options. She'd have liked to do a better recon but this is what she had. Go or no go?

There was only one point where things would look suspicious. Other than that, she was just an innocent girl walking down the street. She figured she could always speak in her fluent French and fake some broken English to confuse the issue. Car trouble would be her first excuse, and her last excuse would be that she was an escort, discreetly parking down the street and heading to a generous older gentleman's bedroom. As a worst-case scenario, she probably outgunned anyone in the immediate area and had surprise on her side.

Fifty-eight rounds of 9mm ought to be enough to fight my way back to my rifle. If I can make it there, I have six thirty-round magazines and a seventy-five-round drum of 7.62 Russian for the AK. I can extract myself.

And attitude was a good shield. If you obviously sneak around, looking over your shoulder, running from cover to cover, people will immediately know you're up to no good. But stride along like you own the place and no one will question you. That's what she did, walked down the street like she had every right to be there.

The only thing out of place was the kilo of cocaine in the small bag under her arm. And the wrecking bar in her hand. And if someone looked closely enough, the lock picks in her pocket.

She walked past the mayor's house, down the middle of the street. Some of the houses showed lights, candles and lanterns, and a couple of dogs barked, but nothing unusual. She was really more afraid of feral dogs coming after her than someone's pet or guard dog. But she was unmolested.

The garage door was open at the mayor's house. *God, that's too easy*, she thought.

She kept going another two blocks, turned, and came back. The first pass was the scouting mission; this was the real thing. The mayor's garage was detached from the house and set further back in the yard. As she got to the far edge of his driveway, she turned abruptly and strolled up it.

It made sense when she thought about it. There was no electricity here. The garage door could be manually raised and lowered, but that involved the possibility of getting dirt or grease on your hands. If the mayor was in nice clothes, he wouldn't want to touch the thing and risk soiling them. And no one wanted to get out of a car in inclement weather to open the garage door. So, the door stayed open.

How about the car?

He drove an older-model Lincoln, since all of the cars that ran were older models. She planned to either stash the coke in the car or in the garage and let the state police handle it from there. If nothing came of it, she could always come back in a few months, do a thorough scouting job, and figure out how to take him out.

The car, too, was unlocked. She opened the back door and had a moment of panic when the dome light came on. She thought she was busted for a second, and then groped for the switch in the door jamb that would turn it off. As long as she kept it pressed in with one hand, she had a free hand to slide the bag containing the coke under the driver's seat. She had also tossed a thousand dollars in gold coins into the bag. The coins were dated with the year in which they were minted, and the year was the current one. There was no way the mayor could make some wild claim like the coke was in there when he got the car. No, she had blocked him out of that excuse.

Okay, done!

She closed the door partway and pushed it the rest of the way with her butt rather than slamming it shut. Older cars like this were built with thicker sheet metal than newer ones, and the door didn't dent. Then she strolled down the driveway, down the street, and to her truck.

One more plan to execute. Tomorrow.

Chapter Forty-Two

TAYLOR KNEW WHEN THE truck was supposed to arrive at the house so it was simple to back that time off a half-our or so to figure when the cop had to be there to escort him in. And she had a good guess as to where. The county line was a reasonable starting point.

The question, besides "is the truck coming at all", was whether he was going to escort the truck coming up with the drugs or the truck coming down with the cash. They were both supposed to arrive at the same time. Normally there were two deputies and a police chief, but yesterday she had cut their manpower down to one. She'd bet on the cash. The cash was more valuable. The drugs were wholesale; the cash was retail.

Even if the surviving deputy had brought on someone else to escort one of the trucks, what she really needed was the police car. And what she was interested in was the cash truck.

She started cruising the stretch of I-20 early, an hour early, and made passes back and forth until she spotted the cop on the side of the road. She pulled over in front of him and backed up to have their vehicles close together.

She figured the cop would be on edge, what with the killings and the burning stash houses and almost getting shot himself yesterday. He wouldn't want any damned civilians interfering with this delivery, so she had a secret weapon.

That was exactly the corrupt cop's attitude when he saw her pull over. "Shit. What does this asshole want?"

When Taylor stepped out of her car, his tune changed to "Holy shit!"

She had short, short, shorts on. They had started out as blue jeans but now they were about bikini-sized. The sides had been cut up so high that the belt loops barely remained. Her usual panties were too big to wear under the skimpy little shorts so she simply wasn't wearing any. Her top was a tight shirt that didn't appear to be buttoned at all, just tied so that her tummy and a substantial amount of cleavage was exposed. She didn't have a huge bust, was average at best, but guys would definitely check it out. They would look at anything a girl wanted to show. When the breeze blew with that skimpy clothing on, she felt like she was naked. Out in public, almost naked. It was actually kind of enjoyable, a naughty little thrill.

The cop thought that maybe he could give her some attention after all. A redhead, at that. He'd never had a redhead. He wondered if the carpet matched the drapes.

He got out of the car. The girl was still walking towards him, and she dropped her keys. She had already taken a step past them, so she had to turn around and bend over to pick them up.

"Mother of God," the cop murmured under his breath, admiring the excellent view he got of her tight little ass, with at least half of it hanging out of those shorts.

Keys back in hand, she walked up to him with a distressed look. "It's making a noise. Can you look at it?"

"I'll be glad to," he replied, hoping that the truck wouldn't be early.

They got the hood up and the girl leaned over, displaying a considerable amount of cleavage. And most definitely no bra. The cop didn't hear any engine knock, and certainly wasn't looking anywhere but down the girl's shirt.

"It's not doing it all the time," she said. "Hold on. Listen to it in a second." She went back to the driver's compartment and the cop looked around at the engine for the first time. He couldn't see anything obviously wrong.

"Don't move! Keep your hands where I can see them!"

The dirty cop jumped, startled, then did what she commanded. The girl, the beauty, the *chica* he was trying to figure out how he could fuck all afternoon, was gone. In her place was, as the center of attention, an AK rifle pointed right at him. The *chica* was suddenly a very different person than a few seconds ago. She still had the same clothing on, but a whole different attitude. He realized his mouth had dropped open and closed it, then just had to open it again to talk.

"Now look —" he began, using his calming voice.

"Don't talk. The safety's off and this is a nice, smooth trigger. I'm running a hundred and twenty-three grain hollow points alternating with heat-treated steel penetrators at about twenty-three hundred feet per second. If the seven point six two by thirty-nine hollow points don't cut right through any Kevlar you might have on, the penetrators definitely will. Now, reach down with your left hand and unfasten your belt. Slowly and carefully."

He did as she ordered and his pistol, cuffs, and everything dropped away. His mind was racing. Bad news: she sounded professional. She was holding the rifle like she knew what she was doing. She wasn't clutching it like she was afraid of it, but she had it under control.

The majority of criminals barely know what caliber they have. In contrast, this girl was intimately familiar with everything about her weapon. The corrupt cop's stomach twisted. The chief and the other deputy had been killed by a shooter using an AK. He'd found the empty casings in the house. And there were six or seven people missing that shouldn't have been missing. He assumed their bodies just hadn't been dug out of the ashes of the two houses yet. Holy shit!

She ordered him to sit down beside the car.

"Do you radio the truck or use hand signals or what?"

"You're going to kill me, aren't you?" He had started to sit but suddenly he was up on his feet, turning and running at her, screaming like a maniac. Startled, she pulled the trigger until he dropped at her feet, five or six rounds.

"Shit!"

She didn't need a dead body lying on the side of the highway but that's what she had. Not that there were many cars. Reduce the population by ninety percent, fry the computers and circuit boards in all the cars, reduce everyone to subsistence level farming for survival, and that tends to reduce traffic. No vacations, no road trips, no going to games or taking the kids to college or visiting Grandma. But commerce was coming back, and there were occasional cars and trucks. She had to do something, and fast.

Putting him in one of the cars was out. It is very difficult to put a dead body into a car. Anyone who has tried to move a passed-out drunk friend knows this. She dragged him as close to her truck as she could, hoping that would shield him from view since she intended to leave the truck here. The next thing was to disguise the fact that he was a cop, so she stripped his uniform off.

The situation was a lot better now. Anyone coming by would see a cop car behind a suspicious vehicle or something, but a situation that was under control. They wouldn't see a cop shot on the side of the road. No good Samaritans should stop to offer assistance and interfere with things.

The uniform and the equipment belt went into the police car. She grabbed her gear out of her truck. That and her AK also went into the cruiser. Standing on the side of the road, she pulled on a pair of dark blue jeans over her skimpy shorts. She untied the dark blue shirt, buttoned it up, and tucked it into the jeans. Lastly, she put sunglasses on. She hoped the illusion would work. The guy in the truck would see someone in a cop car in what appeared to be a dark blue police uniform.

Even if he got a good look at her and didn't recognize her, that shouldn't matter. She was in a police cruiser in the right spot at the right time. That should be enough to get the truck driver to go along. If not, then she'd bring Mister AK into the conversation. Or another option was to back off. She was sure the police car had more acceleration that a delivery truck, so if there was a guard in the truck or the driver was armed, she could always take off at a higher speed than the truck could match. If it came to that she could stop and set up an ambush.

The truck had to stay on the highway. As long as her ambush was before any off ramps, she had him.

Now she just had to hope that the truck was actually coming. Communications were still fractured but someone could have gotten a message out, warning them off because of the danger that she was causing. She was banking on Big Tim being the only point of contact in town and the only one that would know who to communicate with and how to do it. She kicked herself for not asking him that exact question. But if the truck wasn't coming, then why was the cop sitting here? Did he not get the memo? Or were they shipping in a team of shooters? In which case she might find herself up the proverbial creek without a paddle.

All she could do now was sit and wait and see what happened.

Chapter Forty-Three

TAYLOR HAD HER EYES glued to the rearview mirror since that is where anything would come from, and there it was. A white box truck that flashed its lights at her in groups of three. Flash, flash, flash, then a few seconds pause and another group of three flashes. When the truck got close it did the same thing with its horn, a couple of groups of three as it approached and passed. She hit the gas and took off after it, fishtailing a bit as she came off the weedy shoulder and onto the pavement.

Was she supposed to be in front of the truck or behind? She didn't know, and didn't want to do something wrong, so she was just going to shut it down right off the bat. If she could.

She cruised past the truck, looking hard, and there was just the driver in it. So far so good. She passed the truck and pulled in front of it, letting off the gas and putting her right turn signal on. She stuck her arm out the window and pointed to the side of the road a couple of times and then rode the brakes down and pulled off. The truck matched all of her moves.

At the end, she jammed it into park and jumped out with her AK. She ran back to the truck and was at the driver's door before he even had the truck stopped completely.

"HANDS UP! HANDS UP!" she screamed, aiming right at him. She was glad to confirm that he was the only occupant. There could have been another guy, armed, that was just sleeping or something, scrunched down by the passenger door. But there wasn't. She wrenched the door open.

"Shut it down! Put the parking brake on! Get out!"

"I'm just the driver!" he protested.

"Get out! Now! Hands up!" She was keeping him disoriented with constant screamed commands, not giving him time to think. She hustled him off to the other side of the truck, away from the highway.

"Up against the truck! Assume the position!"

She let the AK dangle from its strap and pulled her pistol, which she then pressed up into his crotch while she frisked him left-handed. If her pistol was at his back, he might be able to swing an arm around and knock it away, but that maneuver was not so easy in her current position. But she thought she'd make it clear to him.

"You feel where this pistol is? Don't try anything or my first shot is going straight into your balls. A nine-millimeter vasectomy, *comprende*?"

"Yes! Yes! Please, don't shoot!"

He was clean and she stepped back and switched weapons back to the AK. There was no sense in standing close enough for him to make a grab for your weapon. The whole idea of having a projectile weapon was to allow you to hurt the enemy from some distance away.

"Open up the back." He was in the mode now. She gave the orders and he jumped.

"Wait. There's nobody back there, right?" Taylor had a moment of apprehension.

"No, just me. There's no one in the back."

"All right, here's how we're going to do this. You stand in the middle and I'm going to stand off to the driver's side of the truck. Now when I tell you, you open the door."

While she was saying this, she moved into position directly behind the driver and slightly to the passenger side of the truck. If anyone was in the back and was going to shoot at her, they had just heard her say she was going to be on the other side. She was going to use the driver as a shield. The other good thing about that position was that it put him and anyone in the back in her line of fire at the same time. That was a lot better than having one guy in front and one to her side.

But there was no drama. He opened the door to an empty truck. Almost empty. There was one pallet with four steel ammo boxes strapped to it.

"Hop up in there and slide those boxes out here to the door. Then you go sit down at the front."

Once he did that, she slung the AK and cut through the wire and lead seal that would reveal any tampering. Inside, the can was full of bright, shiny gold coins stacked and wrapped in paper.

"They don't tell me how much it is, but I did the math once." The driver was feeling talkative all of a sudden. "I bet that's close to two million dollars. A million five for sure. Maybe two five. I didn't have a scale; I was just estimating the weight. You don't have to shoot me. I don't know nothin'. I'll tell them it was three guys that stopped me. I have kids —"

"I'm not going to shoot you," Taylor interrupted. "Put these boxes in the police cruiser and then we're done here. You have a watch? I want you to take a nap in the back of the truck. Fifteen minutes at least."

"Yes, ma'am."

"Actually, there is one more thing." She tossed him a little notebook with a ballpoint pen stuck in it. "Write down the address where you pick this stuff up. And the time. And how often."

He looked up at her, apprehensive. Giving out that information could mean his life. But that was something for the future. Pissing this girl off could also mean his life, but right here and right now. That was the critical difference. He started writing.

With the gold in the cop car, the driver in the back of his truck, and the door closed, she took off. She gunned it, enjoying the acceleration. Almost all of the vehicles she had driven had been practical work trucks and SUVs. This was different. It was fast and fun. Too bad she couldn't keep it.

She made a U-turn as soon as the highway allowed it and raced back, past the box truck, past her truck, until she could make another U-turn. Once back at her own truck, she took everything she wanted from the cruiser and put it in the truck, and innocently motored off down the highway.

The smuggler was still on his nap when she went by. Specifically, when she went by, a million and some, maybe two million dollars richer.

Chapter Forty-Four

SHE HEADED SOUTHEAST TO San Angelo, a couple of hours down the road, using a Texas map that was undated but showed William P. Clements as the governor. He served a term from 1979 to 1983 and then another from 1987 to 1991. Even at the later date the map was considerably older than she was, but it didn't affect anything on this route.

The roads and highways didn't look like they did pre-Hexen, though. Back then there were entire crews of men whose sole job was to mow the medians and the shoulders and keep fallen trees and branches cleared off. Other crews patched potholes and cracks and fixed other issues. When Hexen hit, nine out of ten of them died and the rest had to turn to farming or ranching to eat.

Not that it mattered. The highways were jammed with dead cars, hopelessly impassable to anything but people on foot or on bicycles. Gradually, slowly, painfully, the roads were cleared. Older equipment was repaired or made to run again and once mass starvation seemed to be held at bay, attention eventually turned to the streets and highways.

Usually, they opened one lane for traffic in both directions, with plenty of "wait-a-minutes". That was a gap with both lanes open for a short space. The idea was that if there was oncoming traffic, someone had to pull over in the wait-a-minute and let the other vehicle by. That gradually expanded to where, years later, most or all lanes were open.

The dead cars had to go somewhere. If there was a parking lot nearby, they were usually stacked there, sometimes in a huge pyramid, if the workers had a big crane. Out on the interstate highways, there was usually a junkyard of stacked or bulldozed cars every mile or two, just a field commandeered by the highway department. Simply pushing the vehicles to the side of the road would have been faster, but would have increased the rate of erosion of the shoulders and then the roadbed.

The road crews, the new ones, spent almost all of their time on repairs or maintenance of bridges and overpasses. They had to preserve those because no one was going to build any more for a long time. The consequence was that weeds, vines, bushes, and saplings grew on the shoulders unhindered, so that driving down a highway was like going through a green tunnel.

The interstates were mainly pretty good, now, for the most part. There were some that were effectively down to one lane due to plant growth and debris on the shoulders, but those were the ones in more remote parts of the country. Driving in mountainous areas was prudently done very slowly or during daylight hours due to rock falls, but any road could be a hazard when larger wild animals decided to cross. Absolutely no one wanted to slam into a twenty-five-hundred-pound longhorn steer at speed, and even the deer and feral hogs that weighed a tenth of that or less could kill you.

Smaller roads out in the countryside were anywhere from very good to virtually impassable. The typical one was effectively down to one or one and a half lanes due to the plant growth on the shoulders, and frequently featured obstacles such as downed limbs and whole trees, livestock or wild animals in the road, and occasionally roadblocks that the locals used to keep outsiders out or charge tolls.

Taylor's route down US-87 was in good shape. There were none of the tall pine forests that dominated east Texas. Pines tended to fall across roads or to sprout rapidly growing seedlings everywhere. Here the climate was much more arid and supported mainly grasses and low, stunted trees and bushes. The highway was two lanes in each direction with paved shoulders on both sides and was well-maintained. She made good time.

***

In San Angelo she found a combination garage and car dealership, parked her truck a half-mile away on a busy street, and walked back. The owner was sitting in a chair outside the office with an open bottle of beer.

"Good evening, ma'am," he greeted her. "Please don't think badly of me, drinking a beer. It's way past five o'clock. Can I offer you one?"

She laughed at his little joke. "Thank you. I will take one. I have to get to Tulsa and back, so I need something reliable." She picked that city off the top of her head and added the "and back" to let him know she would return to complain if what he sold her broke down. The AK across her shoulder emphasized the severity of the complaint she could bring, if needed.

He uncapped a beer for her and they clinked the bottles together in an impromptu toast.

They walked his short line of trucks, him talking about the route to take and his own visits to Tulsa while in the oil and gas industry. Besides the trucks, there was a single car. And a Chevy S10 Blazer on the end. That was actually what had caught her eye. It was sort of a gray metalflake paint with a little bit of red accent striping.

"That's cute," she said.

The salesman laughed. "That one's a handful. That used to belong to a friend of mine. This Blazer came with a little bitty six-cylinder motor and it wouldn't accelerate worth a durn. But someone smart made a kit where you could swap a V8 engine into these and once you had that, you could make all of the power you wanted. My friend put in a stock engine just to make sure it would fit and all that, and was going to build it up for better performance as he went along. And then Hexen came to us."

224

Taylor had the door open by now and was in the driver's seat. The vehicle was in great shape. Apparently, the friend had redone the interior and body work, too, in addition to the engine swap. She looked at the shifter knob.

"Six speed, so that would be two overdrive gears?"

"Yes, ma'am, that is correct. I take it you can drive a manual transmission?"

"Yep. Why did you say it's a handful if the engine isn't souped up?"

"It's a pretty stout engine out of a Corvette. One of the older ones, before they put on all of the emission controls and reduced the horsepower. That was way before your time. All it has on it now is headers. But it's a pretty light vehicle with a short wheelbase and a high center of gravity. It can get away from you."

"I want to drive it." She had made sure the parking brake was set and was going through the gears, getting a feel for them.

The guy only hesitated for a second. "I'll get the keys."

* * *

If Taylor had enjoyed driving the police cruiser, she *loved* driving this thing. She was a bit clumsy at first, missing a gear once and squealing the tires a few times, but that was just getting used to a new vehicle. The manual transmission made the power more obvious. This wasn't some lawnmower engine that slushed through the gears automatically and eventually hit forty miles per hour. This was raw horsepower and torque, right here, right now.

And it sounded like it. Not offensively loud, but there was a heavy, throaty roar that thrilled her. It let her know every second that there was a beast under the hood that she controlled and that responded immediately to her every command.

Now she suddenly understood a poster she had seen in the motor pool on the wall of the shop. It was a photo of a very well-endowed girl, very scantily clad, astride a Harley motorcycle. The caption read "Put Something Exciting Between Your Legs." She knew the double entendre was mainly for the sexual part but now she realized the 'exciting' part. This vehicle made driving something you did as a thing in and of itself, not just a way to get from Point A to Point B. It turned a chore into an adventure.

She bargained some with the man but he was glad to have a buyer for it. It wasn't a truck with an open bed, which most people wanted. It also wasn't something the average person could handle, with the manual transmission and stiff clutch and high torque. And this young lady had cash in the form of cold, hard gold. He didn't mind cutting her a deal at all.

She made sure she got a full tank of gas with the little SUV and drove off down the street, to where she had parked her truck. It was full dark now and she felt safe pulling up beside it for the sixty seconds it took to transfer everything from the truck to the Blazer. She threw the truck keys onto the driver's seat, where anybody walking by could see them.

Somebody would take off with it before long. That was fine. She just didn't want it connected to her in any way. And it wasn't connected to the ranch either, since it had never been registered to anyone there. The last owner of record was probably twenty years ago, now deceased, and no one was going to dig that record out anytime soon anyway. All of the databases that contained that information were offline, probably permanently.

Chapter Forty-Five

SHE SPENT THE NIGHT in the Blazer, with the back seat folded down to make the cargo compartment bigger, parked behind an abandoned house out in the country. Her feet were towards the back hatch and her AK and Glock 19 were both close at hand, but nothing disturbed her sleep.

By a little after dawn, she was a brunette again, and on the road to Abilene. There, she found a nice place to stay and took a couple of days off. Well, not entirely off.

There were things she needed to do, so she couldn't just hole up in a room and keep out of sight. Since she would be out in the public eye, she needed to disguise the cut on her cheek. Makeup was out of the question. She was afraid that it would get into the wound and cause an infection or some other issue.

A mask was also a non-starter. Masks hadn't worked with COVID, they hadn't worked with Hexen, and even the last holdouts had stopped wearing them years ago. She wasn't even sure she could find one, now. The guys at the ranch had worn the last ones as dust masks while bush hogging dusty fields and spray-painting things.

With a little shopping, she found a pair of sunglasses with huge lenses that would cover most of the cut. There was still a part where it turned down and went to her jaw that was exposed, but the glasses helped make it less noticeable.

Now with this disguise, she shopped some more and assembled a better one. She already had a hat, a Stetson Black Hawk Outdoor, a cowboy hat with a smaller, flatter brim than usual. It was black, and a strip of black lace, pinned to the brim and hanging down in front of her face, made her wound even less noticeable.

She sent an encrypted telegraph message to MCC, just in case she didn't make it back to give a report in person. Life is uncertain. She wrote up a more detailed report to mail, and also found a funeral home that sold her a child-sized coffin.

She figured a coffin would be more secure. Someone may pry open a box or break a lock, but they would probably shy away from opening a coffin, expecting it to contain what it was designed for, a dead body. She packed the coffin with three-fourths of the gold and Cody's rifle, plus Big Tim's code book and some encoded messages that had been in the boxes with the gold. Everything was tightly wrapped and packaging material filled out any gaps. Taylor didn't want the coffin to make any noises when it was moved. A metallic clink would give away the illusion that it contained a corpse.

Fully packed, she very thoroughly nailed it shut. The hotel owner helped her get it into the Blazer and she sent it off on the train, addressed to herself at Marten Cattle Company. The report went on the train, too, enclosed with some paperwork she'd found in Big Tim's office. She hoped that Eric would not open the coffin. She figured he wouldn't since it was addressed to her, but she didn't need anyone screwing things up for her. The addresses in the code book needed to remain secret a little longer.

She had one more plan to play out, and some shopping to do. But the first thing she treated herself to was a bath. A genuine hot-water-in-a-bathtub bath. And shampoo! She had been using a wet washcloth to bathe with, sometimes even with warm water, for the past week. She got more frequent showers at Marten Cattle Company, but there was solar power there. Out here things were a little more rustic. Deodorant was pretty much a thing of the past everywhere, though.

The bathhouse was just like the ones seen in the Old West movies. A guy was feeding a couple of outdoor concrete block stoves to heat water. Taylor had a girl in her young teens as an attendant, bringing in buckets of the hot water and handing her soap and shampoo and a towel as needed. Once again, she breathed a sigh of relief that fate had pushed her in the direction that it had, and sent her to Dani and Eric. She hadn't ended up as a bath attendant. Unfortunately, she couldn't save everyone, so she settled for giving the girl a big tip.

Laundry service was another luxury she took advantage of at the end of the week. Not for the outer garments, so much. She had put the jeans on fresh eight days ago, and both her shirts only had four wearings, so all of those were good. The underwear was her main concern, her bras and underpants and athletic socks. Wearing clothes multiple times was something else she never even thought about any more. It was just life. There wasn't an excess of clean water, or hot water, or soap to wash clothes every time you wore something. Unless you sweated in it or got it dirty, you wore it again until you did.

Walking around town, she used the screwdriver on her multitool to collect three out-of-state license plates, with colors that were dramatically different from the blue and white Texas plates. She put a New Mexico plate on the Blazer, a screaming yellow thing with red numbers and letters.

She also located a motorcycle shop and bought a helmet with a full-face shield. For something lighter, she also tried a set of goggles, but found immediately that they pressed on the cut on her cheek. The owner suggested motorcycle sunglasses, which had a little bit of foam rubber around the lenses that helped to seal them to the rider's face and keep the wind and dust out. They were smaller than the goggles, no bigger than regular sunglasses, and didn't hit the cut.

Since she had some time to kill, she visited a doctor for the wound on her cheek. He did a little cleanup and pronounced her good. No stitches were required, but the doctor warned that it might leave a scar. Taylor took that news with a head bob to the side. No big deal now, about something that would have sent her and her parents into hysterics pre-Hexen. Immediate plastic surgery required! No respectable young lady would have a scar on their cheek, and — horror of unspeakable horrors — certainly not one acquired in a knife fight!

Here, now, she just didn't care one way or the other about a scar. There were no beauty pageants any more, and she certainly wasn't going to be anyone's trophy wife. She was a badass so it may even be cool.

On the way back to her hotel she thought about her parents and there was no pain. Maybe four years had dulled the ache, but should it be so complete? Dani still mourned her parents. She had once said that she would mourn them forever, but she had to set that aside at times or she could never get on with her own life. Taylor couldn't even dredge up much emotion for her parents. It was only the thought of their reaction to a facial scar that brought them up now.

Maybe I was born for this world, not that one. Destined. Fated. Where else could I do this?

Scenes in slow motion from the men she'd recently shot flowed through her mind. The sharp crack of the gunfire, the high-speed blood spatter, the once-powerful bodies crumpling and falling. The danger that they represented to her blowing away like a leaf in a heavy gust of wind. Their power reduced to nothing, their ability to dominate her, to force her to do things, to strip her of all self-respect suddenly ripped from them.

Taylor didn't hate men. She'd willingly given up her virginity to a man. If their lives hadn't been on other paths, they might still be together. And she'd killed a couple of women, too. It was people doing bad things to other people that she hated. Unfortunately, some people were bad and others turned that way if they thought they weren't going to be caught. She didn't mind killing them at all. She wondered why she'd waited so long to do it again.

Enjoy it.

A shiver went down her spine and she began to breathe heavily. She hadn't had time to savor the memories yet.

Enjoy it.

It was only midafternoon but she loaded up with a lot of beer and some food and barricaded herself in her room for the night. She needed some alone time.

Chapter Forty-Six

THE NEXT SATURDAY, TAYLOR was parked on an overpass west of Weatherford, which is west of Fort Worth, which is west of Dallas. She had figured out the address the driver gave up was a business park, which made perfect sense. The smugglers would want a location that could reasonably be expected to have a high amount of traffic, yet be fairly isolated from prying eyes. A business park just outside of a major metropolitan area was perfect.

FM-4, Farm-to-Market Road Number 4, passed over Interstate 20 and offered a quick route to get onto the Interstate. Taylor wanted something that was some distance from the address, away from built-up areas, and gave her an elevated observation post. She surveyed what the options were and selected the FM-4 overpass.

She sat in the heat, her head sweating under the red wig, with her cowboy hat to shade her eyes, courteously fending off offers of assistance from locals driving by. Just when she was thinking that the drug runners would be idiots to not change the schedule, she spotted a familiar-looking truck. Not that there weren't a million other white box trucks on the roads, but it was when and where she expected it to be. Or was it? Was this just some random truck?

She had to check it out. If this wasn't it, then she'd park on the side of the Interstate and wait for the target truck. The Blazer fired up smoothly. She'd had a mechanic in Abilene go over it from bumper to bumper and make sure it was tuned and lubed and greased and oily where it was supposed to be.

It took a bit to convince him to remove the windshield, but he did it, right before she got into the driver's seat and kicked it out. Taylor put her motorcycle sunglasses on for protection from the wind and took off, enjoying the hard launch that the manual transmission, light vehicle, and powerful engine provided.

She ran north to the service road, then west for a quick half-mile, before merging with I-20. She watched the truck chugging by while she was still on the service road and saw that there was an escort tucked in close behind him. She adjusted her speed to merge onto the Interstate behind them.

From running up and down this section of I-20 several times, she determined she had about a twenty mile stretch to do the takedown. Beyond that, it seemed there was a small community every few miles for some distance. The shooters would get suspicious if she followed them for too long, so things were going to happen real soon. Twenty miles may sound like a lot but she didn't think it was. It was twenty minutes at highway speeds. That felt tight to her.

It would have really been great if she'd had some help, but she didn't want to endanger anyone else. No, this was her deal. And that was going to be her gold, if there was any gold in the truck at all, and not some trap.

If they were smart, they'd have a decoy or two. But was the gold the real goal, anyway? Or was it the adventure? The chance to kill some people? Putting herself into dangerous situations, risking her life, and coming out on top? Winning? She would think about that later. Right now, she felt the thrill of the hunt, the rush, the surge of adrenaline. She laughed a little to herself.

The air blasted in through the missing windshield and out the open windows, the Blazer surged forward with the slightest touch of the accelerator, and she took her hand off of the gear shift to touch the AK, make sure it was where she expected it to be. She didn't have to look down to know where it was.

She accelerated smoothly, not gunning it, to cruise by the escort vehicle.

Three guys. They look the type, but no visible weapons or military equipment.

That was a dilemma. Were they some innocents, maybe roughnecks headed out to their jobs? She didn't want to light up some civilians like that. As she came by them, she was eyeballing them pretty hard, and they returned the favor. She smiled and twiddled her fingers at them and they head-bobbed in return. The guy in the back smiled at her. He could clearly see she was a cute young lady, red hair blowing in the wind.

And when they turned towards her, she could clearly see the gang and prison tattoos they had on their faces.

Seriously, guys, don't put that shit on your faces. That was the kicker. What were the odds that some tatted up ex-con gang bangers would be closely following a truck that was carrying drug profits? *Zero. Zilch. None. Nada.*

Then she was past them and coming up on the box truck.

Are you kidding me? she thought. *I hit that truck, that* exact *truck last week, and they didn't even bother to change the license plates?*

Not that she had deliberately memorized the plate. Her memory was sharp as a razor, almost photographic, and she could pull up the number from last week without any effort. It matched. She moved up a little further to make sure the truck didn't have a passenger and saw that it was even the same driver as last week.

Dumbasses.

She let off the gas and dropped it down a gear, out of overdrive and into fourth to give her some acceleration on tap as needed. The truck and car sailed past her, the gangbangers eyeballing her hard again, wondering what she was doing. She put the Blazer right in the middle of the two lanes, giving her the widest margin of error possible in case she veered to one side or the other, and hauled the AK up into a ready position but still below the dashboard.

She made sure the safety was off, not having to look down to do it. She could operate the rifle in the dark or blindfolded. That was just part of the training, not only operating your firearms blindfolded, but taking them apart and putting them back together.

The driver was watching her in the rearview and the two passengers were both turned around in their seats. Then the one in the back turned to roll down his window so he could lean out and shoot back at her if needed.

They were late to the party. And she already had her window down, right in front of her. The windshield, or rather, the big gap where it used to be. She had a nice field of fire and the seventy-five-round drum magazine was locked in place with the spring wound tight.

She put her knee against the steering wheel, let go of it, and brought the AK up to her shoulder with both hands.

The reaction in the car in front of her was almost comical. The front seat passenger looked astonished but he started bringing a rifle of his own up. It was too long and clumsy for fast maneuvering inside a vehicle. He'd have done better with a pistol. He had to go back and forth with the rifle between the seat and the dash, like trying to turn a car around on a narrow street, and pointing the muzzle at the driver more often than not.

The bad guy in the back seat wasted time turning around to look at her and then couldn't decide if he should go back to rolling the side window down or shoot out the back glass. His rifle was pointed at the side and he tried to swing it around, covering both front seat occupants.

These clowns just might shoot themselves, Taylor thought, amused.

She fired five rapid-fire rounds at the guy in the front seat, since he looked closer to getting his weapon under control. The next five went to the back seat passenger, or at least where she thought he was through the glass that had shattered but stayed in place. She raised her head up from the sights for a quick glance to make sure she wasn't going off the road, and gave both of them another five. It would only take one good hit to put them out of action and she wasn't seeing anything from either of them. There was no movement that she could see and no return fire.

The driver slammed the accelerator to the floor and started weaving a little. He had apparently decided the truck driver could go fuck himself and was over in the other lane now, accelerating past the box truck.

Taylor had to get back on her driving to follow him past the truck, but there was no problem catching up to them, not with her little hot rod SUV. She had been holding back to go as slow as them and easily kept up with him now.

Once past the truck, she put it in the middle of the highway again and went back to the rifle. She ripped ten shots off at the driver to close out the show. In a movie, the driver would have had a spasm or something that would jam his foot down on the accelerator, causing the car to go to a hundred miles an hour until it veered off the road and flipped and exploded spectacularly.

Instead, he clutched up in a fetal position and his foot abruptly came off of the accelerator. The car slowed dramatically, without brake lights to warn Taylor.

Oh, SHIT!

She dropped the AK, pretty much throwing it in the direction of the passenger seat, to grab the steering wheel. At the same time, she was on the brakes hard, but the back end of the car was coming up way too fast. She snatched the wheel over to miss the car, hoping that she was far out in front of the truck enough that she wouldn't catch its front bumper and give herself a PIT maneuver.

At the seventy-five or so miles per hour that she was going, she figured that would roll her vehicle. The best she could expect from that was to be stranded on the side of the road. Death was probably more likely, either from injuries or from some gang member killing her slowly and painfully after dragging her from the wreck.

She missed the truck but now she was headed for the ditch at the side of the road. She steered back, trying to straighten it out, and it fishtailed. It rocked badly back and forth and probably pulled one wheel off the pavement, but it came back under control, tires smoking from the skid.

Once it was straight she got off the brakes, now afraid that the truck would slam into the back of her, but she saw that it was further back and the driver had the brakes down to the floor and was pulling off onto the shoulder. The escort vehicle had drifted off into the weeds between the eastbound and westbound lanes.

"Shit!" she exclaimed, releasing tension from the gunfight and the near-wreck. "Holy shit!"

She rode the brakes the rest of the way down, dropping it into first gear to be ready to run if anyone from the escort car jumped out and started shooting. She groped for the AK while she eyeballed the car. A little cloud of tire smoke drifted by her.

There was no movement and she couldn't find the rifle, so she had to take her attention away from the car and lean way over to retrieve the AK from the floorboards. Thinking back, she totaled up the rounds she had fired, thirty, and figured the forty-five remaining in the drum should be enough. No magazine change needed. And still no movement from either the escort car or the box truck.

Judging that it was safe, she found reverse and headed back to the truck, tires smoking and engine screaming at high RPMs. Traffic would be coming up behind them in the next minute or two, probably. She jumped out and ran up to the truck. The driver didn't know what to do so he sat there with his hands up.

"Hey! Remember me? Go two miles down and then pull over on the shoulder. I let you live last time. I'll let you live today. But don't fuck with me or you'll end up like your friends over there."

Two miles should be sufficient to distance her operation from the shot-to-hell car and occupants, she figured.

"They're not my friends. They're trash."

"Two miles. Let's go." She held up two fingers. She didn't have time for a debate over who was friends with whom.

***

It looked like this was going to go off without a hitch. The driver even knew what to do. There was no one in the back and the driver loaded the boxes of gold coins into her Blazer. She was just about to close the hatch and take off.

It's just when things seem as if they're going great that they usually turn into absolute shit.

Like now.

Chapter Forty-Seven

THE OTHER ESCORT VEHICLE showed up.

If Taylor had seen both of them, she would have never gone after the truck. But it was way too late for that now.

The other car was coming fast, obviously running late and racing to catch up with the truck. The driver saw a truck on the side of the road, slowed some, then slammed on the brakes when he determined it was, indeed, their truck. That was stupid. If he had pulled over without all the drama, the men could have quietly come up around both sides of the truck and shot Taylor down before she could do anything about it.

That was Taylor's first warning, the tires screeching on the pavement, then smoking from the friction, the brakes grabbing unevenly and skidding the car a bit sideways. She had the AK up in a heartbeat, going into a crouch at the same time. The first guy she saw was the one in the back seat, pushing a rifle out through the open window. She fired at his head, and again, and again, and the fourth time was finally the charm. The car had still been skidding when she started and the man's head had moved forward and back as momentum pushed him around and the car rocked forward and then back on the shock absorbers.

But now the car was stopped and men were piling out of the other doors. There was a rattle of automatic weapons fire and bullets sleeted into both the Blazer and the box truck, sending glass flying. Rage surged up inside Taylor as she heard the bullets whacking into her vehicle and blowing out the side windows. She was more pissed off that they were shooting her truck up than the fact that they were shooting at her.

Not that she was going to let them shoot at her if she could prevent it.

She ran back behind the front corner of the box truck and scanned for targets.

If I was running this, I'd come up both sides, around the front of the Blazer and the back of the truck, she thought.

She had been taught small unit tactics by Eric the Marine, and had practiced it for years with paintball and airsoft games that were a lot more training sessions than games.

The box truck driver panicked. He had hit the ground when the shooting started and now jumped up and ran, first down the shoulder of the road, then taking a sharp right and plunging into the thicker underbrush on the shoulder when he spotted the men.

One of the men ran up and threw his rifle to his shoulder, sighting on the truck driver's back. He had apparently seen a target and fixated on it, forgetting Taylor. Or maybe he thought the truck driver was the guy to shoot and had never seen Taylor. Things were happening fast. Maybe he hadn't gotten the memo, but if he was going to make a mistake, she wouldn't complain.

She got the sights on him and fired two shots into his ribcage, bullets that slammed through his heart and lungs. He dropped, his rifle hitting the pavement and clattering away. He had never fired a shot at the truck driver.

She danced back a couple of steps and dropped into a low crawl beneath the truck. Weeds were growing through cracks in the pavement and she lay down in their small bit of concealment. She kept her head on a swivel, scanning for targets. Nothing. That was bad news.

Then one ran up in a sprint, to stop behind the front tire of the truck. Another sprint took him to the back corner. He was working his way around the truck, hoping to come up behind her. She expected one to come around the other way. That meant she was going to have to turn her back on one of them. She raised up a little and changed position slightly, her knees trembling, expecting to be shot at any moment.

The guy made another sprint to the other corner and swung his rifle up, expecting his sights to be on her back. They weren't. She was no longer standing beside the truck. That was so ten seconds ago.

She fired into his thigh from three or four feet away, three times, as fast as she could pull the trigger. The bullets shattered the bone and severed the artery, the leg collapsing immediately. He hit the pavement hard on his hip and she blasted two bullets into his chest, swung the muzzle a little, and added one to the face. Something flew out the back of his skull and he was no longer a threat to anyone. She spun around and pressed down into the weeds, still expecting to be shot, scanning desperately for targets.

One more, or two? Perhaps even three if she was really unlucky. And if they were smart, they were moving to catch her in a crossfire. That would put her in a position where she could only defend against one, while giving the other one an easy shot at her. It was a cat-and-mouse game that only the winner walked away from, and even that wasn't a guarantee. The winner may just turn out to be the last person to bleed out.

A couple of long seconds went by, then a couple more. She was trying to sense the man's presence, trying to feel him, hear him, smell him, anything. There was no movement except a breeze. No sound. No traffic. No birds. Nothing in sight.

Even if she had wanted to retreat, the options were the same. Any movement could put her running into danger rather than away from it. And she wanted that cargo in her bullet-riddled vehicle. She hoped it still ran, but that was something for later. Surviving this fight right now was the priority. Everything else could wait.

This is where the rabbit panics, when the tension becomes too much, when the waiting is unbearable. The risk of death is preferable to doing nothing. At least the uncertainty will be over.

A sound rose up in volume until she could identify it: tires humming on pavement, squeaky brakes, an air horn blowing, an engine being downshifted, and then a truck went by, slowly, because the escort car was stopped in a lane of traffic. Taylor sank lower into the weeds, if that was possible, and peered through them, seeking her target. She was thankful that the drum magazine was shorter than the usual thirty-round stick magazines because that meant she could get closer to the pavement.

Then she heard a voice. She couldn't make out what he was saying, but they were single words, three of them. Not a sentence of three words, but one word called out, a pause, then another word, and another pause and word. Questioning. The silence returned and stretched out again.

Names, she thought. *He was calling out the names of the other guys. Does he not know the one guy is in the back seat with a hole in his head? Or is there another one out there? Were there four or five guys in the car? Shit, this is like Dirty Harry asking the punk if he feels lucky. The problem is, I'm the punk.*

Suddenly there were blasts of automatic weapon fire towards the front of the Blazer, the space between the vehicles, and the back of the truck. Then it swept back, hitting under both vehicles, a full thirty-round magazine dump. When the shots came under the truck, something slammed into Taylor's shoulder, hard. She grunted at the impact and tears came to her eyes.

OH SHIT! I'M SHOT!

Air hissed out of the tires right beside her and the truck bed started to settle, lowering down on her. She turned her head enough to get a look at her shoulder and couldn't see any blood, and was able to flex her fingers, so those were both good signs. She wiped the tears from her eyes and started scanning for targets again, but there was the slam of a car door and the escort vehicle was taking off, obviously with the accelerator down to the floor. A rifle slid off of the hood and clattered onto the pavement.

Either he got scared and is hauling ass, or there is one more guy left and he's waiting in ambush for me to come out, thinking it's clear.

She hesitated just for a second, the thought going through her mind that these guys just weren't that good, not smart enough to lay a trap like that.

But if this is a trap, they expect me to come out on the left side of the truck. I can't get a shot from the right side, so let's do the unexpected.

She took a deep breath and moved.

Someone was about to die.

Chapter Forty-Eight

TAYLOR SCRAMBLED TO THE passenger side of the truck, her body bent to keep it from hitting the underside, but her legs extended as much as possible to give her better mobility. A quick glance to both sides and then she was out in the open air, straightening and advancing with the AK at her shoulder, her head high. That gave her better visibility than a tight cheek weld against the stock, and anyone she encountered now would probably be at arm's length and would not require precise aiming.

But no, no one at the back of the truck and no one along the side.

I'm not shot yet. So far, so good.

Rifle still up and all senses on high alert, she moved quickly to her vehicle. At the driver's door, she spun in a complete circle, scanning, the muzzle following her gaze. No enemies. She could tell at a glance that the tires were good on the Blazer, no flats, and a quick look under the vehicle didn't show any fluids pouring out. The truck driver was probably still hiding in the weeds, but she had stopped the guy from shooting at him, so he could crawl out at his leisure. Or not. She didn't care.

Now to catch this guy.

She slammed the back hatch closed, jumped in, fired it, and took off. The Blazer smoked the tires most of the way through first gear, fishtailing the back end a little but Taylor didn't back off the throttle. She banged through the gears like a pro, the tires chirping at the gear changes. The speedometer maxed out at eighty-five and the needle went a little beyond that and hung there, at its limit, as she tore down the highway at over a hundred and accelerating.

Her target vehicle was a big four-door boat of a car, a mid-1980s Impala in a sexy pea-soup green that was sure to attract the ladies. Not really. Eric would call that color a BCD, a Birth Control Device, meaning that if your car was that color, you were never going to get laid, much less get anyone pregnant.

The guy in the BCD did have a head start but his horsepower was about half what Taylor was packing, unless they had done some performance upgrades. They had not. The car was only intended to follow the truck and they didn't need any extra horsepower for that. They needed something big with four doors with some fuel economy, not a race car. Still, it could maybe do a hundred if pushed hard enough. He was definitely pushing it, but it was no match for her hot rod SUV in an acceleration contest.

The wind slammed through the hole where the windshield had been, pushing her head back against the seat, sandblasting her skin with any stray item in the air — dust, leaves, insects. She'd pulled the motorcycle glasses on, but wished she'd gone with the full helmet and face shield. No chance to change it now.

The steering wheel vibrated in her hands. She looked down and saw that the tach strapped to the steering column was past redline and backed off of the accelerator. The extra speed wasn't necessary to overtake the car up ahead, and she didn't want to blow past it.

She had put the AK in her lap when she started, and the next step now would be to take it in her hands, ready for action, but she couldn't make herself take her hands off of the steering wheel. The thought of steering with her knee again was terrifying. This wasn't cruising along at fifty-five like it was earlier. This was twice that, probably more. One slip, one mistake, could send her rolling over and over until the vehicle, with her inside, was wadded up like a discarded beer can.

She forced her hand to let go of the steering wheel, keeping it hovering there in case she had to grab it with both hands again. Surprisingly, she was still alive and the Blazer was not tumbling. She reached down and grabbed the AK, dragging it into position, slowly and carefully so she didn't make some move that would bump the steering wheel and send her to her death. She got the drum propped up on the dashboard, immediately saw that it raised the muzzle too high, and pulled it back so that it dropped off and now the forearm rested on the dashboard.

Since there is no way in hell I am letting go of this steering wheel, I'm just going to have to aim the whole vehicle like a fighter pilot aiming at an enemy aircraft.

The BCD was ahead of her going straight down the center of the two lanes. She matched that and started firing off rounds to try to see where it would hit. Nine rounds later, she'd hit the back window exactly once, low and far over on the passenger side.

The dashboard and everything is vibrating way too much. I need to get closer and risk my freakin' life. Do I really need to kill this guy? He never saw my face. He has no idea what I look like. He's only seen the Blazer. But I want to keep the Blazer, so I guess he has to go. Damn it.

She came up with a plan and did it before she could second-guess her decision.

Accelerating quickly, she closed the gap. Ten feet from his rear bumper, she got off the gas and rode the brakes down hard. The speed dropped to a level where she felt safe taking her other hand off of the steering wheel. That gave her both hands to bring up the AK and start launching some aimed shots.

The BCD had kept at its speed but hadn't been able to open up that much of a gap yet. It was certainly nothing that Taylor couldn't overcome. She fired off five aimed shots, shooting quickly but not just ripping off as many bullets as she could. Accuracy was more important here, for a moment, until she grabbed the steering wheel again and made sure she wasn't about to crash or lose control.

But no, everything looked good, so she accelerated again. She counted her shots, trying to remember what she'd fired, figuring she'd used about fifty-something rounds at this point. Maybe a couple less, but call it sixty. That meant she could do the chase-brake-shoot thing three more times before she had to reload.

She didn't have to.

As on most highways now, they had been passing broken-down vehicles with some frequency. The vehicles now, the ones that actually ran, tended to break down, and it wasn't unusual to see them stranded or out of gas or abandoned.

The BCD slowed and drifted off to the right. Taylor looked up ahead, beyond the car, and saw the trailer, the big boxy part, of an eighteen-wheeler just ahead. The car was heading straight for it, still moving at probably eighty-five.

Oh, shit!

She could envision the car hitting the trailer and the back end whipping around and taking her out with it. She jumped off of the gas and got back on the brakes, edging over to the left lane as far as she could as quickly as she could without sending her vehicle out of control.

She couldn't do it. She couldn't get stopped in time so she reversed her feet yet again, off the brakes and back on the gas. Maybe it would be better to clear the area as quickly as possible.

The BCD slammed into the corner of the trailer and parts exploded in all directions. Things clattered against the side of her vehicle, and she saw something coming towards her, wishing she still had a windshield to take the impact instead of her face, but it whipped by over the roof of the Blazer.

And then she was past it.

She tried to look back in the rearview mirror, but the interior one was awry and the side ones didn't give that good a picture of the wreck, which was rapidly disappearing in the distance. If she had to guess, she would say that guy was gone. He'd been hit by one or more of her bullets, and then he hit the trailer. If he survived all of that, then *vaya con dios*. Go with God.

There was an exit before too long, one that crossed the interstate via an overpass and then looped back down, effectively a big U-turn. She got headed in the right direction and stopped on the side for a moment. Her first order of business was to reload. Next, she checked out her shoulder. There was a bruise forming, with some burst capillaries and a very tender area. The good news was that there was no blood, no broken bones, and no bullet holes in her.

Then a more careful visual check of her vehicle showed that nothing was leaking or on fire, always a good thing in one's transportation. The bad news was that they had shot up her cute little Blazer. The side glass was gone and the bullet holes in the sheet metal made whistling sounds as she drove down the highway. She pulled the full-face motorcycle helmet on, being careful with the cut on her cheek. The helmet was better to keep the wind off of her face, and it did mute the whistling some.

Not enough to keep it from pissing her off, but some.

Chapter Forty-Nine

From Weatherford to Tyler is roughly 160 miles. Taylor had enough gas to make it without stopping, so she put the pedal to the metal. She remembered a tire shop they had cleaned out and found it with only one wrong turn. She was through the broken front door in a heartbeat, hauled one of the overhead doors up manually, pulled the Blazer in, and dropped the door. There was a huge metal platform that formed an interior second floor overlooking the shop floor, where the shop had stored their tire inventory. They were all gone now, but the rubber smell remained.

She stayed up there throughout the rest of the daylight hours, not attracting any attention, yet able to keep the Blazer under her immediate control. That meant under the barrel of her rifle.

She had the time to take a more thorough look at her arm. It was bruised badly although the skin wasn't really broken. Thinking back, the tires had collapsed on that side when the guy emptied his magazine. Apparently, a bullet had gone through the truck tires and been spent by the time it hit her. She didn't pray but she closed her eyes and breathed a word of thanks out into the ether, glad that a full-power bullet hadn't shattered her arm and either left her crippled or caused her to bleed to death out there on the shoulder of the highway.

***

Once it got dark, she fueled up from the one can she had left, swapped the license plate for an Oklahoma tag with green lettering, and headed for home. She wanted to make this last leg under cover of darkness to prevent as many people as possible from seeing a shot-up vehicle headed for MCC. She figured that someone would be awfully pissed off at her after losing three or four million in gold, to say nothing of the guys she had killed.

But if the state police got all over it, maybe they'd think it was them all along.

Criminals tended to think that everyone was dirty. It would therefore be a pretty logical conclusion to think that state police would shoot their guys, burn their houses, and knock over a couple of trucks full of money and then turn around and launch an official investigation into who did it. That way they would profit personally from the gold and have some nice busts on their professional record. They'd never think that some teenaged *girl* would come waltzing in and take down all of their guys all by herself. Their *machismo* would never allow that.

But never tempt fate. There was no reason to not be stealthy on the final approach. No reason to point an arrow at MCC if anyone came looking.

***

Taylor took a roundabout route to the ranch, and came in what she considered a back gate. To the west was a more built-up area, to the east was more residential. She went the residential route, figuring that since it was dark, people would be inside and maybe sleeping already. Also, the motor pool was closer to the east side.

A lot of the motor pool was really nothing more than a junk yard and Eric had put up tall fences around it. He didn't want to look at a bunch of junk trucks every time he went by, which made it a nice spot to hide the shot-up Blazer. Provided she could get inside, that is.

With it being after dark, there was no guarantee that anyone would be there. The duty NCO would have a key if they needed a vehicle, but going by the office would wipe out any stealthiness she had achieved by coming in the back. As she got closer, though, there was a brightness that indicated an electric light was on. Closer still and she saw the gate was open. Success! She pulled in and drove over to the side furthest from the stall that was lit.

She started to get out, then stopped, pulled her wig off, and stashed it in her pack. Her real hair was still pinned up, but she wasn't obviously in disguise.

"Bear" was the nickname for their top mechanic. He gave unflinchingly of his time, keeping everything running, giving classes to a new generation of mechanics, and then helping people build and fix their own vehicles after hours. Sure enough, he had three young guys around him and they had been deeply into an old truck but were now interested in the newcomer.

Of course, they recognized her as she came closer to the light. They exchanged greetings and made small talk for a minute until she could ask Bear to take a look at something for her.

At the Blazer, he fired up one of their rare old incandescent flashlights. "Damn. You weren't driving it when they shot it up, were you?"

"No, I was at the back."

"Well, damn, that's where all the bullet holes are at! You'd have been safer in the driver's seat, Miss Taylor."

That was a Southern thing, a level of familiarity between formal and informal. 'Taylor' was a familiar, casual form of address. 'Miss Marten' was formal. Southern culture offers 'Miss Taylor' as an intermediate option to show respect. It is also used for distance. An older man can refer to a younger female this way to indicate that he is not trying to be too familiar with her.

She laughed. "It wasn't a choice for me. But I want to get it fixed, and I also want to kind of keep the bullet holes secret. Maybe not the fact that there are bullet holes, but the fact that they're fresh."

"You been getting into trouble again, Miss Taylor? That's where that cut on your cheek came from?"

"No, it was good. Very good, actually. And I love this Blazer. I want to get it repaired, replace all the glass, and fix where some of the bullets went through the trim and the seats. Plus, I'm thinking roll cage. I almost rolled it in a panic stop. And muffler cutouts, like you did with your truck. I'd like it to have a nice sound but then if I need to be stealthy, pull a lever and have it run through quiet mufflers. Extra lights, winch, brush-buster bumper. And maybe do something with the engine. The guy I bought it from said the engine came out of a Corvette but it was stock. I'm thinking maybe we can improve on that?"

She could see Bear's big teeth shining even without the flashlight. He loved anything high-performance. He was already thinking of camshaft specifications, dual-plane intakes, and he was certain he had a set of aluminum heads that would probably be perfect for this little beast. Plus, wider tires to take advantage of the additional power.

"And this isn't an official request," she added. "I guess I'm asking you to do this in your spare time, so I'll pay." She handed him a paper-wrapped roll of gold coins.

He hefted the weight in his hand but he knew what it was. "No, no, you don't need to do that." He tried to hand it back but she crossed her arms.

"Nope. You're not handing it back. If you don't want it, then donate it somewhere. Give it to one of the churches. Help out the hospital. Do something good for the kids. Throw a big party."

He looked at the paper tube in his hand and hefted the weight a couple more times. "How much is this?"

"Ten thousand."

"Oh, no, no, no. This is too much." He held it out to Taylor to take back.

"Divide it into ten pieces and make ten people happy. As a matter of fact..." Taylor spun on her heel and walked around to the rear hatch. She did something there and then started walking towards Bear's office. "I'm gonna put this on your desk. You decide who gets what."

"What are you doing?"

"This is another forty thousand. Don't tell anyone where it came from."

"Oh, no, no, no."

"If you need any help, talk to Liz Mitchell. She can help you decide what goes where. Just don't mention my name. She'll think it's coming from Dani."

Bear followed her, shaking his head but bowing to the inevitable. Liz would know what to do. He'd drop it all on her desk tomorrow, the sooner the better.

After Bear agreed to fix the bullet holes himself, they threw a tarp over the Blazer and removed the Oklahoma tag. Taylor signed out a truck from the motor pool and loaded it up with all of her stuff and the boxes of gold coins.

She wasn't about to go to the house this late and risk waking the baby so she headed for the office. There were some built-in bunk beds there for people that just needed to stay temporarily or had the next guard shift or whatever. It was called 'The Doghouse' because the joke was that if someone got in trouble with their wife or girlfriend, they could come there and sleep.

Taylor secured her stuff in a couple of lockers and joked that she'd "cut herself shaving" when the duty NCO asked about her cheek. It had been a long day and her arm hurt. She racked out for the night, fully clothed except for her boots, with her rifle beside her.

Chapter Fifty

TAYLOR WAS UP BEFORE dawn and drove to the house. She knew Eric and Dani would be awake. Eric didn't like to burn daylight and Dani was sleeping when she could, due to the baby. She was up at all hours and napping when the opportunity presented itself.

They were happy to see her when she came through the door and immediately concerned about the cut on her cheek.

"Oh, my God, *chica*, are you okay?" Dani exclaimed.

"It's nothing. I think it'll add to my swashbuckling persona," she joked. "And I have a nasty bruise on this shoulder so I might not use my left arm much for a few days. It hurts."

"What happened?"

"It's a long story. The summary is that I found the guy and his little stash house and followed things up from there. To their big stash house, and dirty cops and dirty mayor and trucks running cash back down to Mexico. And their location outside of Weatherford, Texas. I know where it is but I haven't seen the place. I'm gonna leave that one to the police."

"How about the other places?"

"The last time I saw the two stash houses they were on fire with dead bodies inside."

"Holy shit. You better give us the whole story. Wait, let me call the office and tell them to reschedule a meeting." Eric headed for the phone.

While he was doing that, Dani looked at Taylor, concerned.

"You were just supposed to make a buy and ID the guy. You know, confirm that he was the one. What's all this other stuff?"

Taylor tossed her head to the side, her version of a shrug. "That guy was small-time. If he got arrested, they'd have him replaced in an hour. Besides, the police were all dirty there. They wouldn't have arrested him in the first place unless the state police were standing right there looking over their shoulder. I questioned him and moved up the line to more important targets."

"You questioned him," Dani parroted, but clearly asking for clarification.

"I ran a torch up his leg and around his balls until he talked, Miss Cheese Grater." That last bit was a reference to Dani's own history. She had needed answers once and didn't have time to ask nicely, so she'd used a cheese grater. Dani took the hint. She couldn't exactly bitch about Taylor doing something that she had done herself.

When Eric got back, she went through the long story. Dani and Eric mainly kept quiet. They were not squeamish people, having had to fight their way up to his house from Houston, close to a couple of hundred miles. They had had several run-ins with people that wanted to rob, rape, and presumably kill them. Those individuals had obviously all failed and their bodies had been left where they fell to feed the buzzards and coyotes. Dani had made a particular habit of shooting all of them in the head to ensure that they were very thoroughly dead.

But this was Taylor, not them. And they had to question the legality of it. In the immediate aftermath of Hexen and the EMP lots of legal niceties had been overlooked. Survival was at stake and if someone didn't get read his Miranda Rights before he was hung for attempted cattle theft, for example, nobody cared. But that was four years ago and things were supposed to be getting back to something that more resembled normal.

Unfortunately, that 'normal' was still a far cry from twenty-first century normal. More like nineteenth century, early twentieth. That meant there was a distinct lack of any watchdog over the police or local government or anyone in charge. People couldn't get incriminating evidence on audio or videotape, so any abusive authority had pretty free rein.

On the other hand, if Taylor got in and out without leaving evidence, she was more than likely home free. As long as her fingerprints weren't in any blood or on shell casings, there was no evidence, and no one had her fingerprints on file. Even if they did, there would have to be something that specifically pointed at her to get a comparison initiated.

Taylor wasn't that stupid. She'd gone in with the intention of pushing this investigation further than they had initially discussed. She had worn wigs and makeup that changed her looks and, to tell the truth, had killed most of the eyewitnesses. No one had seen her shoot the dirty cops. She'd never checked in with Marten Oilfield Security so no one knew she was in the area. She'd travelled under a false name, not that names were recorded for train tickets anyway. Cash is anonymous. There were no credit card records, surveillance videos, cell phone GPS tracking, nothing.

She was a ghost.

A wealthy ghost, as a matter of fact.

"I had the driver load the boxes in my truck and I took off." She was telling the part about hitting the gold truck.

"How much was it?" Dani asked. She was all about the business. Eric would rather not worry about the money.

"I don't know. I sent three of the four boxes here in a child's coffin."

Eric laughed. "Oh, thank you for not sending a real body in that thing. I debated what to do with it and figured you wouldn't do that. But I put it in your room just in case you did, so that you could deal with the smell."

Taylor laughed, her first laugh of the morning. She had been on the defensive, with the attitude that Dani and Eric were putting out.

"Want to open it?" she asked.

"Let's carry it out to the shop versus doing it inside." Eric knew better than to open it in the house and make noise that would wake his now-sleeping daughter.

"We can get the other boxes out of this truck, too." She hooked a thumb over her shoulder to indicate the truck she had driven that morning.

"What?"

"I hit the gold truck twice. That's why I wasn't back last week. I had to hang out until the next delivery."

"Holy shit," Eric said, almost under his breath. He drew both words out. There was admiration there, if one listened for it. To hit the truck once was one thing. To dive right in the following week and hit it again showed serious guts. Or insanity. He was impressed.

"That one was a little messier. They had an escort car with three guys in it. Then there was another escort car that came screeching up with four guys in it." Taylor had a thousand-yard stare on her face. "It was... exciting, but they were amateurs. No concept of small-unit tactics. I can't imagine they were any good at anything other than a drive-by shooting. Which, by definition, is a stunningly poor way of trying to whack someone."

"Oh, God, baby, I wish you wouldn't do things like that." Dani was almost in tears. Taylor just smiled at her.

"Were there any witnesses to all of that?" Eric asked, concerned.

"There was only one truck that went by."

"What vehicle were you in? Did you ditch it?"

"No. I found a cute little hot rod Blazer. Bear is fixing the bullet holes in it."

Eric stood up, very concerned now. "Fuck me! Are you kidding me? You brought it here after that?"

"I hid out in Tyler until it was dark, and I came in the back way."

"Shit. Shit. *Shit!*" Eric was heading out the door.

"I want that Blazer! Don't do anything to it!" Taylor was upset and was standing up now.

Eric turned to face her and glared at her for just a second until his features softened.

"Taylor, you pissed someone off bigtime when you hit their cash truck twice. They are going to come looking for you. And the biggest thing they have to look for is that Blazer."

They stood there staring at each other for a few seconds.

"We'll build you another one. A better one. Well, not another Blazer, but something you'll like."

Taylor's head dropped and she turned and sat back down, pouting. Dani commiserated with her while Eric went to go kill her Blazer.

***

Dani distracted her by suggesting they count the money. They also got the coffin outside and cracked it open. Taylor now had Cody's AR rifle to play with. It was a 6.5mm Grendel, which is about fifty or sixty percent more powerful than the usual 5.56mm AR chambering. Ammunition for it wasn't plentiful but it was something to have fun with.

And the gold. Taylor was now officially a multimillionaire, with well over three million dollars in cash. She gathered up ten of the ten thousand dollar rolls of gold coins and pushed them across the table towards Dani.

"Do something with that. I'll make donations every year. Not that big, maybe, but something. As for the rest... I hope you'll agree with what I want to do."

***

Bear looked guilty when Eric stormed into his office.

"Nobody saw it. It's under a tarp, and it's hidden," Bear stated, trying to get ahead of one of the famous Eric ass-chewings.

"That's good but it needs to be gone. Totally and completely. Any suggestions?"

"I'm sure we could bury it someplace but you might not want someone to dig it up later on. We could stash it in a building somewhere in Tyler. Hell, leave it somewhere with the keys in it. Let someone take it and then it's their worry. Leave it on the side of Interstate 20."

"Yeah, that may do the trick." Eric considered the options. "Tonight, after dark, clear this place out. I don't want anybody here to see anything. I'll be back and we'll load that thing up on the flatbed tow truck, still wrapped in the tarp. We take back roads to get to I-20. We drop it on the shoulder and burn it. Bring a few cans of gas."

"Can I pull the engine and trans? Taylor said it was a pretty strong piece out of a 'Vette."

Eric had to think that one over. "Not unless you can bolt another one in. If anybody looks at that vehicle, I want them to think that it broke down or something and the driver burned it and took off in something else. If we drop it out there without an engine that scenario won't wash."

Bear smiled. "Not a problem. I'll be glad to bolt one of these old boat anchors in if we can keep that engine."

"And obviously you have to do that swap without a bunch of damn people seeing that Blazer. I guess I need to send some people over to stand guard. Tell people it's a secret project."

Bear shrugged. "It's really not that much to swap one of these old engines. I can do it by lunchtime, and have it hooked up just like it was runnin'."

Eric paused again. "Okay. I also have a very disappointed young lady at the house who is heartbroken that I'm destroying her cute little Blazer. Do you have anything we can replace it with? Not another Blazer."

Bear grinned this time, ear to ear. "Our priority, set by you, is trucks and SUVs. But I just happened to spot something about six months back that I couldn't resist. I had to throw it on the truck. It doesn't run now but that engine from the Blazer will drop right in there. Nineteen eighty-two Camaro Z28. Kind of a dark, smoky gray. Hey, that's almost the same color as the Blazer, now that I think about it."

"How soon can you have it running?"

"By the end of the day tomorrow. The only problem is going to be the shifter. The one that's in the Blazer is going to be too long or have the wrong bends in it for the Z28. We might have to cut it down or something. It might be an issue finding the right one for it. Other than that, it'll be the interior. Mechanically we can do anything it needs. Doing a new carpet or seat covers for it will be the holdup."

"What's the paint look like?"

"Oxidized, but let me put a guy on it with a buffer and we'll see."

"Put this one on high priority. Your guys can probably start on it right now, can't they?"

"You bet. Let's walk over there and point them in that direction. They can go ahead and pull the bad engine from the Z and check the brakes and rear end, maybe get some temporary seats in there until the stock ones can be reupholstered." They had made it about halfway when Bear decided to say something else. "Miss Taylor said not to mention her name, but did she tell you what she did? The fifty thousand?"

Eric stopped. "No. What?"

"She gave me fifty thousand dollars last night when she pulled that Blazer in here and told me to donate it to something. She didn't care what. Told me to choose, or to go to Liz Mitchell if I needed help deciding. She said to keep her name out of it."

Wow, Eric thought. *Taylor gets that money and the first thing she does is start donating it.* She wasn't really his little sister, not by blood, but his throat tightened up with pride.

"We need to do that car up really special for her, Bear."

"We sure do."

***

When Eric got back to the house, Taylor apologized for bringing the Blazer into the ranch.

"That was stupid of me. I figured we were almost two hundred miles from where I hit the truck and I didn't stop for gas. But I should have been more cautious. I'm sorry."

"Hopefully there won't be any repercussions from it. Better to err on the side of caution in something like that, though. And we're working on saving the engine and transmission and putting it in something else. Something for you."

"Really?" Taylor brightened up instantly. "What?"

"Do you want me to tell you or do you want it to be a surprise?"

She thought it over. "How about a hint?"

"It's a car, not a truck. Something sporty."

"Oooh!" Taylor's eyes danced with excitement. "When do I get to see it?"

"I guess you could go take a look at it now if you want. Bear says he can have it running by the end of the day tomorrow but it's not going to be perfect. It'll need a new interior and some more work."

"I'll wait. I'm excited!"

"And if you don't like it, I'm sure we can come up with something else. If nothing else, you're rich now, aren't you?"

Her face dropped. "No. No, please don't call me that. Don't treat me any differently. I don't want anything to change."

"We can't tell anyone, anyway, for the same reason you're getting rid of the Blazer," Dani pointed out. "We have to keep it a secret, where she got that money."

"Well, that's a great point," Eric mused. "I was focusing on the Blazer, but I guess we can't say anything. What are you going to do with —"

260

"Meet our new business partner," interrupted Dani, making a dramatic two-armed gesture to indicate Taylor. "She's investing over three million dollars in the company. We'll get the attorney to issue her shares of stock with no mention of money changing hands. It'll look like we just granted her a block of stock. Plus, we'll wait six or eight months to do it so there is no paper trail that anyone could ever tie into... anything."

Eric grinned broadly at Taylor and reached out to shake her hand. Before he released it, he looked her in the eye and said "There is no one I'd rather have as a business partner."

She blushed and looked down. "Even if I do stupid things like bring a shot-up Blazer into the ranch?"

"Blazer? I don't think we have any Blazers here at the ranch."

***

In the morning, Taylor was tempted to tread lightly around Dani and Eric. She knew she'd pushed the envelope with her solution to the problems in Midland, and she'd truly screwed up by not ditching the Blazer. But she couldn't hide in her room until they left, so she mentally prepared herself and walked out into the kitchen. They were eating breakfast and invited her to join them, as usual.

She loaded a plate and as she was sitting, Dani looked at her excitedly.

"We want to do something that involves you," she started. "Some reorganization, that I guess is not really a reorganization."

"Should I be apprehensive?" Taylor asked.

"No, no, I think this is a good thing. Over the past five or six months, I haven't really been much good in the office. What with the pregnancy, and now Elena is only sleeping in little increments and keeping me up, you've been running everything. And Eric is only here about half the time." She looked at him.

"Yeah, you know how it's been. I'm here a week and then in Austin or on the road for a week, home for two weeks and then gone for ten days. So it's spotty. If

261

I was here every morning and gone in the afternoons or something, that would be workable. But I can't really commit to a definite schedule at this point."

"So, to repeat, you've been running the ranch," Dani picked the conversation back up. "And we think you should continue to do that, but with the actual title and pay and all."

Taylor looked surprised, and fumbled for words. "But, but what... What are you going to do? You're not going anywhere, are you?"

"What we want to do is focus on the strategic direction," Eric answered. "If you can take over the day-to-day management of the ranch, and that's what you have been doing for months, and doing it perfectly, then that frees us up to expand our operations.

"In my travels and work for the governor, I meet a lot of people, and I get offered a lot of business opportunities. I have taken advantage of some of them, which is why we have as many partnerships as we do. I mean, partnering with the oil executives got us into oilfield security, and that has expanded into the agricultural arena. Partnering with the bankers got us into the very lucrative banking and money exchange business. Of course, Dani took that a big step further by negotiating the deal sweeteners with Louisiana and the other states that gained us all of the books and oilfield supplies and equipment and so on.

"Anyway, if we don't have to pay attention to managing things here, then we will have the bandwidth to take on more opportunities. And as Dani says, if we have more, we can help more. We are, effectively, running the state's largest orphanage right here. We don't really look at it in those terms, but that's what we're doing. We have dormitories full of kids who we are keeping safe and comfortable and well-fed, sending them to school and then teaching them a trade.

"With you in charge here, that gives us, me and Dani, the ability to meet with these businessmen much more easily. We trust you. You know what to do. You've lived and worked with us every day for years."

"I'm honored," Taylor said slowly, getting used to the idea. She turned to Dani. "That means, obviously, that you'd be travelling with Eric."

"Not now, anyway, with a newborn. But coming up in the future, yes. It's very likely that we would set up a house in Austin and stay there for a week or two at a time. We don't know. Things may change."

"I can see the possibility of us setting up an office in Austin," Eric put in. "The necessity, I should say. That's where the power players are. That's the one city that is being kept running, to use the term loosely. The downtown is actively policed and kept clean, and some of the buildings are powered up with solar or generators. I guess we could combine things into a big house with some offices in the front, an admin assistant, and a bedroom upstairs for us when we're in town. The admin would stay in Austin full-time, keep the office open, pass messages on to us if we're here at the ranch.

"But the focus right now is on Taylor. What do you think? And if you need some time to think things over, please feel free to do so."

"I guess I'm more upset about the thought of both of you being gone." Taylor stood and went to first Dani, and then Eric, hugging them both. "I can do the work. I can manage this place."

"Of course you can. We have every confidence in you." Eric smiled at her.

"Also, this is an opportunity to give you the share of the company from your investment," Dani mentioned, hesitating only slightly on the last word. "Along with your promotion comes a block of stock. We'll have paperwork that will show where it came from. The actual cash you provided will be gradually filtered into our system in the course of our normal operations and will be untraceable." She smiled broadly. "It certainly helps that the IRS is gone and there is no electronic banking that records where every cent came from and where it went."

Chapter Fifty-One

THE Z28 WAS A hit. The paint had polished out better than expected and the bad spots would soon be repaired and repainted. The interior had deteriorated but there were plenty of cars sitting in new car dealers' lots that could be pirated for carpet and seats and it wasn't difficult to find nice wheels and fat tires for it. Bear was only too happy to equip it with headers and loud mufflers and other performance parts and keep it in top tune for her. Taylor cruising in her "Z" became a common sight, usually with a few of her friends, some of the younger girls that she mentored.

She gave as much time to the girls as she could, almost as much as her day job. The underage kids that hadn't been adopted stayed in dorms, grouped roughly by age. Taylor played big sister to them, listening to their troubles, preparing them for the world, and giving them the knowledge and the skills that they needed.

Those ranged from her usual classes in firearms and self-defense to soccer, dancing, hair styling, and more. She shepherded them through their proms and dances and *quinceañeras* and weddings. She also served as the rebellious young aunt, giving many of the girls their first experience with alcohol. Technically, she wasn't old enough to drink in the state of Texas herself, being under the age of twenty-one, but that was one of the laws that was routinely ignored.

Dani, then underage, had seen nothing wrong with a fifteen-year-old Taylor having an occasional beer or glass of wine. Now nineteen, Taylor stubbornly maintained that she was teaching the girls what alcohol would do to them,

264

which was much better than having some guys get the girls drunk and take advantage of them.

And Taylor could get alcohol whenever she wanted. She didn't flaunt it, like bringing sixteen-year-old girls into a bar and demanding that they be served, but she could get drinks or buy as much beer for carryout as she wanted. There really wasn't anyone on the ranch that would tell Taylor 'No'. Not that she was a bitch or threatened to sabotage them in some way or anything like that. On the contrary, she always went out of her way to help people, and they returned it. Rules just kind of didn't apply to her.

Eric hadn't been real happy with underage girls drinking but he was up against Dani on that issue and decided that was not a battle he wanted to fight. He couldn't force morality on everyone, as many leaders before him had discovered. As long as it wasn't flaunted, there were many things he had to ignore, like the 'friendly girls'. That was something he delegated to the medical officer and didn't want to ever hear about. He had demanded that they be adults, operating on their own free will, and have regular medical checkups.

***

Taylor modelled the short, short shorts exactly once and only for Dani, just so they could have a big laugh over it. Dani squealed and called them one of the sluttiest things she'd ever seen. Especially on Taylor. She just didn't dress like that.

After that one showing, the cut up remains went into a rag pile at the motor pool. One of the mechanics found a couple of the pieces, enough to arouse his curiosity, so he went through the bin until he could tape the whole thing back together. That sent the whole motor pool into a couple of days' worth of speculation regarding who had worn them.

That had some cold water thrown on it when one of the guys was holding the reconstructed shorts and wondering aloud what girls' waist would fit. Some smartass asked "Why do you think it was a girl?" The guy immediately dropped the shorts like they were contaminated and kicked them back in the direction of the rag bin while the others laughed.

***

Taylor stripped the AK down to the barrel and trunnion. The barrel is pressed into the trunnion and pinned, so they are a unit unless disassembled with a hydraulic press. They had presses in the shops but it just didn't matter. They had more than enough rifles. She took the AK parts and the barrel from the baby Glock and wiped them down to remove all fingerprints, then wrapped them in paper. A few days later she tossed the parts off one of the Texas Highway 155 bridges into Lake Palestine. The lake is not very deep but it isn't exactly clear and no one was doing any scuba diving there.

If she had stepped over the line in Midland and on the highway, there was no sense in being stupid about it. No reason to keep incriminating evidence around.

Chapter Fifty-Two

In Austin, the governor sat with Eric Marten of Marten Cattle Company and Ray Schmidt, Director of the Texas Department of Public Safety. That organization included the Texas Rangers, the Highway Patrol, and divisions for Criminal Investigations, Emergency Management, Intelligence and Counterterrorism, and a number of others.

"Ray, I want Eric to tell you what he told me just now," the governor began, as the Director settled into his seat.

"Ray, as you know we run security for oil and gas operations all over the state. One of our people received this message from an anonymous source regarding a danger to our operations in Midland. We also had an incident recently in which a couple of our people seemed to have succumbed to temptation and bought several ounces of cocaine for processing into crack. We have them up for prosecution and the information that they gave up ties in with the claims from this anonymous source. I therefore have to think that it's good, reliable info. I'll give you this message but what it says is that the mayor and entire police force of Midland is dirty and cars and properties should be searched. They are solidly involved with drug smuggling. This one address listed in here is a way station for drivers running drugs to refuel and rest before continuing to Dallas.

"The informant that sent this message has actually been inside this stash house and has seen the drugs, has seen the mayor with drugs, and has seen the local police escorting the drug shipment trucks. They also list another address and several names, or at least partial names, of people involved. This next sheet is apparently a roster for guard duty at the stash house. In addition, there is an address for what is supposed to be a larger stash house, a warehouse or something, outside of Weatherford." He handed the pages across the table.

"I can't tell you how much this pisses me off," the governor growled. "Drug smuggling is one thing, but when you're the elected mayor of a city? That just infuriates me. And I understand there were some shootouts there in Midland with some police officers killed. And last but certainly not least, I don't have to tell you how vital oil and gas operations are to this state. We cannot have people distributing drugs to oilfield workers. That could cause catastrophic accidents."

"Oh, I know it." Ray hated drugs for what they had done to a niece of his. He wasn't exactly happy with people like Eric pushing him into specific investigations but he was the governor's buddy and it would be a waste of breath to even say anything against it.

On the other hand, resources were tight. If Eric wanted to finance an investigation, do most of the leg work and point the DPS in the right direction, then step away and let them finish things off and take credit for the arrest, that was not exactly a bad thing.

"I'll get people on this as soon as I get back to my office. Is your guy, the one who was contacted by the informant, available for questioning?"

"I'm sorry, Ray." Eric really did look contrite. "They are no longer in Midland. I understand that individual is mobile right now, but if you have any specific questions, I can relay them. I don't know how long it might take for them to get a message." Eric thought *I just made three statements. The first is true. The second is technically true if you define "mobile" as "Taylor doesn't have a broken leg", and the third is true since I don't know specifically when a message would be sent, therefore I don't know when it would be received. God, I'm turning into such a politician!*

Ray translated all of the verbiage as "no". He hadn't expected anything else, but Eric's birddog had pointed at specific addresses and names that they could check out.

***

Two weeks later, he had his top investigator back in his office for a status report.

"What's the thirty second summary? Let's start with that," he asked.

Delbert had worked for Ray for years and knew his style. "My opinion is that a vigilante group, maybe no more than two or three people, decided to clean house. They took it upon themselves to take out the drug dealers and corruption in their city. The other option is that a rival gang wanted to take over, but there is no evidence of that. The opposite, in fact. The same gang is trying to rebuild their operations in Midland with a new stash house. They're having a hard time because the local guys are scared to work for them now.

"With the guard roster that we received, we were successful in running down some street names and started questioning people. We got some to roll over and give us everything that they knew, which wasn't a lot. Midland was mainly a truck stop, a place for truck drivers to rest and refuel. Drugs come up from Mexico and continue to Dallas. Money comes down from Dallas and goes to Mexico. Nothing stayed in Midland for any length of time except for some small amounts for local use."

He hadn't timed it, but knew he was close to the half-minute mark.

"What about the police and the mayor?"

"Unfortunately, it appears that all of the police officers may have been dirty. We found that all of them had amounts of money, certainly in excess of what they should have had. Two of them had drug stashes, one big enough to be called sales weight. Of course, they're all deceased now.

"We performed a traffic stop on the mayor and found a kilo of pure, uncut cocaine in his car, plus a thousand dollars in cash. In his house, he had cut recreational cocaine and some marijuana and other party favors. Now, of course he claims that he has no idea where that kilo came from, but the other items tell a different story. He is under arrest."

"Do you have a line on the vigilantes?"

"Very little. There are three persons of interest I'd like to talk to. One is a young woman that was seen with one of the dealers that ended up dead with his house burned. She came looking for him, by name, in a bar that he frequented, and they left together. She might have been bait to get him to go where someone else could grab him. The other is one of the stash house guards that disappeared. Of course, it's possible his body was dumped somewhere, and we just haven't found it yet. The third was the girlfriend of one of the men that was killed, but reportedly she's an addict so there's no telling where she is now.

"We have shell casings that have all been wiped clean, no fingerprints. We have lots of fingerprints from other places, houses, but nothing to match them with. No database. I guess I never really appreciated computers sufficiently when we had them.

"With information from the people we picked up, we were able to bust their new truck stop house and we also took down the truck coming up with a load of narcotics. We also tried to get the money truck but there seems to be a change with it. They altered the route or the schedule or something."

"Related to that shootout on I-20?"

"Yes, sir. The word is that the corrupt cops were escorting the trucks in to the house. The one cop's body was found at the county line, on the afternoon that the truck regularly came in. That means someone knew that truck was coming in with money and took down the cop that was waiting to escort it. Presumably they also took the truck down. That could have been an inside job with that stash house guard that's missing.

"Now we come to the following week, on the day that the next money shipment is going to Midland, and what do we get? A shootout on Interstate 20. Seven dead cartel men, some of them just chopped to bits by gunfire. I mean shredded. I'm assuming automatic weapons. We have a lot of AK-47 rounds fired at the first shooting but no shell casings. That makes me think they were fired from inside a vehicle. That sounds to me like a driver and a shooter or two, so again I am back to two or three vigilantes. In this case, they pulled up behind the car and fired a bunch of bullets into the men inside.

"A couple miles down the road, they had a shootout while stopped. There were two bodies there, plus the truck carrying money. It was empty and some tires were shot out on it.

"We have a third crime scene a few miles further down the road, two cartel men in a car. Both were shot and their car slammed into a parked eighteen-wheeler trailer at high speed.

"At the second scene, we have some AK-47 casings that were wiped clean, no fingerprints. We also have AR-15 casings and we recovered the rifles that fired them. Now these boys that met their maker out there on the interstate were a different level than the Midland guys. It looks to me like a gang allowed the locals in Midland to operate that house but when they needed to send in some shooters, they called in a different crew. These guys were all ex-cons, heavy-duty bad guys."

"But not heavy-duty enough that they didn't all get killed," Ray pointed out. "Apparently without even wounding anyone on the other side."

"That's true. That may mean that the vigilantes are some serious people, too. Maybe ex-military guys with real combat experience. Hell, we were sending men off to war a lot in the years before Hexen. The Global War on Terror. There are plenty of people out there with the skills."

Exactly like Eric Marten, Ray thought. *It wasn't him, though. Not personally. But this is his style. Just kill 'em. He sent that artillery strike into the gang in Dallas and then shot anyone who tried to run away from it. Or who surrendered. Eric does not accept surrenders. And that wife of his is famous for shooting people in the head to make sure they're dead.*

The governor said he'd seen a demonstration of the guys, and girls, too, at their ranch. All kinds of weapons, sniping, close quarters combat, hand to hand. He's been training them in infantry tactics for years. It doesn't matter how young they are, ten, eleven years old, he'll start training them.

That sonofabitch sent a team in there and whacked all of these people. I'd almost bet money on it. And there's nothing I can do about it.

Or want to do about it, for that matter.

Politically, trying to prosecute any Marten people that Eric didn't want prosecuted would be bad. Nobody in power would want the scandal, what with the close ties between the Martens and the governor. And the close ties with all — not some, but *all* — of the surviving oil and gas executives in the state. And the bankers. And the ranchers. And... well, at some point, you just don't need to lengthen the list any more. Be happy that you made some good busts and write off the possibility that a good guy might have gotten a little too enthusiastic.

Don't poke the bear, in other words. It will go rapidly downhill afterwards and is not likely to end well for you.

"Delbert, I have to say, man to man, that I don't really care about any vigilantes. I would rather you spend all of your time going after the drug dealers. That is especially true if the local boys are out and the cartel is sending hardcore members up here to run things. The vigilantes are probably just some good ole boys who got fed up with the local government's corruption and inability, hell, unwillingness, to protect them. It's not good that they took matters into their own hands but they wouldn't have done it if the druggies and the corrupt officials hadn't been doing bad things in the first place."

"I was actually hoping you'd say that."

They looked at each other for a moment, neither speaking, but communicating. Both nodded, and any further investigation regarding the vigilantes was quashed.

"How are you going forward?"

"We have surveillance on that warehouse in Weatherford and I'm coordinating with —"

Chapter Fifty-Three

Two months later, in the Kansas City area, a young man named Mike stood in front of the congregation of a Baptist church.

"Brothers and sisters, I come before you a sinner," he began. "A sinner. I'm talking felony-level sinning. And I would still be doing that same sinning today, except that I met the Devil. I met Satan himself not long ago. I am not speaking of a vision, or a dream, or of some evil person with hate and malice in his heart. I mean that I met Satan himself in the flesh, and I devoted my life to Jesus that day. That is the only reason that I stand here now, is that Jesus protected me. I saw six men die that day, and heard two others die, some that were friends of mine, and some that I had known all my life.

"Satan was there, walking the earth, in the form of a beautiful young woman. I looked upon her with lustful thoughts and she offered me pleasures of the flesh. And then over the course of a few hours, she murdered those men and forced me to watch." His throat clenched up on him, and tears streamed down his face. "Tortured and murdered and burned their houses down. I did not have the strength to witness it all. But I put my faith in the Lord, and I live today only because of that.

"What I want to tell you today, brothers and sisters in the Lord, is that sometimes the Devil throws pillows. Sometimes the Devil throws pillows. Now we think of the Devil as some hideous creature with horns and cloven hooves for feet and a forked tail. Something really frightening. But when the Devil, in the form of a beautiful woman, offered herself to me, that was a pillow. She was trying to lure me in. And it worked.

"She used me to get to other people and kill them, right there in front of me. If you try drugs and they make you feel great, that's one of the Devil's pillows. But the feeling goes away pretty quickly and now that person may have an addiction, or an infection from a needle, or may have to steal to support their habit. That pillow becomes the devil's pitchfork. That pillow that you thought was so comfortable comes with a price. You get the nice pillow to lure you in, and then the sharp steel, the tines of the pitchfork, stab right into your body, into your very soul."

He actually had the gift of gab. He just never could resolve in his mind why the Devil had saved the girl from the burning house. It was an inconvenient truth. He was telling the story, so he got to leave that part out, but it always bothered him.

Mike had a career ahead of him, and some minor degree of fame and fortune. But also nightmares that had him screaming in the middle of the night, along with an absolute refusal to be anywhere near hot dogs on a grill. *Ever.*

He had his eye on a good woman here, and as he concluded his sermon he looked at her and they smiled at one another.

"So, brothers and sisters, we all have the opportunity for redemption. Our sins can be forgiven by our Lord and Savior. Our sins can be cast aside. I was saved. We can all be saved. No one is beyond saving."

***

Taylor was in her room that same night, washed and brushed and ready for bed. She was thinking of the money.

My money, not my father's. Three point something million is not a huge amount, but I'm young. There's time for me to increase that. The Marten companies should grow. The banks are bringing in huge profits every week, plus the agriculture and the oil wells, to say nothing of the stock we own in the oil companies. I think I would go to college at this point, if there were any in operation. Maybe in a few years. But I can scan the personnel records and see who has skills that I may be able to learn.

But her planning was being interrupted. She was still thinking about the events that had occurred recently, still getting flashes of memories, like videos that suddenly popped up out of nowhere. She didn't feel guilty about what she'd done, but killing someone and having men try to kill you are pretty intense experiences and the memories come back for a while, sometimes forever, for some people.

I know that I probably did no more than put a temporary kink in their operations, but we can only do what we can. We can't simply throw up our hands and give in to criminals. And especially the corrupt cops. If they take the oath to uphold the law and then become criminals themselves, then they're even worse scum.

That led her to think about her performance and what she could have done better. That led to covering her tracks and disposing of evidence after the action. And that led to thinking about Mike, not exactly an innocent bystander in the whole affair.

She had shot three other guys who were doing exactly the same thing as him. Four, if you included Hulk. So why not him? Underneath, though, Mike was a nice guy.

She went back and forth a bit on that. Maybe she should have taken care of him. Weren't the others probably nice guys underneath it all, too?

Irritated with herself, she ended the speculation with a conscious effort. If Mike had taken her advice and left Midland, she probably had little chance to track him down and kill him now, not that she would. And there was still the girl. And the truck driver. If she was going to kill them, she should have done it while she was face to face with them. She didn't do it then and couldn't now, so she determined to stop thinking about it.

The trip to Oklahoma came to mind, and that made her think about sex. Maybe she should have invited Jason into her bed. And then abruptly, a mental image of Antonio came up.

WHAT?! No, no, God, no. He was married and had kids. No, she was absolutely *not* going to lure him off into a tryst. Not that there was anything wrong with him; just the opposite. He was strong and handsome, and he'd replied to some of her furious interrogation, back at the train station, with calm and reason. And never held anything against her. Well, except for that hug he'd given her when she got back. That hug that was a bit tighter and a few seconds longer than she would have expected.

Okay, calm down. You've been through a trying time. Just relax.

Instead, she thought again about those she had killed and savored what it felt like to stamp out those bastards. Feeding the small, terrified young girl inside her with power. With safety. With kills.

You want to come up against me, you bastard? Let's see how big and strong and dangerous you are when this bullet hits you. When your flesh ripples from the impact like a pond with a rock thrown in it. When the blood gushes out of the hole and you scream and writhe and cry and curl up into the fetal position in a growing wet, red pool of your own life substance. Or when this chunk of lead and copper slams through your skull and bounces around inside like a ping-pong ball, turning your brain into mush. Lights out, motherfucker. You think this little teenaged girl is just a piece of meat? She'll leave you in a pool of blood before you know what hit you.

Tears formed and ran down her cheeks. She lay on her bed and curled up into her own fetal position, mentally cradling that terrified little girl inside her.

I will *protect you. I* will *protect you. I* will *protect you.*

Tears streamed out of eyes that blazed with determination. She reached over to grab her rifle, checked that it was fully loaded, one in the chamber, on safe, and placed it on the bed beside her If she needed to, she could just reach over and lay her hand on it.

It was both the worst and the best teddy bear she'd ever had.

Epilogue

TAYLOR HAD ALWAYS WORKED hard, ever since she'd arrived at the ranch, and now that she was managing the place, it was no different. But things occasionally came up. Sometimes the only real way to end a problem is to end the thing that is causing the problem. She'd done that before.

She didn't know, yet, that trouble was brewing up in Louisiana that would affect the rest of her life.

About the Author

Al Hagan is a retired IT project manager. His career also included a four-year tour of duty with the Marine Corps and a number of years in the intelligence community, working in Washington, D.C. and in foreign countries.

More from Cannon Publishing

Join the Crew!

SIGN UP FOR OUR newsletter for the latest news on new releases and more.

Follow our authors at their Amazon Pages!

Shane Gries (Dragon Finalist)

Lucas Marcum

Al Hagan

James Copley

Jason Kyle

G. Scott Huggins

Michael Morton

Charles Hackney

Jon LaForce

Jason Weiser

Kal Spriggs

Brian Gifford

Charli Cox

Dan Kemp

Jonathan Shuerger

J.R. Wise

Steven Vickers

More Books from Cannon Publishing

Irregular Scout Team One

In July of 2016 a plague swept the world, and the civilization collapsed and fell. For a lone National Guard sergeant, a veteran of the wars overseas who had settled down to a new life, the nightmare began on a hot summer evening at the barricades. Orders and chaos, gunfire and being overrun, his unit dwindles away in the face of the infected. Months later, living in the ruins, the thud of helicopter rotors followed by a crash and the rescue of a downed pilot leads Sergeant First Class Nick Agostine back into the arms of the US military. From his experience comes the idea of teams, military and civilians experienced in dealing with the undead and barbarism of the wilds. The first Irregular Scout Team leads the way for Task Force Liberty to advance down the Mohawk Valley in Upstate NY, making contact with survivors and clearing out the infected with stealth and firepower.

Volume 1

Volume 2

Volume 3: Civil War

Volume 4: Bad Company

Volume 5: End of Days

The Line

When the world descends into chaos and anarchy with an unbelievably swift plague, turning victims into ravenous maniacs, the soldiers of America's storied 1st Infantry are asked to hold the line. From the brutal streets of urban combat to the bloodied, desperate defense on the plains of Kansas, they fight a war against an unrelenting enemy who used to be their fellow citizens. As civilization falls, can they hold the line?

The Thin Dead Line
Dead Storm Rising
The Big Dead One

Fallen Empire

What's a soldier to do when the war is over? When he's only known conflict his whole life? Since time immemorial the solution has been to find another war, this time for pay. Whoever has the credits and wins the high bid gets the experienced fighter. Sometimes, though, the credits aren't enough to cover the price. Empires rise, but Empires also fall. The Terran Union has spent five centuries under the control of the alien Grausians, like a barbarian tribe under the thumb of Rome. Now, after almost two decades of civil war and succession struggles, the formerly subject races have settled back in their ancient territories to lick their wounds and re-arm, leaving hundreds of settled planets to exist in a political vacuum. Into that space steps the free companies, mercenary units that fight for gold, honor, power and glory. Veterans who can't get the wars out of their souls, new recruits looking for adventure, corporations with their own agenda. Join us in a 27th Century that echoes history.

The Irish Brigade

Overrun

Silent Violence

Doom Company

Athenaeum, Inc

The Professor has problems, and not just what decades of soldiering did to his back and his knees. His boss just died, leaving him as CEO of the extremely discreet intelligence contractor Athenaeum, Incorporated. His old buddy the Operations Director is a highly skilled Army Ranger veteran but his finance chief is slightly unhinged and spends her money on highly inappropriate work outfits. The surviving old men on the Board of Directors are stuck in the 1970s. Running Athenaeum out of an old Cold War bunker and keeping their roster of experts together is expensive, but the government contracts are drying up or going to bigger, flashier corporate players.

Door Number Three

Doubling Down

Off World

When nuclear war erupts on Earth, the American colony in the Alpha Centauri system is left stranded. As the new day dawns, a furious attack by the native inhabitants threatens to overwhelm the colony's defenses. It's left to the thin red line of the US Army's 9th Regiment to stem the tide and ensure humanity's survival in this harsh new world. From two time Dragon Finalist and author of the best selling series "Irregular Scout Team One" and "Invasion" comes a new tale that tells of the struggle for survival on a brutal planet.

Offworld: Ragnarok
Offworld: Expeditions

Cannon Fodder: Tales From the Gun Crew

Fifteen stories from Cannon Publishing Authors, each taking from the universes of their novels to bring you perspectives and deepen their world. From 27th century mercenaries fighting on distant planets and young soldiers riding with Arthur to defeat Saxon hordes, to enchanted weapons dealing damage in hands of Fae, we bring you the best of Science Fiction and Fantasy!

Valkyrie

Humanity engages in a desperate struggle with an alien species for this side of the Orion Arm. Space ships die in instantaneous bursts of light and turn into vapor, but on the ground Marines scream and lie wounded in the mud and blood, praying for the Valkyries to come save them. They aren't wishing for death and a Nordic goddess to take them to Valhalla, the wounded are praying for the men and women of the '348th Field Hospital MEDEVAC to dive through fire and hell to come save them. Because they know that ...Valkyries never die!

Valkyrie
Valkyrie: Rebellion
Valkyrie: Attrition

High Caliber Awards

The Cannon High Caliber Awards are an annual contest for new writers. In it we ask them to submit a novella length story of Science Fiction, Military or Fantasy genre to challenge their skills.

2024

2025

The Wishkiller Saga

While on patrol Captain Aethal Paaling discovers evidence that an ancient terror has reached the rich soil of his home: the Lotus, a prolific growth whose addictive leaves devour their victims from within turning their hosts into horrible, terrifyingly violent mockeries of humanity. Created at the dawn of history by the twisted power of a godly relic called the Well, the return of the Lotus may be a harbinger of even more horrors to come. Carrying the fatal news to the capital, Aethal discovers that even in the face of death itself, the Lords Paramount of Verlaen will fight to keep their secrets and their power. With only the guidance of his legendary Greater Rifle and the aid of the Pheonix Lancers, the soldier must find his way through the halls of a forgotten holy order and into deep dens of crime seeking answers. He must find the truth as quickly as he can, because the Lotus may have already taken root among those he loves... and fighting it may cost him everything, including his soul.

A Cold and Mortal Spring
War of the Shattered Moon

Hexen

When nine out of ten people in the world have died in a brutal plague, what do those who remain do to pick up the pieces? Does the creed, "Duty, Honor, Country" have a place any more if there's no country left? On his way across the devastated remains of Texas, Marine Corps veteran and survivor Eric Marten rescues a young woman from a vicious attack by men who have turned into savages. As Dani slowly learns to trust him, they try to stay alive in the deathlands that America has become, using all their wits to survive a post-apocalyptic nightmare.

90% Death Rate: A Post Apocalyptic Thriller
Angel of Death: A Post Apocalyptic Thriller
The Bloody Princess: A Post Apocalyptic Thriller

Hell Train

A single train carries what might be the last vestige of civilization through a hellish nightmare. A few hundred alive out of millions, lights going out all across what was once America as the possessed arose from the dead and murdered the living. A few hundred survivors travel across the country in an armored train, seeking some place to shelter in a fallen world. All that remains is a dystopian nightmare marked by rains of blood, impossible horrors, and portals to Hell opening in the skies.US Army Captain Jack Zamora is responsible for their safety, a self-imposed burden that wears on him every day. Fighting off undead, protecting the survivors, keeping the train running and supplied as his team desperately plans their next moves. Starvation and disease threaten. but it gets worse, because the ancient gods have sent their emissaries, horrific beings of myth and legend that walk the Earth. Things that can drain a man's very life essence or even that of an entire city.

Hell Train: All Aboard

The Path

Sometimes a hero isn't what you expect, and the one you need comes from the castaways of society. Nearly broken and at the end of his rope, former decorated scout pilot and prisoner of war, Red has finally accepted the inevitable. He and his kin have no future in the Human Confederation of Worlds, being gene mods and barely human themselves. With the help of his friend he flees Terra for adventure and fortune out in the reaches of the galaxy. Along the way he's dragged back into conflict that calls on all his piloting skills and he learns the deeper meaning of Kin, as his crew becomes his family.

Path to Freedom: The Path, Book One

Invasion

More than a decade after the Confederated Earth Forces were defeated, their commanding general, a boyhood protegee, lives in exile and disgrace. His life on an isolated farm is forever changed when two strangers show up at his homestead, and the war comes crashing back down on him. The problem though, remains the same. How do you fight an enemy that is technologically superior and holds the high ground?

Invasion: Resistance

Invasion: Day of Battle

Invasion: Total War

Military Sci-Fi/Fantasy Anthology

The military experience is timeless, and echoes down from our past and into our future. Along the way, not everything is as it seems. Thirteen stories from established and new writers in the field of Military Science Fiction and Military Fantasy bring you tales of the terrors of combat and the even greater fear of the unknown in Cannon Publishing's first Bi-Annual Military Anthology.

The Hundred Worlds

Fifteen classic Science Fiction stories from both masters of the craft and up and coming new writers! A tyrannical United Nations pulls the strings of its colony worlds, ruling with an iron fist. Corporate interests take precedence, and brushfire rebellions smolder on the edges. One system, home to the only alien species yet discovered, with human allies throws off the yoke and calls itself Independence.

MECHA

Feedback from the slight pressure of a hand closing sends a powerful mechanical arm smashing into an opponent. A neural link hurls blustering plasma fire from your suit's shoulder mounted cannon. Your reactor levels scream with overload as return fire smashes into your armor, and damage alarms wail while you hurl your twenty ton body sideways for cover. You're a Mecha, a mechanical fighting machine with a human pilot. The guy that the infantry curse at in training and pray for in combat. The machine that the last hopes of your people ride on. The construct that strikes fear deep into alien hearts as they hear your turbines power up. The one able to pass through hell and come out the other side victorious, or die trying.

Under A Different Sun

In the near future, massive empires rule the stars, and west of the Reach, they are battling for control of new systems. In the no-mans land between the front lines, Captain Nate Meric and the crew of the privateer Lexington fight for prize money, and loyalty to their ship and their friends. Beneath it all, though, runs a hidden dream. To see America restored, and take her rightful place among the stars.

Sea of Fire: Demonrise

Brian Corel, former slave, gladiator, ex-fiance to an Empress, exiled Captain of the Taland Royal Guard and now owner of the frigate *Widowmaker,* does the best he can to balance the lives of his crew with his own desire to live life as a free man. Skirting the border between being a privateer and an outright pirate, Corel stumbles into a war with a religious cult intent on corrupting the kingdom of an old friend and has to set things right while grieving over his lost love. Along the way he signs a dragon into his crew and has to risk everything to rescue his brother from the grasp of a demon that has destroyed an entire continent.

Chosen by the Sword

There are some things a PhD doesn't prepare you for, like running two feet of steel through the guts of a flesh-eating monster straight out of a nightmare, while ducking razor sharp claws. Or having the sword critique your fighting style while you do it. Dave Howard had a problem. Last week, he was out looking for a teaching job in the middle of a wrecked job market. This week he was neck deep in green blood and hellfire. Dragged into it by the very sword, his grandfathers' mysterious possessed blade, that was now walking him through hacking up a ghoul without getting his own head cut off. This wasn't exactly what he had gone to school for, and the University he had just taken a job with seemed to be anything BUT an academic institution. More like some kind of monster hunting bunch of weirdo nerds. Maybe his degree in Personality Psychology might be useful there, at least. The fighting though ... as he dodged another swipe of claws and awkwardly tried to follow the instructions the sword was screaming at him, he shot back at it, "Hell, I'm Canadian! Swordplay isn't in my cultural DNA!"

Beyond the Wall: A Novel of Post-Roman Britain

The legions are but a memory, the glory of Rome only a shadow of crumbling ruins and broken walls. A darkening tide of barbarism was washing across Britain's shores and the lights of civilization were slowly flickering out into darkness, only kept burning by the legendary Red Dragons cavalry unit. Led by their Tribune, Arthur, who serves no kingdom but goes where the fight is hardest and most crucial, they wage desperate battles to keep back the tide. The Red Dragons ride the length of Britannia to fight the invading Saxons, Scoti and Picts, wherever they show, from across the seas or down from the Highlands. At sixteen years old Peredur of Gwynedd has listened all his life to the stories of his father Pelinor fighting with Ambrosius Aurelianus. When word comes that his older brother has been slain in battle with the Saxons, his desire for revenge leads him to follow in his father's footsteps as a warrior, becoming a cavalryman with the Red Dragons. Along the way he may either find himself a warrior and leader worthy of Arthur or be left lying forgotten in the dust of history.

Hell's Bells: War & Love Downrange

Two souls collide in the middle of a deadly war.

Sergeant Sylvie Lyons of Her Majesty's Royal Engineers wishes she'd listened to her grandda's advice and stayed away from the military.

USMC Sergeant Hondo Cassidy wants nothing more in life than being a Marine and fighting. Hondo and Sylvie find themselves thrown together when his artillerymen are assigned to provide security for her engineers deep in the desert of Afghanistan.. Amidst death, destruction, cultural misunderstanding and the inevitable that happens when you mix an all male unit of Marines with an engineer unit that is mostly female, Sylvie and Hondo find in each other a reason to live. That is, if they can survive.

Semper Die

The dead rose expecting a feast. What they got was a firefight.

Sergeant Alex Slaughter and the Marines of Alpha Squad were on a routine training exercise near Quantico when everything went silent. No comms. No command. No clue.

What they find when they return to base is worse than anything they trained for: a bioweapon has unleashed a zombie virus that has shattered civilization, and now they must survive the Collapse.

But as the squad pushes deeper into hostile territory—through the death-choked streets of Arlington and into the rot-stained corridors beneath D.C.—they discover that the undead aren't the only threat. Desperate survivors, rogue military units, and darker truths buried beneath the weight of secrecy will test their loyalty, their mission, and their very humanity.

Written by USMC veteran Jonathan Shuerger and set in J.F. Holmes's brutal and unrelenting Irregular Scout Team One universe, Semper Die delivers pulse-pounding action, authentic military detail, and a terrifying vision of what happens when duty and apocalypse collide.

Lock. Load. Semper Fi. Semper Die.

Troll Hunter

In a world ravaged by endless war between humans and trolls, Gabriel Cullen, a grizzled hunter gifted with the rare ability to track by scent, is captured by the very creatures he hunts.

Bound both by his captors' chains and by an ancient prophecy, Cullen glimpses a chance to end centuries of bloodshed—if he can trust the trolls who butchered his kin. When a sinister force from the deep dark threatens both sides, and even trolls tremble at its approach, the tracker is forced to question everything he believes.

Unaware of her father's changes in hearts, his daughter, Isabo, a fierce warrior driven by duty and vengeance, vows to rescue him, leading an army that wields a devastating new weapon to crush the troll clans. Yet her quest risks igniting a deadlier war. As Cullen allies with a young troll warrior and a blind shaman to confront a demonic evil from a forgotten age, both father and daughter face wrenching choices between peace and betrayal.

In a land where hope is fragile and blood stains every blade, their sacrifices will forge a new world—or shatter it forever. Troll Hunter is a raw, gripping saga of loyalty, loss, and the brutal cost of survival.

More from Irregular Scout Team

Volume 1

In July of 2016 a plague swept the world, and the civilization collapsed and fell. For a lone National Guard sergeant, a veteran of the wars overseas who had settled down to a new life, the nightmare began on a hot summer evening at the barricades. Orders and chaos, gunfire and being overrun, his unit dwindles away in the face of the infected.

Months later, living in the ruins, the thud of helicopter rotors followed by a crash and the rescue of a downed pilot leads Nick Agostine back into the arms of the US military. From his experience comes the idea of teams, military and civilians experienced in dealing with the undead and barbarism of the wilds. The first Irregular Scout Team leads the way for Task Force Liberty to advance down the Mohawk Valley in Upstate NY, making contact with survivors and clearing out the infected with stealth and firepower.

This is a remastering of the best selling Zombie Killers series, combining the 2017 Dragon Awards finalist "Falling" with book 11, "Patient Zero", placing the story in proper chronological order and connecting the stories together.

Volume 2

A year has passed since the plague destroyed most of civilization around the world and the U.S. military is slowly starting to move out into a devastated country. From their bastion in the Pacific Northwest mechanized task forces take the fight for America onto the offensive.

In front of the military, deep into the wild ruins, go the Irregular Scout Teams. A mix of hardened military veterans and experienced civilians who can operate for long periods of time on their own. Checking the road, rail, and water transportation infrastructure, identifying groups of survivors for reinforcement or evacuation, running rather than fighting. The Teams have all the might of their task forces' firepower on call but it's better to be unheard by the infected and unseen by the lawless.

IST-1, the first team and the most experienced, is ordered to operate on their home ground of the ruined Upper Hudson Valley. Sergeant First Class Nick

Agostine, the Team Leader, driven to fulfill his oath to the Constitution and his county while haunted by the memory of his dead family. His fellow NCO and Team Medic, Doc Hamilton, trying to keep everyone alive. Ahmed Yassir, a man without a country or tribe, deadly at a thousand meters with is calm shooting. Isaiah Jones, a giant of a man with a machine gun and a booming laugh, who grew up surrounded by violence. Brit O'Neill, the fiery red head with the ice blue eyes, who is just as ready to take off an infected's head with her shotgun as she is to put at teammate into their place with her sarcasm. Former Serbian soldier Sasha Zivcovic, who is a born killer living in his preferred element, war.

As the eyes and ears of Task Force Empire, it's their job to save the lives of thousands of soldiers by providing accurate intelligence. That's the mission, in theory, but incompetence, the fog of war and politics get in their way, putting the entire teams' lives at risk.

This isn't a book about the Apocalypse. It's a book about the men and women of Irregular Scout Team One and how they lay their lives on the line for each other in the face of incredible danger. A book about how a bad decision or just plain bad luck can put yourself and the ones you love at risk. In the end, though, it's a book about ...

... Hope.

Volume 3: Civil War

Three years after the Undead virus / parasite infected the world, civilization struggles on. The United States is scraping by as a nation by the skin of its teeth, with forty million people crammed into the Pacific Northwest, living in squalid refugee camps. Army units have made inroads into the ruins of the rest of America, working on clearing the major cities.

Outside America, England survived, as did other island nations. The survivors are struggling back to their feet, fighting a long, exhaustive campaign to regain the Japanese Islands and Europe.

On an island in the Hudson River, thirty miles north of the nearest Army outpost, several families have homesteaded. Mixed military and civilian, planting crops and salvaging the land, they are survivors of the Army's elite scout teams. Children are born, old friends mourned, rivers run clean and trees grow in the ruins. The fight, though, still goes on ..

Irregular Scout Team One, call sign "Lost Boys", is working clearing operations in support of Task Force Liberty, designating targets for Close AIr Support. Their assignment is interrupted by the Task Force commander, who gives them an off the books mission that will plunge the nation into civil war.

This book contains the original books four and five of the Irregular Scout Team One series, "Civil War" and "Endgame". The entire series has been remastered and put in the proper order.

Volume 4: Bad Company

The world has fallen, swept away by plague and civil war. In a quiet corner of what remains of the United States, former Scout Team leader Nick Agostine struggles to adjust to peace, wanting to raise corn and kids with his wife. He has a good crop of both growing when the reality of violent war shatters his precious peace.

Called back to active duty, Colonel Agostine is tasked with planning reconnaissance missions for the Scout Teams to take out the leadership of the rebellions Mountain Republic. A final strike to end the last war, but when nuclear weapons become involved, Irregular Scout Team One travels to Florida in chase of a renegade traitor. Disaster overtakes the Team and Agostine sets out on desperate search to find his missing wife.

Through it all, the question runs, what price loyalty, and does the dream of America still live on in the hearts of men, or has it died in the ashes of barbarism?

Volume 5: End of Days

The plague has come and gone, followed by Civil War and the ruin of America. Still, the torch of hope is held aloft by those who haven't forgotten their oath...

As the Federal government battles the remnants of the Mountain Republic, Colonel Nick Agostine settles into a calm life of running a trading post and farm north of Albany. Feeling restless, after the harvest, he sets out with most of IST -1 to explore a long valley north of the remains of New York City, searching for survivors and looking for places where refugees can resettle.

Along the way old hatreds thought long buried resurface and the Team finds itself caught in a brutal ambush. As bullets fly and grenades crack, casualties mount and a shot sends the Scout Team leader spinning to the ground. He awakens to find himself facing torture and death in his most desperate situation yet. It could be ...

The End of Days.

More From the Fae Wars

Get the full series!

Onslaught

What would you do if America and the world were invaded tomorrow by a relentless and brutal enemy? In an alternate 2015, a US Army Special Forces Team, part of the legendary black ops unit "Delta", is in midtown Manhattan to take out a Chinese spy and his handlers, sending a message short of outright conflict. All goes smoothly until they find themselves in a full blown shooting war through the canyons of the City. Portals from another world have opened in Central Park, making a way for figures out of historical nightmare to invade. The Fae, creatures banished from Earth thousands of years ago and now only part of our legends, have returned with Dragon fire, spell and sword to conquer and take revenge. The first volume of The Fae Wars covers Team Three, G squadron, Special Forces Detachment (Delta) as they fight their way off Manhattan and then join the defense of the refugees as the Fae assault the bridges. The fabled 69th Infantry puts up an epic fight against superior weaponry and then the war descends into the asymmetric hell that the Delta Operators know so well. Along the way they find new allies and old powers that come to their aid.

The Fall

For the first time in two hundred years an enemy has stepped foot on American soil and war has come to our cities. The US military is rocked back on its heels and driven into a fighting retreat as each defense line falls. The foe is unstoppable and ... Fae. Creatures from a legendary past who have come to reclaim the Earth in the name of magic and revenge. In the hills of Pennsylvania a ragtag, devastated army prepares to make a last stand against dragon fire capable of melting an Abrams tank and wizardry that stops fifth generation fighter jets in mid-air. Inevitably it comes down to shining steel verses human will, and Sergeant Oliva Acevedo transforms from a hospital clerk to a hardened fighter. Volume Two of the best selling "Fae Wars" follows the fighting retreat of the US Army as the Fae establish control of a shattered America.

Futures Past

Two thousand years ago the Fae were banished from Earth and they've spent that time plotting return and revenge. When their portals open around the world and start crushing the human's military with spell encased steel and dragon fire, it becomes a massive struggle between technology and magic. When the Fae Invasion hammers the West Coast, Captain James Powers and his California Army National Guard artillery battery is caught on its way home from Annual Training. In a running battle the unit is smashed by combat with orcs and elves, leaving their commander struggling to keep his people together and alive. Along

313

the way a dying priest with a strange ability to see the future manipulates people and events to bring Captain Powers to his true calling as a Seer. As they run and fight, the humans gain new allies, Fea tinkerers who love all things mechanical and hate the elves. With their help they begin to take the war to the enemy in a brutal mayhem of ambush and assassination. Book Three of the Fae Wars series following the bestselling "Onslaught" (set in NY City) and "The Fall" (Pennsylvania)

Tales From the Occupation: A Fae Wars Anthology

Wars end, enemies are defeated and territories are conquered and the combatants have to return to a life changed. America and the rest of humanity have fallen to the Fae, ancient mortal enemies of mankind. After building their strength for two thousand years, the Elves have claimed their vengeance and now rule Earth with an iron fist and dragon fire. Down but not out, a human resistance is building, but first daily life needs to be lived. An anthology of stories exploring life during the Occupation in the best-selling Fae Wars universe.

Insurgent

Wars come and wars go. Eventually even the most belligerent of combatants will arrive at some kind of living arrangement, either through exhaustion or slaughter. Kill enough, down to the last child, and there will be no more war ... until the next one, of course.

In August 2015, the war started, portals opening up between their world and ours, allowing the Fae to return to our (or their) home world in blood, fire and magic. Conventional forces fought back as well as they could, but the invasion had been planned to hit us in the middle of our civilization. America's military was scattered overseas or concentrated in large bases that were quickly overwhelmed by forces that were dropped right in the middle of their units. The fighting was brutal and horrific, magic overwhelming technology. It took six weeks, and the President surrendered to spare the civilian population. A puppet government was put in place and the Fae started to divide the conquered lands into principalities run by their Great Houses, slowly turning America into a land of feudal slavery. Thing is, though, the Fae had lived in their exile for thousands of years, fighting wars among themselves and against various races that populated their new home. Pitched battles where there was a clear-cut winner and loser. They had never fought an insurgency and had no idea how bloody it could get. Major David Kincaid. United States Army 1st Special Forces Operational Detachment–Delta, soldier of a defeated but unbroken nation, was going to show them. If, that is, he can keep the faith. The follow up novel to the bestselling "Fae Wars: Onslaught" by J.F. Holmes.

Ghost

There are wars, and then there's War. The all-encompassing thing that is fought on many levels, and with many kinds of weapons, many kinds of warriors. Even ghosts.

Alex was no one, a man just trying to get by at his paperwork job at the new Homeland Security. A man grieving for his wife, who had died in the Invasion. Someone just trying to keep his head down while the elves appointed him to do the paperwork of putting their boots on the necks of a conquered American people. Thing is, even a nobody paper shuffling clerk has a weapon, one that had lit the fires of revolution in America hundreds of years ago. His mind, and his words. The internet was still up and running, somehow and someway, and Alex takes to his keyboard. Inspired by his hero Patrick Henry, soon the words of the "Ghost" start inciting attacks on the Fae and the District of Columbia rings with explosions, gunshots and cries of Freedom. The Resistance notices, and Alex is soon assigned a bodyguard and a handler, an ex-police officer who is running from her own hidden past. Together they work to keep the flame of resistance alive and escape from the tightening net of the Fae. The consequences are, as always, Liberty or Death.

Northwest Front

Fae Wars returns on a new front as war rages in the Pacific Northwest!

Corporal Erik Doherty isn't some kind of special operations super soldier; he's just an infantry grunt trying to get by in what was once the United States Army, now an enforcement arm of the Fae overlords. When orders come down from a chain of command more interested in boot licking their new masters than protecting American citizens, he has to make the choice. To serve and live, or run and die? Ashleigh Greene is a teenage girl with a price on her head, the Fae looking for retribution for the killing of one of their nobles. As her hometown burns behind her, she flees into the mist shrouded forests of the Pacific Northwest, her family killed by dragon fire and her world destroyed. On separate paths, each human comes face to face with a haunting legend that has lived for thousands of years. One that has been waiting, watching, and hating the old enemy that has finally returned. Together, they bring war to the Fae in a battle for honor and revenge. Book seven in the best-selling Fae Wars series!

Vendetta

The echoes of the Fae Invasion have died out in the Midwest when a new thunder rumbles across the plains. Tukor, former warband leader of the Red Arrow Clan, now rides with a motorcycle club of humans and orcs against his former masters. It's hard to tell which challenges Tukor more though; being the new chief of all the orcs in the free city of Wichita Falls, Texas, or being engaged to the tough and lovely human woman Misty.

Throw in an elven duke that's still pissed at Tukor for murdering his sons, a motorcycle club that'll follow the chief to hell and back, and a newly arrived orc matron determined to prove Tukor and Misty wrong about their future. The Fae occupation of the Midwest just got way more bloody.

Featuring orcs on choppers, magic ammo and a whole crew of Army SpecOps, the tale of Tukor and Misty is a front seat view of the occupation in the Southwest that no one expected, least of all Tukor himself.

Relics of Empire

In a world shattered by elven conquest, where magic crackles and dragons soar, the Navajo Nation stands as a defiant refuge. Living there is Ben Yazzie, a battle scarred Marine veteran who wants no more war—until a brutal encounter with elven oppressors at a remote gas station ignites a spark of rebellion. Alongside Maria Hernandez, a grieving widow fueled by vengeance, and a band of unlikely allies, Ben is thrust into a fight against an empire wielding arcane power and ruthless ambition.

As ancient ley lines awaken, unleashing chaos across the American Southwest, Ben uncovers a legacy of resistance tied to his ancestors and a mysterious relic from a forgotten era. Magic surges and the earth itself stirs, forcing Ben to embrace his destiny as the Coyote, the elusive and mysterious warrior leading a desperate stand against an otherworldly tyranny.

From the dusty trails of Arizona to the neon-lit chaos of Las Vegas, *The Fae Wars: Relics of Empire* is a pulse-pounding tale of courage, sacrifice, and defiance against overwhelming odds. Will the old ways and a warrior's heart be enough to reclaim a shattered land?

The rebellion begins here.

Authors

John Holmes

J.F. Holmes is a retired Army Senior Noncommissioned Officer, having served for 22 years in both the Regular Army and Army National Guard. During that time, he served as everything from an artillery section leader to a member of a Division level planning staff, with tours in Cuba and Iraq, as well as responding to the terrorists attacks in NYC on 9-11.

From 2010 to 2014 he wrote the immensely popular military cartoon strip, "Power Point Ranger", poking fun at military life in the tradition of Beetle Bailey and Willy & Joe.

His books range from Military Sci-Fi to Space Opera to Detective to Fantasy, with a lot in between, and in 2017 two are finalists for the prestigious Dragon Awards.

In 2018, he launched Cannon Publishing, www.cannonpublishing.us specializing in military science fiction, fantasy and thrillers, with an emphasis on works from up and coming authors.

Lucas Marcum

Lucas Marcum is a critical care nurse practitioner and an officer in the US Army Reserve. When he's not working, or performing his reserve duties, he can be found hiking, reading, attempting to perfect his soft pretzel recipe and spending time with his family.

James Copley

James Copley is a former Non-Commissioned Officer of the U.S. Army, having served over twenty-one years in both Active and Reserve/Guard units, variously trained as Infantry, Communications, and Ordnance specialties before finally retiring from the Army National Guard in 2016. During his service, he deployed four separate times, twice to Iraq and twice to Afghanistan.

He is currently working as a software engineer in Central California with his wife, two children, and two dogs. Reading was his number one passion from a very young age, and more recently he decided to try writing his own. Feel free to join him on his writing journey!

Charli Cox

Charli Cox is a best-selling Military Sci-Fi and Horror Comedy author. She also writes Sci-Fi, Alternate History, and Military Fantasy stories.

If you enjoyed Fae Wars: Northwest Front and want to see more stories about Ash and "Gunny," Cannon Publishing has you covered. Burnt Mountain and Sasquatch will be coming to your Kindle later in 2025. Also, please be sure to leave a review!

Representing #teamandmore, Charli's first published short story is in The Phoenix Initiative: First Missions from Chris Kennedy Publishing. She has stories in Bureau 42 and Express Elevator to Hell, also from CKP.

Look for Whistles of the Wendigo, an Alternate History/Military Fantasy novel set in the Joint Task Force 13 universe from Three Ravens Publishing, due to release soon.

Charli's previous experience has been as a Realtor, HVAC Business Manager, IT Office Manager, and freelance bookkeeper. Professional skills such as drafting strongly worded emails transition surprisingly well into writing fiction.

An animal lover and #boymom, she lives in SW Oregon with her Leg husband, two sons, an Arabian mare, and two Husky mixes who think they are hooman.

Learn more about Charli and sign up for her newsletter on her website. Hang out with her on Facebook, Instagram, and/or TikTok.

Jason Weiser

Mr. Weiser has been a government contractor for the last eleven years, and before that, a writer working odd jobs trying to get by. He has a BA in History from CUNY Brooklyn. Mr. Weiser released his first novel in 2025, with Cannon Publishing, but before that, released a short story in their 2018 Spring Military Sci Fi Anthology.

Mr. Weiser is also an avid wargamer and has been published quite a bit in the hobby, having most recently run "Military Miniature" magazine as it's editor in chief from 2021-2023. Before that, he wrote for EpochXperience (a division of SJR Research) as a contributing writer for their blog on wargaming and military history topics from 2020 to 2021.

He also wrote two scenario books on Cold War wargaming topics, "Red Star, Burning Streets" and "Red Star, White Lights".

Mr. Weiser encourages all his fans to visit Cannon Publishing at their website

Brian Gifford

A military veteran with more than 25 years of service in the U.S. Air Force and Army (in an order that would surprise you!), Brian is a lifelong science fiction and fantasy nerd of the highest order. A student of the hard sciences and the arcane arts of cybersecurity and IT alike, Brian has spent a lifetime accumulating his unique view of the world, which he now insists on sharing with everyone else. He is a husband in awe of the magnificence that is his wife and the proud father of three awesome sons, and looks forward to retiring from the military in the near future to focus on his family and his writing.